C000090668

A
SHOT
from the
SHADOWS

As ever

Mike Atherton

Also by the same author

The Long Shot

A
SHOT
from the
SHADOWS

MICHAEL ATHERTON

Copyright © 2016 Michael Atherton

The moral right of the author has been asserted.

Apart from any fair dealing for the purposes of research or private study, or criticism or review, as permitted under the Copyright, Designs and Patents Act 1988, this publication may only be reproduced, stored or transmitted, in any form or by any means, with the prior permission in writing of the publishers, or in the case of reprographic reproduction in accordance with the terms of licences issued by the Copyright Licensing Agency. Enquiries concerning reproduction outside those terms should be sent to the publishers.

This is a work of fiction. Names, characters, businesses, places, events and incidents are either the products of the author's imagination or used in a fictitious manner. Any resemblance to actual persons, living or dead, or actual events is purely coincidental.

Matador
9 Priory Business Park,
Wistow Road, Kibworth Beauchamp,
Leicestershire. LE8 0RX
Tel: 0116 279 2299
Email: books@troubador.co.uk
Web: www.troubador.co.uk/matador
Twitter: @matadorbooks

ISBN 978 1785891 823

British Library Cataloguing in Publication Data.
A catalogue record for this book is available from the British Library.

Printed and bound by CPI Group (UK) Ltd, Croydon, CR0 4YY
Typeset in 11pt Aldine401 BT by Troubador Publishing Ltd, Leicester, UK

Matador is an imprint of Troubador Publishing Ltd

MIX
Paper from
responsible sources
FSC® C013604

For Baby 'Olaf' whatever you are,
you're going to be very welcome at Granddad's

Foreword

A Shot From The Shadows is fiction; the places and most of the times mentioned in the book are as they were. Events described did happen but I'll leave it to the reader to decide which ones are fiction and which are true.

One thing that is fact and irrefutable is that there were over thirty attempts to assassinate Adolf Hitler between 1921 and 1945, and these comprised of bombs, poison and even shootings; the two things that they all shared was that they were credible attempts, and all failed. He was clearly either very lucky or blessed with foresight. I'm not sure I believe in either, in his case.

We also know Hitler had a doppelganger who stood in for him, Gustav Weler. He was executed at the end of the war to confuse the advancing Russians.

The Commonwealth War Graves Commission (CWGC) continue to do a fantastic job all over the world by ensuring that the fallen from both wars are treated with the respect and dignity they so rightly deserve. Maintenance of the CWGC cemeteries is a never-ending task. If you have never visited one, I urge you to go and visit. They truly are peaceful, reflective places and are kept immaculate, albeit built on a foundation of so much pain and suffering.

The memories of the men and women who lay there deserve the best we can offer and sometimes that's as much as a simple visit and a moment of reflection.

CHAPTER 1

1916, the Beginning

It was his shaking hands that gave away the fact his mind was in a dark place. He wiped his forehead with the trembling forefinger of his right hand. With a blank stare, he looked at the cruciform body lying at his feet. Life had little or no meaning here in the trenches. He had seen many men fall and die right in front of him, but this one was different. In life, Hauptman Berger had impressed him, but in death he felt disgusted by him. In truth he had heard about him before he had ever met him, and he only met him yesterday. One young corporal to hand over a trench line of over 200 metres seemed a little extreme, but these guys were very good and had spent a lot of time facing the British. He would be back with his own regiment tonight, back in the line away from all the madness for just a short time.

He looked down at the dead officer, prostrate at his feet. As he wiped the remains of Hauptman Berger's brains from his face he looked into the dead man's eyes: they had become 'squint' with the impact of the bullet that had left a neat hole exactly in the centre of his forehead. A second bullet had taken his voice. There was very little of the back of his head left, death had been swift; it was probably more than he could have expected and certainly more than he deserved.

Hauptman Berger had been standing on top of the trench, very much in harm's way. He was in a rage; his sadistic sport had been spoiled. The British officer who had been caught and trapped on the vicious barbed wire had gone. He had delighted with his malignant depravity in slowly killing the officer, taking pot shots over the past couple of days aimed more at antagonising a response from a rescue party than killing him swiftly.

Clearly there was a rescue mission taking place, and if Berger could just see where the rescue party were hiding with his wounded prey, he could call in the artillery to obliterate the area out in no man's land. He hadn't expected that he, the hunter, had now become the prey. His hunters were two elite snipers, Jack Adams and Albert Hagerman, one British one German, now joined together as brothers in arms fighting together against a common enemy, him.

There had been a storm of lead from the British side that was both extremely accurate and intense, it had claimed quite a few lives in the German trench.

It was with a mixture of emotions that the 27-year-old corporal cleaned his face of the dead man's splattered and now dribbling brains. Anger and fear are uncomfortable bedfellows, but today was a turning point in the young Adolf Hitler's life. Yesterday he was a normal, relatively balanced, respected soldier. Today he was broken. Like a twig snapping, the switch of sanity had been flicked.

From today he would be a different man, a bitter, twisted, damaged individual, the latest victim of this abhorrent war.

The consequences of this particular casualty would be felt by the next generation of warriors, in a different war, but for Adolf Hitler this chapter of his war was over.

He could hear cheering. As he looked around, the bile of hatred rose in his throat, his comrades were cheering; they were cheering because the man lying dead at his feet had been killed. The realisation that Berger had been unpopular, hated even, hit him as hard as a slap in the face. How dare they dislike or disrespect an officer of the Imperial German Army? If he could he would make them pay, every last one of them.

CHAPTER 2

The Somme, France, 1994

The darkness was impenetrable; there was no light in this dark cavernous shell, it died along with hope a hundred years ago. Its inhabitants had all perished here in a different time, a lifetime ago and were now just bones, guardians of the dark. Their uniforms would have shown that they were a mixture of French and German soldiers who had fought and died for the land above in the war to end all wars, or so they had thought.

The dead lay witness to the true carnage, and the victors of the hand-to-hand fighting who had taken this concrete bunker and had been dealt a mighty blow, for just as they had celebrated the hard fought victory a massive howitzer shell exploded close enough to collapse the entrance to the huge room and entombed them. Condemning the victorious to a long and lingering death.

The wooden roof struts that had taken the weight of the bunker's ceiling and the soil above for nearly a hundred years first creaked, then cracked and finally splintered before falling completely and collapsing.

The result of the collapse would have far reaching

consequences; above, a cemetery belonging to the Commonwealth War Graves Commission was undermined and had fallen into the void. Bones fell from above as if to offer a change of guard to the dead below. The bones of the dead, buried with such reverence in the 1920's, rained into the bunker. The bodies of the dead long since forgotten below now had some company.

CHAPTER 3

1994 The Somme

Andrew Phillips stood at the edge of the crater looking into the void. "Do we know how many fell in, Magnus?"

"We think nine. We won't know for sure until we go down. According to our records there are four that are named but the others are unmarked."

Andrew nodded, that seemed about right for this area, most of the graves belonged to unknown soldiers.

In the distance they could see the huge monument that was the Thiepval memorial. It had stood in defiance of the wind, rain and sunshine for decades. Designed by Sir Edwin Lutyens and opened in 1932, it was a magnificent tribute to over 72,000 men commemorated on its walls, all of them missing without a known grave. It was somewhere for the families of the missing to come and remember the fallen. It was yet another reminder to Phillips as to why he loved this area so much.

Magnus Roche was the local agent for the Commonwealth War Graves Commission in this part of France and had worked with Phillips many times before.

Andrew Phillips had been with the commission, man and boy, for twelve years now since starting as a headstone checker after leaving university with a history degree. He loved his job, it was his father's dream job, but his father had been too old to follow his dreams and had passed the idea onto his only son. Now Andrew Phillips was head of the Commonwealth War Graves Commission for the whole of France, responsible for ensuring the upkeep of getting on for a thousand cemeteries. Still young at thirty-four, he had a passion for this work. Andrew respected all the dead, regardless of nationality and treated them with a reverence bordering on obsession; along with Roche's dour sense of humour and down to earth nature they made a great team.

They were, of course, only part of the recovery operation, and from a makeshift office which was in fact an ex-military tent erected on the edge of the cemetery, came Robert Deville the French forensic pathologist. He had been called in to help 'tag and bag' the bones for identification and reinterment, but only once the area had been made safe from further collapse. The rules on corpse identification had changed in line with the medical advancements available to the modern world since the initial protocols of the Imperial War Graves Commission. There was a national register in all the post combative countries apart from the United Kingdom for DNA sample analysis; however, this was in discussion with the British government.

"Bonjour, Robert." Phillips liked to try to speak French but was always happy when the French replied in English.

"Hello Andrew, quite a mess here. Are you going down?"

"Yes, Oui. I am just waiting to make sure the engineers say it's safe to go in."

Robert nodded and walked back into the tent. Inside there were ten fold-out tables with the appropriate paperwork ready to start the process of putting the skeletons of these few men back in some order. It would be unusual to have mixed bones. Normally when a body was found buried in the battlefield they would be more or less in one piece and relatively easy to reassemble, but today was not going to be like that. The bones would have become mixed up so it was highly likely that the wrong parts would be assembled, but he would try to do his best and ensure the right bones were together.

Magnus handed Phillips a high-visibility jacket to go along with his bright yellow hard hat. They checked the headlights and torches. The team had already had a look inside the crater with fibre optic TV cameras and a gas monitor showed there was no danger of gas.

The TV showed what looked like a concrete bunker, the area was riddled with them, and recently there had been two others that had finally collapsed into themselves. Heavy rain over the past two years had been to blame, and erosion was proving to be more and more common. The field archaeologists loved it. Each new collapse helped them draw a new part to an already existing land map. This new map was slightly different in that it reflected an underground world they had little knowledge of previously. They knew it was there but there was a lot more they didn't know about the tunnels, mines and now bunkers, and slowly their maps were being filled in, like a jigsaw puzzle. They would have a look in here only after the nine headstones and the people they belonged to had been removed.

A florescent *break and shake* light tube, similar to those used in the nightclubs by kids, had been dropped down into the darkness. As Phillips sat in the cradle above the hole he could see it down below, much further than anticipated; this bunker must have been quite a size.

Phillips thought about the glorious weather they were enjoying today and the horrendous conditions the men below had to endure getting on for a hundred years ago. At least today was dry and warm and he started to sweat in his protective jacket.

"We're sure there's no gas aren't we?" He knew the answer but smiled as everyone nodded and watched him swing his feet over the edge.

He really shouldn't be doing this, it wasn't really his job but he loved being hands on. He knew that Magnus would have his back and look after him. The rope creaked as the pulley above his head slowly lowered him a few inches at a time. His headlamp seemed woefully inadequate initially but slowly as his eyes adjusted, the beam of light from the LED lights illuminated the darkness. The descent seemed long, and after every metre the man at the top of the rope called down to him how far he was down.

"6 metres, can you see the bottom yet?'

"I'm nearly there, I can see the bottom." he called back.

The beam from his headlamp was like a frozen rod of light, sharp and bright so that he could easily see his surroundings now. The harness was cutting into his bum and he swivelled round to ease the load. He could just make out the fallen headstones on the floor now not so far below.

He felt his feet touch the ground, the stretch of the rope bounced him and he lost his footing and landed with a bump right on his arse. He regained his balance and stood up.

"I'm down." he called and clicked on his radio and camera. "The floor is dry, it's a bunker as we thought."

He shone his light around the room: it was approximately 15 metres long and nearly 6 metres wide with a high ceiling. The air was stale and dry but the walls were in remarkable condition. A noise above him made him look up, it was Magnus with a tripod and light, a bit like a security light that just fitted onto a battery pack. Within a couple of seconds the whole room was in a brilliant white light. The headstones were all in the same area, and scattered around them were the remains of the bodies that had rested inside the small wooden cases used as coffins. These coffins had disintegrated years ago, but there were bits of wood here and there; such a mess.

Over the other side of the room there lay more bones, but these were still in uniform and it didn't take the pair long to realise they were a mixture of French and German uniforms.

"There are other remains down here, we are counting about half a dozen but I will confirm that, wait out." The radio clicked off and Phillips went to investigate his new charges.

"Six," said Magnus, "plus the ones that fell in, a total of fifteen."

Phillips thought about who would need to be officially contacted later, but before any of that could happen Robert would need to come down and confirm the dead were old war victims and not recently deceased, a formality, he could see that, but a necessary one.

What in the name of God had it been like in here all those years ago, he let his mind drift back in time. There had been a battle in this bunker and the casualties of it lay here in front of him. What must it have been like in this place? And why were these men here? No doubt the answers would pan out to be simple but for the moment it remained a puzzle.

CHAPTER 4

Germany, 1924

Albert Hagerman was at his office in the *Rathaus* (Town hall). These were difficult times in Germany but nowhere was worse than here in Tuttlingen.

Less than a year ago that madman Adolf Hitler had been involved in a major fracas in Munich, less than 300 kilometres from where Albert now sat. Hitler had been caught by the authorities and incarcerated in Landsberg jail, but he was back on the streets now and spouting his vile brand of politics on an ever-eager population.

Things had been very hard since the war, the poor were poorer, the hungry more hungry, nothing much had improved since the end of 'The war to end all wars'. Albert thought this was a stupid title for an insane situation that he felt Germany had been implicit in starting.

Now the powers that be needed someone to blame for Germany's defeat, and no one was excluded from the probing scrutiny, the Jews, the Communists, even the emperor had been accused of betraying the German army of a defeated nation. No one would be spared inspection, and fear had become a common feeling amongst normal folk.

Surgical instrument makers had replaced the simple farmers and toolmakers traditionally found in the area. Small family run businesses that together formed small collective cooperatives. Each household would manufacture some part of an instrument, and then a master instrument maker could assemble each part. Things were getting better here and all Albert wanted was for people to leave his small town alone, show them no interest, let them grieve for their lost sons and let the community grow collectively.

Unfortunately the *Nationalsozialistische Deutsche Arbeiterpartei* (National Socialist German Workers' Party) was very interested in everything they did here, but Albert was certain, as mayor, that it was a dark interest. He could see no good in the Nazi party and he had seen the worst in people before.

He knew it wouldn't be long before the *Sturmabteilung* or *Brownshirts* as they were being called, arrived in force. Some had already been in the town for weeks, sneaking and bullying, pushing their weight around and all the time hiding behind an ugly officialdom. Albert rubbed his eyes; he could feel a familiar foreboding, a slide back into the old times. So much of what was happening now in this part of the world was similar to the ridiculous posturing and bullying that had happened just a few years past.

That episode had led to a war; a war in which everyone seemed to lose. He had lost a son, and nearly been killed himself on more than one occasion. He could see Germany heading for another war, had they learned nothing? He shook his head and looked at the picture on his desk: Monica, she had changed so much in the years since his return. When Hans went to war he took his mother's heart along with him and neither Hans nor her heart had ever returned. Albert returned from the war a decorated hero, but he felt as though he had a huge hole inside his heart; in this hole the pain and misery of his lost son gripped him tightly, like a rope being twisted. It was there every day but today it seemed worse, perhaps it was foreboding. He looked at the picture of his family taken at their farm just ten years ago, Monica, Hans and himself and once again the rope tightened. The day ended at 5pm, Albert had a short bike ride to get him back into the woods on the outskirts of Tuttlingen then another half hour before he got home. There was a good road to his area because the woodcutters often came this way with the lumber they had cut that day.

Albert felt uneasy, as he had done for the whole day, again the familiar uneasy feeling that reminded him of his past, his senses were telling him something was wrong but he couldn't quite identify what it was. He was perhaps being over cautious, he had seen a lot of the *Brownshirts* in the area for the past two days and frankly he didn't like them or what they stood for.

By the time he approached his house he knew he had been right to be worried, there had been a motor truck up the road, he could see the tracks in the dirt. The woodcutters used horse and carts; who would have come here in a truck?

He rounded the final bend and everything he loved

ended. There on the porch at the front of the house lay Monica, she looked lifeless, he cried out her name and pedaled faster than he thought possible. He dropped his bicycle and ran over to her, there was blood on her face, and bruising around her eyes, her nose was broken and her clothes were torn. She groaned as he folded her into his arms. Confusion ran amok in his mind, what could have done this, had she fallen from the roof? He let his hands stroke her hair as she opened a bruised eye, she reached down to her skirt and he tried to help her sit up, it was then he noticed her underwear had been discarded and as he moved his hand he saw it was now covered in fresh blood. When he looked he could see Monica had been shot, she had a bullet wound in her side just under her right breast and she was wheezing as she tried to speak.

"What has happened Monica, who did this?" his eyes had returned to the cold dead eyes of a killer, there was no expression, no life; no emotion in those killers' eyes.

"Four men, dear husband, *Brownshirts* in a uniform. They said you were a traitor. Said you had betrayed the Fatherland, worked with the Englishman in the war." Her breathing was becoming shallow and Albert Hagerman knew that death was about to visit him once more.

"They used me and then shot me, to shame you, they thought I was dead but I didn't die, I wanted to tell you how I know you never did those things."

Albert felt a tear of rage drip from his nose.

"No tears husband, it is my time to go back to meet

Hans, he will be needing his mother. I am not afraid." She breathed slowly then coughed, bright frothy blood erupted from her mouth and splattered onto Albert's face, some went onto his lips and he could taste the bitter, metallic elixir of life as finally Monica Hagerman closed her eyes for the last time.

As he held her in his arms there was a reincarnation of a life gone by in years past. He knew once more he was a killer and he savoured the feeling, cherished it as he would an old friend, as if it was his own lifeblood. Revenge and vengeance were as good as any reason to live and if that was indeed the case he had never felt so alive.

CHAPTER 5

Adolf Hitler

The pain in his jaw had kept him awake for three nights. On the fourth day he could stand it no longer and went to see his dental doctor to have the offending tooth removed.

As he sat in the chair, he refused any form of anaesthesia; paranoia is an underrated analgesic and the fear that ran through Adolf Hitler would demand full consciousness. Strangely, he didn't do well with pain and avoided the dentist as much as possible, but this was something else. The pain gnawed at his very soul, constant and agonising. Worse his regular dentist was away on holiday and consequently he had never met this dentist.

"Herr Hitler, this must be excruciating, the gum is badly infected and I'm afraid I cannot save the tooth. It must be extracted at once if we are to avoid further infection."

Abraham Meir was a senior dental surgeon who had gained more experience in the last war than most doctors would in a lifetime. He had even worked in England after the war; working with plastic surgeons repairing the mutilated faces of the injured soldiers before taking the skills he had learned back to Germany.

Hitler nodded. "It is a distraction Herr Doctor, please remove it quickly." Hitler instantly took a liking to this man, a trust he didn't afford many.

Meir tried to convince the recumbent patient to have some form of pain control but Hitler would have none of it; there was no doubt he had a high pain threshold.

Meir picked up the scalpel and passed Hitler a small section of wooden broom handle to grip.

"Squeeze this, it will help. I have to tell you this tooth is very deeply embedded and it's going to be quite an ordeal for you whilst I get it out. At any time you can raise your hand and we can stop, or if you prefer I can give you some gas that will temporarily put you to sleep. I do understand your reluctance Herr Hitler, but the offer is there should you change your mind."

Hitler nodded again and sat back, he knew this was going to hurt. Meir made his incision into the gum; the blood ran freely and was sucked away by the *Yankauer* suction pipe, quickly turning to pus as the large abscess that had formed in the tooth root burst: the relief was instant. The tooth was gripped by a set of forceps more akin to pliers than a medical instrument and with a twist left to right and then right to left, the tooth was extracted. The gum was sutured, neat and tidy, and the bleeding stopped very quickly.

Adolf Hitler sat in a pool of his own sweat, he was groggy because he had passed out; he was furious because Meir had let him.

Abraham Meir dropped the extracted tooth into a sterile glass bottle, he labelled it and slid it into the top drawer of his desk. He could have no idea of the importance this tooth would prove to be in the future years ahead.

CHAPTER 6

On the Bench, 1994

Robert Deville looked at the tables in front of him. There were sixteen tables, and on each table lay a jumble of bones. Six of these jumbles were still in uniform, four French and two German. All the remains had been respectfully placed in boxes that resembled small coffins. Andrew Phillips had overseen the collection and boxing down in the bunker but only after Deville had confirmed they were ancient remains. Each box had a label with an identification number, and numerous photographs and a video had been taken prior to any movement; the whole process had been recorded for analysis later in the comfort of the head office and not here in the field under less than ideal conditions.

The remains had been brought here for initial viewing and for Robert to confirm, yet again, to the local *Gendamerie* that the bodies were archaeological remains and not new remains or recently deceased. This was standard procedure to ensure that no crimes had been committed and that the remains were treated with all the due diligence and respect afforded to the dead of both world wars. Once he had signed the paperwork, Robert would have the remains moved to his forensic antiquities laboratory in Peronne, near *La Grande Guerre* museum.

The broken headstones that had marked the final resting place of the fallen had been recovered from the bunker but they were badly damaged and would need to be replaced. The task of matching the remains of the skeletons with the broken headstones would be very difficult and in all honesty, Robert wasn't sure how he was going to manage that. All the remains were carefully examined and once again multiple photographs taken to forever capture this stage of their journey to eternal rest.

Once all the correct labelling and paperwork had been completed they were packed into large polystyrene boxes for transportation.

★

Back at the laboratory Carrie, Robert's laboratory assistant, would receive each sample. She was English but had worked and lived in France for ten years. Blonde and bubbly her girlish looks belied her age: she was forty but looked much younger, a natural youthfulness that benefited hugely from the mild climate of France. She was highly respected, and even desired by all the male members of the staff in both the lab and museum. She liked to be thought of as a bit dizzy but everybody knew that she wasn't: it added to her charm.

Despite her desire to be in the background her professionalism in her chosen career often highlighted things most other people in her trade would miss, and she was often at the forefront of any archaeological investigations. She tingled with excitement as the boxes were unloaded and carried to the workbench in her laboratory. Today was going to be a long day and she would carry on working well into the night; she didn't mind, no one waiting for her besides her dog, Bud. She liked the single life, the men she shared her life with were laid out here in front of her, and that suited her just fine. Carrie took her new charges and placed them individually on the scales. Each skeleton would be weighed and each bone would be examined.

Things had changed massively in the sixty years since these men were buried; before their second interment samples for DNA would be taken as was now routine. Each DNA sample would be compared to the national database for most of mainland Europe, although this scheme hadn't been adopted by the United Kingdom it was now a routine part of the forensic profile for newly recovered remains. On average there were about fifteen new discoveries a year. In the last two years the identities of previously unidentified casualties had numbered eleven, nine French and two German. Families who had long since given up any hope of finding the fallen relatives of the First World War had received a phone call and ultimately had been given the news that their long dead family member had been found. This simple change had reunited the families of long forgotten dead from both world wars. It was getting more common to find a match, and when it did happen each hit was a success and seriously celebrated.

Carrie removed a tooth from each skull, it always surprised her how many teeth had survived given the year they had died. The state of the dentition revealed a lot of history about a skeleton, but more about the years that the man had been alive, how well they had been nourished, and what kind of food they ate when they were young; all evidence that needed logging. Carrie was nothing if not fastidious especially when it came to the detail of the long since departed.

After she had extracted the samples they were sent to the main testing facility at the laboratory in Paris. The sample results would be returned within a few days, then the results could be entered into the national database held by Interpol. Nobody expected any returns from the skeletal remains of the ten skeletons marked only as British. The results would be recorded and stored. It was hoped that in time, the United Kingdom would adopt the European way and a fuller DNA database would be available and only then would they be able to try to trace the living relatives of those who had fallen so many years ago. The other six, the four French and two German may well find a match, it was all the encouragement she needed.

Carrie informed both Robert and Andrew by email with what she had done today. Tomorrow her job would be to examine the injuries to the bones and match the individual bones to a particular skeleton. The remains of any uniform would be handed to a different department for further examination; they were after all in remarkable condition considering they were so old.

The next day work commenced on making up the skeletons for reburial, although it would be months before the groundwork at the cemetery would be completed and prepared ready for reinterment. The investigations on the sixteen sets of bones would take quite a few weeks, but the initial investigations would start today. Looking at the remains that had been in uniform was easy, each one had an identification tag and so these remains would be inspected and a file with the details of injuries started. Carrie thought it was best to do the four French bodies first, politically it was a shrewd move and she might need a favour in the future, you just never knew when.

The lab was very clinical, more like a hospital pathology unit really. The photographer was due in anytime to start recording the process of the identification procedure and bone autopsy. Carrie was also expecting Robert to arrive soon. Carrie opened a file for each casket: *Eric Doule, born 1893; Florian Bonaire, born 1893; Paul Gustard, born 1898; and Arnoud Sherett, born 1889*. It seemed strange to Carrie that these men were now laid in front of her on a table. *What was their story?* There were no obvious injuries, no fractures to any bones.

She examined their clothes; there was very little damage to the material, no bullet holes or shrapnel tears, no bayonet rips. Just old cloth that happened to have been sat underground for eighty years or so. The uniform of the French soldiers showed that they had belonged to the *178 Régiment d'Infantrie*. The military historians seconded to the department had quickly been able to say when the regiment was in the area during the war, 1917; these men had been missing for eighty-two years, but had now been found. With some luck and a bit of research these soldiers would have a story to tell and within a week they should be able to tell it.

The German remains were just as easy to identify, each had a small metal disc with a name and unit stamped into the metal. The cord which had been round each soldiers neck with his disc had rotted over the years but there was enough left to hold the discs in place, sort of. The details were remarkably clear and easy to read. Armin Stumph and Konrad Knutt, had both died in the same place as the French. There was signs of damage to these skeletons though, head injuries and broken bones, ribs and fingers snapped cleanly. Carrie had seen these types of injuries in other combatants. These men had died violent deaths, fighting for their lives. They had ultimately lost the battle to survive and had died fighting. Both had belonged to the same German regiment: the 74th (1st Hannover) infantry regiment. It was all there on the tags, as clear as if they had been stamped yesterday.

When Robert arrived, he looked inside the skeletons and found remains of the weapons that had killed them: in one, Konrad Knutt, there was a 10cm piece of bayonet tip, snapped off in hand-to-hand combat; there was a wound correlation in the ribs where the bayonet had been driven with enough force to snap it.

Skulls had massive crush injuries where they had been bludgeoned with clubs or rifle butts, all the signs of hand-to-hand combat, ferocious fighting desperate and vicious. These men had been involved in a terrifying fight to the death. There were no prisoners to be taken in this fight, and the fact that the French soldiers' remains were virtually unmarked would suggest that they had overwhelmed the German bunker with grenades, before sending in some men to clean up and make sure there were no survivors. It must have been carnage, and Robert found he had tears in his eyes. All these years later and with all the experience he had, it still upset him greatly when he used his considerable skills and imagination to piece together a jigsaw puzzle like this.

Clearly Carrie had taken the samples for DNA but they wouldn't be needed really, not for any of the uniformed remains. Each had been identified and families could and would be found in time for the reburials. Robert wrote his notes and conclusions to be sent to both British and German governments and his head of department. He did have an odd feeling that something didn't quite add up though; he couldn't quite put his finger on it.

CHAPTER 7

London, 1924

Julian Rosewood was getting too old for the city life, what he really craved was a quiet life in the country but today wasn't going to allow for any day dreaming. Major General Rosewood had a meeting with his boss Sir Hugh Sinclair.

Sir Hugh was director of MI6, and the meeting today was being held in a meeting room in Whitehall Court, an unusual occurrence, because politicians rarely came to the offices of MI6. The whole meeting was unusual, one that had Rosewood feeling uneasy.

The Secretary of State for foreign affairs, Lord Curzon, chaired the meeting. Also gathered around the table, looking very solemn sat: Lord Derby, Secretary of State for War; Mr. Leo Amery, First Lord of the Admiralty; Rosewood; and finally, Sir Hugh.

There was only one subject on the agenda today, the rise and rise further of Adolf Hitler and his Nazi party. There was mixed emotions about the whole affair, some thought Hitler was a calming influence to counter balance the Bolsheviks who were, after all, a troublesome lot plying their poison throughout Europe.

Others thought that Fascism was maybe even worse, and that the Nazi party were a growing problem for the future and maybe should be nipped in the bud.

Lord Curzon lit a large cigar, and blew a long plume of blue smoke towards the ceiling, he took a drink from a heavy whisky glass and said: "The world's gone mad, the problem is lack of breeding in the working classes. We fought the damned war only a few years ago. The Germans are moving, gentlemen they are a nation who sees a recovery and have an axe to grind. The damned Americans and French hit them too hard at Versailles, we said it then and I'll say it again, you mark my words, the German people are going to rise like a phoenix. It'll end in war again, mark my words." He took another drink and sat back in his leather chair.

"What do you say, Derby? This is your area and department."

Lord Derby sat and looked at the gathered forum, he was serious faced and had a weight on his shoulders that almost felt physical. He leaned forward and picked up his pen, rolling it around in his fingers.

"Gentlemen, let me make this abundantly clear to everyone, nobody wants another war. It would be the end of us. We can neither afford it financially nor do we have the manpower, or indeed the heart to fight another conflict. However, it is clear to me that there is trouble brewing in Germany, this fellow Adolf Hitler concerns me greatly. We have to face facts gentlemen, we got it wrong after the last show. The bally French and our so called new allies the Americans have pushed their noses into Germany's business more than they should ever have been allowed too, but that's by the by and we have to live with the consequences of that mistake. Lloyd George should have been firmer with them but we can't undo what has been done."

He stopped and took a sip from his glass.

"However, I think there might be an answer, at least in part. We have to cut the head off the serpent, and let us be in no doubt we are looking at a nest of serpents in the Nazi party with this upstart Hitler being the main one. If we take his head, I believe we might well avert another great catastrophe, as I said we can't afford another war, not yet."

The men sat contemplating, each with his own agenda and each with his own plan for the future.

Leo Amery cleared his throat. As First Lord of the Admiralty he carried a lot of responsibility; the Royal Navy still ensured that Britain was master of her own destiny.

"I see it as a simple solution. We either get Herr Hitler on board and he tows the party line, or we remove him completely and put someone we can work with in his place. Rosewood, what have you got in the way of *assets* that can assist us?"

Julian Rosewood didn't like being ambushed, and as he sat there amongst the cigar smoke he definitely felt ambushed.

"Well sir, we do have men capable of removing Herr Hitler. It would depend on a number of things."

"Depend on a number of what things?" said Lord Curzon.

Rosewood moved uneasily in his leather chair.

"Is it an official removal, sir?" he said, "or is this something you might like to keep close to one's chest?"

"Ah I see," said Amery, "I understand what you're saying. It might be better for everyone if we kept this quiet and amongst ourselves."

Rosewood was dreading what the next words were likely to be; he knew that the darker secrets behind the word *removal* actually meant assassination. It wasn't something that he approved of.

"Put a plan together Rosewood, and we will all meet again in a month or so." Said Lord Curzon. "In the meantime I will see if we can't pull this blighter in by the horns a bit, might save us popping him off, eh?"

CHAPTER 8

More Than There Should Be, 1994

Robert Deville picked up the phone; something very obvious had occurred to him in the middle of the night. He dialled the number and waited for the ring to be answered. Carrie jumped when the phone rang, she was quite happy down here in the lab, but once she was into her work it was easy for her to become totally engrossed. It was 9am in the morning; she had been at work for two hours already. Time meant very little to her and she enjoyed being here as much as anywhere in the world. Work was her world.

The shrill ringing startled her back into the present. She picked up the receiver.

"Hello, Path Lab, Carrie here, can I help?"

He wished she wouldn't do that, it was so, well, English.

"Carrie it's me, Robert, can you do me a favour please? I know you might think I'm going bonkers, but how many remains do you have in the lab?"

"Hi Robert of course, we have sixteen in total, why?"

"Sixteen?" he asked, "Are you sure?"

Carrie pulled a funny face, like there was a bad smell, "Er, yes sixteen".

31

Robert could hear her pulling her face. It made him smile.

"You're sure there are sixteen, that's the point. Why are you so sure there are sixteen?"

"It's the skulls Rob, it's a bit of a giveaway", she giggled. There were indeed sixteen skulls. She had spent the best part of three days photographing them, measuring them, cleaning them and generally getting very involved with a group of men who had, in all fairness, been dead for nearly a hundred years.

"That's one too many." There was a hardness in his voice, Carrie knew instantly there was something wrong.

"Rob, there are sixteen. I've been here for days working on them. There are ten sets of British bones from the collapsed graves, and then there are four French soldiers who we have names for and have been identified plus two German skeletons, also identified. All those in uniform had ID tags. I know there are sixteen for a fact. What do you mean there's one too many? How can that be?"

Robert held his breath; he looked at his notes in front of him sat on the coffee table. There it was as clear as daylight, nine headstones from the cemetery, seven with names and two marked 'known unto God' these were British burials, and if nothing else the British were meticulous with the details of their war dead.

"Carrie, we have ten British skeletons, yes? Then four French in uniform and two Germans also in uniform, is that correct?"

Carrie felt stupid, she had checked the bones a hundred times, she knew how many there were. She could even tell how many individual bones there were as she had examined each one at least three times. Still, she counted them again.

"Robert, we have sixteen sets of bones in the lab, I can confirm this because I've just counted them. I don't understand, what are you saying?"

"We only have nine headstones Carrie, there is no record of a double burial. I will check with Andrew as soon as I finish on the phone, but there is no mention of a double, we have one body too many. It must be an admin error."

He said his goodbyes and hung up the phone. Carrie felt a tingle of doubt; a shroud of worry overwhelmed her. She loved a good mystery but this felt very strange, even a bit weird. She went to count the skulls; she had some more work to do, more tests on the bones.

One test would disclose an age or a near enough age at time of the death, these tests were all part of a routine, pointless really. They were all young men; the shape of the pelvis proved each body was male, but apart from that and without some further testing, there wasn't much else to be learned.

Robert rang Andrew Phillips, it was still early and if he was lucky Phillips would still be in his office.

It was normal for Andrew Phillips to go out and visit the ground works out in the field. It was part of his routine and he felt it kept him grounded. Just as he shut the door to his office his desk phone rang, *damn*, he thought, he knew he would have to answer it; it would bother him if he didn't.

"Hello, Andrew Phillips"

Robert hoped he had this right. "Hi, Andrew, it's Robert Deville. I think we might have a slight problem."

CHAPTER 9
Berlin, 1924

Things in Germany were becoming worryingly hostile towards the Jewish contingent. Abraham Meir was very much aware that a move abroad was inevitable, but where should he move? Vienna was the obvious choice, he had friends there and he would easily be able to get work at the highly respected clinic. Indeed he had already been asked and had delayed his answer. Meir was highly thought of in his field and any hospital would be proud to have him on their faculty.

Would he take his parents, indeed would they want to leave? He asked himself if he was being a little paranoid, but it was obvious there were changes happening all around. The *Frontbann* were everywhere, intimidating if not openly bullying people. These so called patriots were nothing more than political thugs and up until recently had been known as the *Sturmabteilung* but had been made to change their name. Still they were thugs and no name change could alter that. He would have another talk to his parents at dinner, he was sure it was time to leave Berlin and perhaps even Germany. He wasn't being paranoid, he knew things were changing and it wasn't for the best. He would go to Vienna. He would write to them tomorrow and accept their offer. His parents would surely want to stay here but he would try and convince them tonight.

He put on his hat, scarf and overcoat; there was a chill in the air this evening. He said goodnight to his assistant and stepped out onto the stone steps that led down to the street. There was so many things going on in his mind he didn't even see the two men stood in the shadows opposite, and in all honesty he shouldn't have seen them at all as they were professionals. Like the police but not the police, these were much worse, these were Nazi thugs, Jew haters every one, and they knew Abraham Meir was a Jew.

They followed him down the street, they needn't have bothered because they knew exactly where he was going, he didn't deviate from the same route he took nearly every day. It didn't take long to catch him up, he didn't hear them, and he never saw them either because with a minimum of fuss the two men threw a cloth bag over his head and crashed a hard rubber cosh across the base of his skull. There was no sensation of pain, it just all went black and he collapsed in the street, unconscious.

CHAPTER 10
Who is He? 1994

Phillips knew instantly there was a problem; Robert Deville wasn't a morning person. It took at least two espressos and five *Gauloises* before Deville's day really got going. The smell of the cigarette smoke was distinctive and not altogether unpleasant even to Andrew who had never smoked in his life. The smell reminded him of his grandfather who smoked all his life and ultimately died because of it; the memory was a very distant one because Eric had died when Andrew was only two and he certainly couldn't remember what he looked like, but he did have a familiar fond memory when he smelled cigarette smoke.

Now sat in Phillips office, Robert looked for an ashtray. Andrew pushed a clean one over the coffee table. Both men sat in leather Chesterfield chairs with a coffee table made from an old knurled oak base with a beautiful chestnut table top sat immaculately square on top.

"Now tell me again, why do you think there are more skeletons than there should be?" Andrew had a slight look of amusement on his face but it was a deadly serious question, there would be no attempt at French today.

37

"I know, I know, you think I'm mad, but hear me out Andrew, there must be a simple explanation. There are nine headstones, and as far as I am aware all the burials were single. How do you say, singletons? Is that right?" his question was met with a nod.

"We also know that we have four French and two German soldiers, each has identification confirmed by tags. Now I know that makes a total of fifteen."

Andrew Phillips looked at the files he had in front of him, inside the folders were all the reports of the site with photos of the bunker and everything inside it.

"Yes, that's exactly as it should be isn't it?"

This time it was Deville's turn to nod.

"We have sixteen skeletons, Andrew."

"What! Sixteen are you sure? Sorry, of course you're sure, but how, why didn't we notice?"

"We weren't looking we were recovering bodies, human remains and we messed up. I don't know how I missed it, it only occurred to me when I was reading my forensic reports for the coroner. Let me assure you we do have sixteen and the only possible explanation I can think of is that there has been an administrative error in the past, and one of the graves is a double. It has to be in with the bones, because the other remains are all uniformed and have identification tags in place. You saw the bunker first hand, it was dry inside."

Andrew Phillips just sat, stunned. In all his time in post he had never had an anomaly like this, he had interesting cases, even mysteries, but never anything like this. He wasn't even sure if it was a problem. Sure, the fact that it had slipped everyone's attention, that there was one body too many was a problem but only an admin error, surely. So why did he feel like someone had kicked him in the testicles.

Phillips phoned his colleagues at the Commonwealth War Graves Commission head office back in Maidstone, Kent. The original records for all interments were kept here dating back to the 1920s. After several checks everyone was positive all the graves involved were indeed single grave plots, indeed there were no multiple interments in that graveyard. There was nothing else he could do, the whole event would remain a mystery, clearly there had been a mistake, or so it seemed.

Events over the next two days would rock his world.

★

Back in Peronne, Carrie collected the mail from the post room, there was several letters for Robert and lab reports for various tests that had been sent over the past few weeks. One letter was slightly bulkier than the others and she knew this one held the results of the DNA tests she had taken from the men downstairs. All the remains had been placed in purpose made cardboard coffins, tagged and labelled ready for burial at a date yet to be decided but no one was in a rush, the cemetery had been repaired and the bunker sealed. Once the *Grande Guerre* archaeologists had finished all their investigations on the plot a date would be set for the funerals of the British soldiers. The French soldiers would be released to the French authorities, as would be the case for the German soldiers who were to be buried in the local German cemetery.

She sat at her desk with a coffee and set about her filing such as it was, she ripped open the envelope and tipped out the sixteen reports. As expected the two German results had *hits* as did the French four. None of these results really mattered as families had already been informed in both countries relaying the information that each family's long lost relative had indeed been found. These families would all be invited to the future interments. She looked at the small pile of reports for the British results, she shook her head in frustration that despite the great quality of DNA she had managed to collect, none of the results would find a match. The families of the named soldiers would be invited to submit samples for comparison and at least she would have some satisfaction. It was the last group that was the most difficult to reconcile her feelings with, the unknown soldiers, this had been their chance for recognition and identification, who knows she thought, in time you might yet be found.

The last sheet was very interesting. It had a German stamp in the top right hand corner indicating that a hit had been found, that didn't really make any sense, but basically it meant that a match had been found on the German database.

It was only when she read the name that a shudder

went down her spine, she felt chilled to the core but knew it was a complete coincidence that the name on the sheet stood out like a sore thumb, it had to be.

The name on the file was Adolf Hitler.

CHAPTER 11
Time to Leave, 1924

When Meir awoke he rolled onto his side and the pain made him instantly vomit. He could feel the broken ribs move within his chest and the pain was excruciating. His head throbbed but there was no blood, not even from his broken nose. Most of the damage was hidden under his clothes he had received a serious beating, and through his swollen and ever blackening eyes he tried to get his bearings. He recognised that he was in fact in his own front room and that made him feel more terrified than anything else because he hadn't got here under his own steam. They had brought him here which meant they knew where he lived. He thought he was alone, terrified, hurting beyond his own imagination but through blurred eyes he could see he wasn't alone. He smelled the sweet pungent tobacco of a cigar and a sinister cold voice spoke to him.

"You're awake then Jew, we didn't kill you?"

Meir couldn't believe he was hearing this, yes he was fully aware of the strong anti-Semitism that was omnipresent in Berlin, but he had never seen it face to face.

"What, who are you and why have you done this? I have never done you any harm, I don't even know you, why, why would you beat me, what purpose does it serve?"

"It's a message, call it an introduction, a taste of things to come. All you Jews are going to be getting a message sooner or later." The voice had no emotion, it was an educated voice but Meir couldn't see who it belonged too. There was a glow from the end of the cigar and a plume of smoke curled into the dim light.

"We will leave you now, give you some time to consider your future. Goodbye Abraham Meir. Make sure we don't ever meet again, it would end badly for you if we ever did. Oh by the way, your parents have already gone, you won't be seeing them again either."

With that the stranger left: just stood up and closed the door behind him, almost politely. It added even more to the feeling of darkness and dread that Meir felt.

He rang his parents but there was no reply, that in itself was very odd and he knew deep down that the stranger had spoken the truth. He would never see them again.

It took three days for the swelling in his face to subside but his ribs were very painful, they went well with his heart. He had tried to find his parents but to no avail, the house was empty and there was no sign of them. He had questioned the neighbours but no one had seen anything or indeed anyone at the house. There was no sign of a struggle. He knew they had been taken and given what had happened to him, he didn't know what to do. The police seemed the obvious choice but bearing in mind the state of Berlin, he didn't think they would offer much in the way of assistance. No one wanted to rock the boat; things were just starting to get back on an even keel after the horrendous shocks of hyperinflation throughout Germany. No one had anything anymore, the rich survived, as they always seemed to but with huge losses to their personal wealth. The middle classes lost everything, the poor had nothing to lose so lost less than anyone but nothing really was nothing, they were starving to death for the price of a loaf.

The Meirs had money deposited in banks in Switzerland and it had remained safe over the past two years. He would need this money if he were to build a new life for himself. Abraham quickly found the deposit books. His mind had been made up for him. He had already spoken to the clinic in Vienna and he would be leaving Berlin within the next few days.

He had collected his surgical instruments from his office and explained to his superiors at the hospital that he was leaving with immediate effect. There was an emotional goodbye to the staff he worked with as he cleared his office and desk of all personal possessions and books including the specimens of medical interest. Amongst these was the artefact collected from the future chancellor of Germany the great Jew hater, Hitler. If only he had known what the future held, if only.

CHAPTER 12
Peronne, 1994

Carrie had called Robert as soon as she put down the results. Robert was instantly dismissive and that had stung Carrie. In truth Robert didn't mean to sound so tetchy and although his English was superb, sometimes he lacked the finesse. It made Carrie smile that she had used a French word to describe the lack of subtly, there she had done it again. She shook her head and thought it would be something to discuss later at the meeting that had hurriedly been made with Andrew Phillips, Magnus Roche, herself and Robert. She was looking forward to the meeting, Magnus was her latest crush and with luck he might ask her out for dinner after the meeting. She felt herself blush.

At the meeting there was an air of calm alarm, there was general concern about the whole situation, but the Hitler revelation was the main talking point. "We don't have any idea if this is *the* Adolf Hitler, does anyone know if it was a common name at the time?" Andrew Phillips was calm but did seem to be a bit confused.

Magnus Roche said, "There were eight in the whole German army, but remember it wasn't really just a German army, there were Austrians, Bavarians and Prussians as well, but there are records for eight including the one we know as the *Führer* but how could it possibly be him?"

Carrie spoke next, her voice seemed to quiver ever so slightly, as if she realised the importance of what she was about to share but not quite sure of why it mattered quite so much.

"We have labelled all the remains in accordance with department protocols, the British bodies were numbered 01 to 10. The French remains have been labelled 11 through to 14, and the German remains 15 and 16. Obviously we have names for all the German and French remains as identified by individual ID tags found on the bodies. We confirmed the identity of the remains labelled as number 08 with the Interpol DNA database, as indeed we did with all the other specimens. However, only number 08 came back with a marker and flagged as *Of International Importance.* This individual has been identified as one Adolf Hitler. Interpol has informed the German embassy of its findings and the Ambassador for the German embassy has been in contact with this department to offer assistance with any ongoing investigations we might carry out. They have asked that we keep them in the loop with any information we establish. They have also asked that we don't release any information to the press, but Andrew will deal with any correspondence with any outside agencies from here on in. It's above my pay scale."

She giggled and looked over her glasses at the men

sat around the table, her girlish looks disarmed all the men sat there. She was glad about this, as the next part of her report would once again shake their world.

"I can confirm that the DNA comparison was 100% match with a sample taken from a tooth removed from Herr Hitler in the early 1920s. This specimen has been held in *Allgemeines Krankenhaus der Stadt Wien* which is the university medical centre of the city of Vienna. A Doctor Abraham Meir left the artefact in the dental and maxillofacial departmental museum in the late 1920s or early 1930 when he was working at the hospital as a dental surgeon. We have a written confirmation from Doctor Meir of authenticity to accompany it. Gentlemen there is no doubt that the man lying downstairs in the lab is the same Adolf Hitler we all know from history."

"You're shitting me, right?" said Magnus "is that for real? How the hell did his body end up in France, and in a commonwealth war grave? I thought he was supposed to have shot himself in the head in a bunker in Berlin in 1945, when the Russians were about to capture him."

"Hang on, hang on!" Robert found he was shouting, the noise in the room seemed very loud, "what did you just say Magnus, just then, say it again."

"You're shitting me," said Magnus.

"No you fool, after that about shooting himself in the head." Richard found he was smiling and Carrie burst out laughing.

"Yeah, didn't he shoot himself in the head?" Magnus said again.

Now Andrew clicked what Robert was trying to get at.

"If he had shot himself in the head, there would be a bullet wound in his skull, either at the temple or through his mouth." With each statement Robert made his fingers in the shape of a pistol and pointed it at the area of his own head.

"There are no gunshot wounds to any of the skulls, absolutely not. I did the post mortem examination and no one had received a head wound. In fact, I made a comment about how well the skulls were preserved. It is in my medical report, look here."

He picked up the file associated with body number 08, sure enough there it said:

The skull is intact and in remarkable condition. There are no obvious signs of trauma to the occipital, temporal or cranial bones. The facial bones are complete and there is no sign of damage or trauma. The mandible is intact but dislocated from the maxilla. Dentition; There is evidence of damage to the teeth and root system with signs of early bone damage associated with gum disease. There are, as you would expect in a man his age, (age estimated as between twenty and thirty-five years) several missing teeth that have been extracted pre mortem.

He closed the file and looked up at the others.

Andrew Phillips looked on, then broke the silence, "Right no one says anything outside this room, am I clear? This stays here for now. I'm sure you all realise the importance of this, its massive and at the moment there are more questions than I can even think of, so keep stum. Robert, I need you to look into this much further please, you need to liaise with your German counterparts to see if you can prove this either way. Find out about this chap Meir, see if it fits. This is a huge deal people, we need to keep very calm otherwise every lunatic, Nazi and fascist right wing nut case will be here trying to claim the fourth Reich has been born. It's simple really, either the DNA sample is wrong or everything we thought we knew about Adolf Hitler's demise is wrong."

He knew he needed to speak to someone further up the chain of command and not just within the Commonwealth War Graves Commission, but probably at governmental level as well. Without a shadow of a doubt this was the most important day of his life.

CHAPTER 13

Langwith, 1924

Jack Adams was invisible, from more than two feet away there was no sign he was there, but he was. Lying in a small rut in the ground he looked down the sights of his trusted rifle. It had come back from the war with him, as had the Zeiss telescopic sight. Over in a wood about 400 yards away high in a tree was his oldest friend. Jim Cunningham sat looking for Jack through a telescope, again a gift from the war. On it was the name of Albert Hagerman.

All three men had once been combatants in the war to end all wars, The Great War some called it but it had been anything but great to Jim. Gassed in a shell hole and medically discharged from the army with a basic pension his best days were behind him. Still he felt like he was one of the lucky ones, you didn't have to go far in Langwith to see the poor blighters who weren't so lucky. Men who had only one leg or one arm, some blind, some deaf, some in chairs but nearly all out of work. The pit had no place for invalided ex-soldiers, but even they tried to collect together enough money each week to pay the rent of former workers and maybe a copper or two to help put food on the table. Langwith was a village with a good heart and no man paid for coal, the pit saw to that, every single household in the area got free coal if they had a wounded soldier living there and charity was freely given to the local community. It was a good village.

Even now the rabbits and deer were being shot for food, not quite poached but shot before the poachers got the chance. Jack was down there somewhere but for the life of him Jim couldn't find him, he looked and searched but there was no sign. It was with a satisfied cough he thought he had taught him well. There was a thud as a bullet smacked into the tree trunk ten feet below him, Jim jumped and lost his balance as he fell from his hiding spot.

"Jesus, Jack, you scared the shit out of me! That was a bit game wasn't it, you nearly shot me you daft bugger." In all honesty Jim knew Jack was nowhere near shooting him, he was just miffed that he hadn't even seen Jack when he had taken his shot, there was no doubt, Jim was losing his touch. He missed things these days, things he hadn't ever missed before, little movements, shadows and silhouettes. Even with this brilliant scope he missed things. Still he had a job and he was good at it, working for Jack Adams was a pleasure and made all the better for apprentice turned sorcerer, Jack looked out for and after Jim and his family, as he did his own.

CHAPTER 14
The Invitation

The colonel was getting old. He had aged rapidly since Tim died and although rarely alone, loneliness was his constant companion. He felt blessed to have an extended family and Jack, Jim and the children visited often. Elizabeth and Albert, Jack's two were wonderful and a genuine pleasure to have around the house. Of course Mrs Millward spoiled them, and so she should. Their fathers had been heroes in the Great War as indeed had his only son, Tim. Poor Tim, he had given of his best they said at the service of remembrance. Indeed if it hadn't been for Jack Adams cutting Tim down from where he had hung on that fateful day that the colonel had found him, hanging in the barn, there wouldn't have been a church service. As it was Jack had sworn Tim was just found dead, a fall from his horse said Jack, and Jim backed him up as a witness. A last kindness given freely for a former warrior.

The Vicar didn't ask too many questions and the local police probably knew the truth but went along with Adams story. 'A tragic accident' it said in the paper. It allowed Tim to be buried in the family plot. Suicide was still a sin; how ridiculous, when men had butchered each other and were thought of as heroes that a poor troubled and greatly injured kind soul like Tim Alcot should be castigated for ending it all.

The house needed living in, especially now that the colonel tended to live in only a few rooms; the house was losing its soul. He had always thought it would be Tim's home with a wife and children to run around and slide down the banisters, ponies in the stables ready to hunt on frosty mornings. If it wasn't for Millward and his staff the house would have been sold after the war, it was too big for one man and he had no family to leave it to.

There was a knock at the door, it was Mrs Millward with the post. *Ah dear Mrs Millward* he thought, she had been with him for longer than he dare think: cook, housekeeper, lover and now carer, but never a wife. Not for her the haughty polloi, she liked what she did and God help anyone who tried to change her. He laughed out loud at his own private thought and waved her in.

"You have a letter colonel, and I have made some tea to go with the scones. Would you like it poured or left to brew?" She handed the letter over to him and pushed the tea service onto the table all set on a silver tray with a side plate and scone.

"Just leave it dear, unless you care to join me for a cup?" he fingered the letter. It had a London stamp.

As he opened the envelope with his trusted letter knife a card fell out onto the desk, it was from Major General Julian Rosewood. A name from the past but a welcome one for all that, it seemed to Gerald Alcot that his and Rosewood's paths had become entwined over the years. From the first meeting during the war to now, they had kept in touch. Rosewood had visited when Tim was laid to rest, but that was the last time they had communicated so it was a nice surprise that the letter contained an invitation for dinner at the General's club in Piccadilly. A room had been booked for him should he wish to stay over.

Colonel Alcot knew the Cavalry club of course, obviously he wasn't a member there having never been part of a mounted regiment. He was a Derbyshire and although he did ride in his position of Commanding Officer he was never a cavalryman.

Major General Rosewood, had been. He was a subaltern in the household division, the *Blues and Royals* and over his career had risen to the highest of high ranks. Seen as a solid officer he had been seconded to various commands and now, although retired, he was working on some intelligence job in London. That was as much as anyone knew and Colonel Alcot knew more than most.

He sat and lit a fine cigar; he was trying to cut back, cigars and brandy or rare single malt, the failings of most retired officers he chuckled. His mind was alive and he wondered what scheme Rosewood was hatching. Damn it, he would have to go just to satisfy his curiosity. He poured another cup of tea for himself and as he helped himself to the other half of his second scone he realised he quite missed all the intrigue and gossip from the clubs.

He flicked the card against his fingernails. He would need Jim to drive him, of course. Johnson his last driver had fallen in the last days of the war, desperate to do his bit, he had gone and fate ensured he never returned. So now Jim did the driving, and apart from a few noisy gear changes he was excellent at it. He really enjoyed it. The position suited him well because these days getting around the woods and fields was becoming ever harder, and in truth Jack Adams was far better off without Jim getting under his feet.

CHAPTER 15

Dinner for Two

The drive to London was full of chat and laughter, Jim was very much on form, and even his gear changes were smooth, unlike the roads. The colonel had bought a new Rolls Royce Silver Ghost in 1922, it was a beautiful machine and very easy to drive. It made for a smooth and comfortable journey.

Gerald Alcot had very little time for pomposity and had bought the car primarily for Tim, but Tim never got to use it. Today was the first time he had gone on a long trip in it, if he had need to travel long distances he tended to use the railway.

He needed a break and a weekend in London would suit him. Jim was anxious about being away from Edith, but the sense of adventure soon overcame any anxiety and now they were on the way he felt as good as he had for as long as he could remember. He would have felt even better if he had known that Edith had travelled down on the train and would be waiting for him in his hotel. A little surprise organised by Mrs Millward and the colonel. It would coincide nicely with the anniversary of Jim's return from the war. It was eight years to the day that Jim came home, wounded and crippled with damaged lungs, but alive. Colonel Alcot had never forgotten, and felt he had a debt to pay because Jim Cunningham was one of his men. Quite a few of his men never came home and he could never repay their debt, but he did look after their families. Money was no problem he had plenty and now there was no one left in his family to inherit it, it could be used in other ways.

When the car stopped, a footman stepped out from the doorway and attended to his door. He wore formal wear with a medal ribbon sewn neatly above the left breast pocket. Colonel Alcott appraised him with the eye of an old soldier and nodded approvingly. The doorman returned the colonel's nod with a slight bow and the colonel slipped a handsome tip into his hand. These old soldiers must be looked after at all costs, damn it the *country* owed them a debt and he for one would help repay it.

The rotating door allowed him easy access to a large hallway with a huge staircase leading up to various offices and accommodation on the floors above. To the left there was a reception desk, manned by another old soldier who, the colonel could tell, had held a position of authority in his military past.

"Good evening, the name's Alcot, I'm expected"

"Good evening Colonel Alcot, sir, the General is waiting in the lounge. I'll have your things transferred to your room." At that there was yet another chap, dressed immaculately to show him through to the waiting General Rosewood who sat quietly contemplating the evening behind a pair of large mahogany doors in the lounge.

"Gerald, good to see you." General Julian Rosewood stood to greet his guest. There was an almost choreographed routine that both men totally understood and adopted instantly, the colonel referred to it as 'breeding'.

"Good trip, old man? Brandy to start the evening before we dine?" 'Old man' was said as a term of endearment and said warmly and certainly received without any problem.

Within seconds both men were seated in sumptuously comfortable leather Chesterfields. All the leather furniture was a warm ox blood red and there was a fug of fine cigar smoke floating just below the ceiling. The smell of leather and cigar smoke made for a heady atmosphere, very masculine and definitely missing the delicate touch of any femininity. This was a man's world, and each man in here had seen things no woman should ever be allowed to see, out there, on the battlefields of history.

The two men eyed each other as would two predators ready to fight. There was no ill feeling or malice, the men liked each other, but once a warrior always a warrior, and both men knew there was an ulterior motive for dinner. There ensued a mental game of chess, the conversation was easy and in time the general would reveal his intentions. The colonel just had to wait and be patient. He likened it to a good trout, just waiting for the fly.

CHAPTER 16
Germany, 1924

Abraham Meir knew his parents were dead, he didn't need any proof, he just knew. They were old and in a very sweet way, naïve. This world was just too evil for their sweet souls and the fear of the intimidation he had experienced would have killed them.

He sat in the train carriage opposite a young lady who sat quietly and smoked a cigarette held in a long holder whilst she looked out of the window. She was delicate and had beautiful smooth skin on her unblemished face. Her lips were perfect with maybe just a touch too much lipstick but it highlighted her stunning mouth shape. Her eyes were blue as azure and crystal clear. Long lashes framed the windows to her soul. Her hair was a light brown and tumbled onto her fox fur that lay over her gorgeous slender shoulders. Truly, she presented as a vision. However, as he looked at her he noticed something else, something deeper, she was crying.

Abraham coughed, he felt uncomfortable as if he was intruding in a private moment. He went to stand as if to leave, and as he moved she looked directly into his eyes and a tear ran down her cheek.

"I'm sorry, I didn't mean to intrude," he said.

"No please, stay, it is I who should be sorry, please will you sit, don't leave," she said. "My name is Eliana, and today has been a dreadful, terrible day. You must think me very forward, I do apologise, please forgive me", at this she started to cry again.

Abraham went into his pocket and retrieved a handkerchief, he passed it over and just for a fleeting second their hands touched and he was smitten. "Meir, Abraham Meir, please, is there anything I can do? Can I get you a drink of something?" He rang the service bell, *he* needed a drink. His heart was palpating, and as much as he wanted to be alone with his private grief he felt compelled to stay here with this beautiful lady.

She offered him back his handkerchief but he shook his head with all the sentiment and sincerity he could manage.

"Please keep it, I have plenty in my luggage. Please tell me why you are so upset?" There was a knock at the door and a smart waiter stood outside and waited.

"Can I get you something to drink? It might help calm you, and I'm having a cognac, please allow me to get you one also." With that and not waiting for an answer he ordered two large cognacs, and with a click of his heels the waiter left to collect his order.

"Now, please, why are you so upset, although it seems like a day for ill tidings, I also have experienced a truly dreadful day. Please allow me to be your counsel, it will help me in my hour of need."

She looked at him and a hint of a smile crept along her immaculate lips. "I am Eliana Bomberg, Herr Meir, and I am very grateful to you for your kindness, I can assure you I am better now and I must apologise for my short outburst. I am a singer in the theatre, not famous but competent and independent. I learned today that my parents have been moved, against their will, out of Berlin. You see I am Jewish and my services are no longer required at my place of employment. I have been advised to leave Berlin. So as you can see it has been quite a traumatic day. Would you care to share with me why you feel your day has been dreadful?"

Meir was stunned, surely this was a cruel jest, or was his mind playing tricks with him. What were the chances of meeting someone on a train bound for another country that shared such a close experience as he? He sat down as the door slid open and drinks arrived, he ordered two more and sat staring in disbelief.

"Mrs Bomberg"

"Miss, I am not married, and please call me Eliana."

"Eliana, I almost dare not tell you what has happened to me, we share almost the exact same experience. Only this week, I have been forced to leave my position at the hospital. I have also been told that I must leave Berlin immediately and my parents have gone missing. Their home is empty and no one knows where they have gone. I was assaulted in the street and woke up in my rooms. A very sinister man made it abundantly clear that if I didn't leave, grievous harm would befall me, and like you I share the Jewish faith. Where are you going? I have been offered a position at the clinic in Vienna, but this changes things considerably."

"I too am going to Vienna, I have friends there who will accommodate me until I can arrange to take a passage to England, I have family there and they will be worried if I don't travel there."

The realisation that his tragic loss might be shared by others hadn't occurred to him, indeed why should it? It was a long journey to Vienna, the train would stop overnight in Prague and commence again in the morning. He had booked a night carriage but didn't know if Eliana had, so in another gentleman's gesture he offered her his ticket. She laughed and he was surprised how joyous it made him feel.

"Herr Meir, this is the sleeping compartment, I think one of us is in the wrong carriage, it must be fate but I would be eternally grateful if you would stay and talk to me for a while."

"Abraham, my name is Abraham and it would be my honour to accompany you, what do you think is happening in Berlin? Why are we being driven out?"

The night that followed was excruciating in both a joyous and yet painful way. Meir knew that Eliana was vulnerable and yet she seemed so assured it just added to the attraction. They sat and talked all night, about their lives and the very fabric that made them who they were. It seemed that whilst they talked all the pain and the problems they had so recently experienced were indeed left back in Berlin.

Not known as a spontaneous man in any way, shape or form Abraham Meir had never made a conscious decision without considered thought in his life. His work was as precise as any surgeon and his results were exemplary, but tonight he really felt that he might have fallen in love.

Neither had a permanent place to stay in Vienna and with an unconsidered wave of his hand he suggested they stay at the Imperial hotel. It was where he was planning to stay, he had a room booked and it wouldn't be any trouble to book another room, maybe just for a few days until they managed to sort things out on a more permanent basis. The future was uncertain, but he felt sure that any future he had he wanted Eliana to be a part of it.

CHAPTER 17
Gun For Hire, London, 1924

Dinner was as expected, first class. Colonel Alcot swore he had never tasted beef so tender; the chef was French apparently, came back to Blighty for surgery after being wounded in the war and never went back. The wine was equally as good, a short, squat bottle of *1914 Prince de Gascogne Rarissime*. It was one of a couple of cases the general had stored in the cellar of the Cavalry club, but it was really getting to the point where he needed to ask what this was all about.

He was just about to speak when Rosewood said: "Well Gerald, I have no doubt you are wondering what I have dragged you all the way down to London for, you have been remarkably patient and I congratulate you. You really must take more time playing Bridge, you have the composure of a card player I have to say. Right then, onto the main subject, do you still have Jack Adams working for you? I know you have, but let me run this past you before you answer. The fact is Gerald, I need Adams to do a job for me. It's a bit awkward telling you like this, but how would you feel about letting me have him for a few weeks?"

Alcot just sat and looked, there was more to come, and he knew it.

"Work for you? In what way would you employ a game keeper and estate manager here in the city?"

Rosewood knew he would have to tell Alcot the truth, there was no point in trying to hide anything from him, and after all it was his estate manager he wanted.

"I need someone with Jack's particular skills with a rifle, Gerald, for a job that is both secret and internationally sensitive. Your man Adams was the top of my list, he fits the bill perfectly. Did he keep in touch with the German, do you know?"

Suddenly dinner didn't taste quite so good, and the wine had become slightly sour.

CHAPTER 18

A Long Drive Home

Sat in the back of the car, Colonel Alcot felt totally alone, bereft and saddened; it was going to be a long drive home.

In the front sat Jim, proud as punch and sat next to him was his wonderful wife, Edith. Looking on from the back seat Gerald Alcot's heart was bleeding, the news he had to take home was as heavy as the weight he now felt on his ageing shoulders. He smiled at the scene before him; this was the happiness he had missed with his long since departed wife. Jim whistled like a milkman and the chatter was a welcome distraction from the memory of dinner and the subsequent meeting with Sir Hugh Sinclair. It had been a long time since Alcot had felt under any pressure from a senior officer and it rankled him that the familiar pangs of resentment still knotted his stomach. He had never taken orders easily and although it had been a 'casual chat' it felt like an order.

He had to relay a message to Jack Adams that his country once again required his particular skill. There was a cloud developing over Europe and it was a dark cloud that the government were keen to make sure didn't become a storm. Alcot thought *that particular phrase sounded very much like Churchill*, and he didn't think much of Winston after the cock-up in the Dardanelles.

In time the car needed to refuel, it seemed like a good time for a cup of tea and some refreshments at a tearoom. It would give the colonel time to talk to Jim privately. Over time Jim and Jack had become as brothers, the relationship had evolved from a friendship to a father and son, and then evolved further to equals and now they were as close as brothers as any men were.

As Jim looked at the engine and Edith went to freshen up Colonel Alcot took his opportunity to have a talk.

"Jim, can I have a word? I need your advice on something."

Jim nearly banged his head on the thick steel bonnet raised in the air as he stood so quickly. Had the colonel just asked for his advice?

"Certainly Colonel, but what can I help you with?"

"It's about Jack. Jim, I need to ask you something about Jack." He knew this was going to be delicate but hadn't appreciated how difficult it was until he had started, and he hesitated with his words.

"The meeting I had with General Rosewood turned out to be more of a sort of interview rather than a social meeting, Jim. I was wheeled in front of Sir Hugh Sinclair, he's the head of some department in the ministry but that isn't the important bit. The important bit is they want Jack to do some work for them. They want me to ask, or rather tell him he should meet them. They think

67

there might be problems in Germany again, and I have to say I tend to agree with them, but I wanted to ask you how would you say it to Jack? God knows he's like family Jim, to me I mean, and I know he is as a brother to you. It's all rather a mess and I'm in a bit of a pickle."

Jim put down the oily cloth and wiped his hands on a clean one.

"What do they want him to do about it, sir? He was never much of a soldier and God above he did his bit. Do they want him to go to Germany and punch this Hitler chap on the nose?"

Colonel Alcot smiled. He really did admire the man stood in front of him.

"Punch him on the nose; not quite Jim, they want him to shoot him."

The trip was quiet from there on, each man was lost in his own thoughts. Edith thought there might have been cross words between the two of the men so didn't say another word for three hours. It stayed very quiet in the car.

CHAPTER 19

Choices, Langwith, 1924

The day after the trip to London the colonel went for a ride on his horse. He couldn't ride to hounds anymore, it was just too arduous but he did like to ride out over the countryside at least once a week. Often he would see Jack out working on some pen or hedge that needed repair but today he hoped he wouldn't see him. He had a meeting to arrange and wasn't looking forward to it, not one bit.

In time he made his way along the old river bank, mindful not to go too close to the water's edge, he didn't want to pull a shoe and the mud here could be as bad as anywhere he had seen. Along the way he could see the smoke from the house he had gifted to Jack after the war, to share with his wife, Alice and now their two children, Elizabeth and Albert. To the colonel they were the perfect family and he knew he was going to be a cad, even if the final decision was Jack's. The very fact that Alcot had to be the bearer of such unwelcome news left him feeling thoroughly dreadful. He ducked under a branch and kicked his horse into a canter.

Jack was working on a dry stone wall when he saw

the colonel riding towards him; he dried his face on the kerchief round his neck and waved. He walked towards the steadying horse and as the colonel broke into a walk he patted the horse on his sweating neck. Jack dipped his kerchief into a water bucket and as he held the horse's bridle he wiped the frothy bit clean. The horse, one of the colonel's favourite chargers was a fine hunter with powerful hindquarters and was really far too much horse for an ageing rider, nudged Jack with his head and Jack fetched him a clear mint he had in his pocket. The colonel shook his head as the animal slavered and crunched on the sweet, he had told Jack before about giving his mount mints but Jack seemed to ignore him; he couldn't be cross with Adams.

"Morning Jack, the wall looks good, have you got much more to do? It's just I need a word and wondered if you could meet me at the house this afternoon?"

Jack looked at the colonel, he was looking older despite being as sharp as a blade, it was a warm day despite it being only late morning, and Jack wondered if the *old man* was doing too much.

"Of course colonel, what time do you want me there? I will have this done in no time. It's only a few toppers then it's done for now. I'll go and clean up before but I can easily be there for just after lunch if that's OK?"

"Come and have lunch with me Jack, I'm sure Alice won't mind. It's man's work I need to talk to you about. I'll have Mrs Millward make some lunch for the two of us. See you at 13:00 hours." Jack smiled at the use of the military time, some things never changed did they?

Jack arrived at the house just before 1pm. He had washed and cleaned his clothes. As estate manager he didn't really have to do much manual labour but liked to keep his hand in and help the lads around the place.

He had a clean neckerchief tied neatly around his neck and Alice had sponged his trousers clean of dust and dirt, a clean shirt had finished him off and he looked as smart as ever.

He was met at the door by the colonel who was full of *bon ami,* and shown into the study for a quick pre-lunch drink. *There would be no more work for the day* thought Jack, the colonel was renowned for his over generous servings when it came to drinks.

"How was your trip to London, sir? Jim said he had a great time in the city." Jack accepted his half full tumbler.

"It went very well, Jack, in fact it's about the weekend I wanted to have a talk to you about. To be honest it was more about you than me, you were what the meeting was about. General Rosewood introduced me to a very important person, and I'll tell you straight Jack I felt a tad trapped by the confounded man. Take a seat and let me tell you what was said."

He then proceeded to tell Jack as much as he dare, he didn't tell all but didn't miss any of the major points.

"So you see Jack, they want to meet you, have a word so to speak, what do you think, will you meet them? Think carefully Jack because there's a bit of an incentive. I'm not supposed to tell you this in case it clouds your mind and confuses the situation, but damn it man you need to know if you accept this little job they have planned for you, you will receive a new army pension, only this time it will be that of a major. You'll never want for money again, Jack"

Jack sipped the strong malt whisky; it was far too early to be drinking hard liquor, it just underlined that the colonel thought this meeting so very important.

"You need to have a chat with Alice but I'm not sure I would tell her all the details Jack, she would only worry. But whatever your decision you need to know that I will look after her and the family, but then you already knew that didn't you?"

Jack knew this was coming, he had been speaking to Jim and in his pocket he held a note, it was a letter from Albert and if he was being totally honest he needed to talk to someone about it, and General Rosewood might just be the best person in the world. Besides what harm could come of it, it was only a meeting.

"Colonel, sir, if this is what has got you all *sweated-up*, let me meet the buggers. I'll be frank, sir, I don't care for the way they have used you to get to me, that's just not fair." Jack could feel the heat in his head, this is what came of drinking hard liquor before food.

"Calm down Jack, I know you have my interests at heart, you're a good man, one of the best I've ever known if I'm honest. I'll arrange for you to meet them but hold your horses Jack, don't go in with all guns blazing, no good will come of it, it never has yet."

With that Mrs Millward rang the bell for lunch and the two men shook hands.

CHAPTER 20
Swings and Roundabouts

"How long have you had this letter then, Jack?" General Rosewood was sat behind his old military desk. That desk had been in his family for over forty years, and he had used it man and boy. Its patina had changed, over the years various marks and scratches mapped out a military career that had spanned the life of the desk. It had belonged to his father when he was in the military based in India and it had been a gift to young Julian when he was a subaltern at the military academy at Sandhurst, he had used it ever since.

"About two weeks, sir. If I'm being honest I wasn't sure what I wanted to do. Albert is a good friend, but what can I do to help him? The funeral has already taken place, sometime last week I believe. I was thinking about asking him to come over here and spend some time with Alice and the family. I know we saw a lot of death in the war but I can't imagine what it's like to lose your wife like that." Jack felt comfortable in this company, it was familiar but still authoritative: it suited Jack.

Alice had been worried when Jack told her he was going to the city to see Rosewood. He had told her a lie, the first time ever, he had said there was something that needed clearing up from the war. Families were travelling to and from the old battlefields all the time now ever since Fabien Ware the new head of the Imperial War Graves Commission had started the recovery of the bodies still laid in unmarked graves and new things were cropping up all the time. So it wasn't a bad lie, he just didn't want to worry her. She hadn't seen Albert's letter, he was sure of it, it would break her heart when he did finally tell her that Monica had died. They had met, just the once, and although neither spoke the other's language they had got on famously. It had been a two-week holiday and Albert had travelled back, with his wife, to England to meet his old friends but that was two years ago, letters seemed to be good enough but now Jack didn't know if he should go to Germany or not.

Julian Rosewood sat and pondered, he liked a pipe of tobacco; a good ready rubbed one that he didn't have to try too hard to get going.

"Didn't expect this one Jack, you know it might be a good idea if you two old rum buggers did get back together, we might be able to kill two birds with one stone here." He took a long drag on his pipe and blew a plume of smoke up in the air.

"Why don't we send Hagerman a telegram and you go and get him, bring him back here to Blighty. Let's hear what he plans to do, who knows, we might be able to help. Leave it to me Jack I'll sort out the paperwork, but I want you to go and fetch him before he does anything stupid."

He had a plan forming in his mind but for it to work it meant putting two *on the shelf* old soldiers back out into the field, back into harm's way.

"There's a sleeper train to Paris, leaves at 17:00 hours, let's get you a ticket to Germany, Jack. It looks like you're going away for a week or so, I'm sure Gerald will smooth things over with Alice." He looked over at Gerald Alcot who knew when he had been beat, it looked like he was going to lose Jack again. Who knew how long for this time?

Jack had clothes but not enough for a week so he was taken to Harrods to look for some more, and a suitcase. The shopping he did in one hour in London he could have paid the rent on Jim's house for over a year. He bought some underpants, and shirts, a pair of trousers and some new boots, socks and a warm jacket and two new hats; he hadn't spent any money on himself for an age. The children needed clothes all the time and although money wasn't ever a problem, if he had spare he liked to spend it on Alice.

Harry, Alice's father was a great help, he doted on the children. Since the death of Elizabeth, his wife, Harry liked to spend a little time in the butchers shop and a lot of time with his grandchildren, not that Jack minded, he liked Harry.

They didn't have a telephone at Jack's house, but the big house did and Gerald Alcot had placed a call to Mrs Millward to go and fetch Alice, he wasn't going to let Jack go without saying goodbye to his wife. When the call was placed Jack and Alice were surprisingly calm. Alice had, of course, seen the letter from Albert but thought it a private matter and wouldn't say a word to Jack until he mentioned it, she knew so much more than he thought. She knew about the bad dreams he had at night, the fear of really loud unexpected bangs, she had seen the fear when he smelled fresh cut hay, she had seen the way he protected the children and the way he never told them what happened. She just knew and she thought she understood but knew she never really would.

"Alice, love, Albert's in a bit of trouble in Germany, it appears there has been some kind of incident involving Monica. She has been killed love, I don't have all the details yet, but I thought it might be a good idea if we brought him back home for a bit of a rest. General Rosewood has offered to cover the costs of me getting him and bringing him home before he does something daft. What do you think?" Jack hated telling lies, he just wasn't cut out for it.

Alice knew instantly that he was trying to protect her feelings, she wasn't hurt by him fibbing, she was quite touched; she was worried that there was more to this story than Jack was letting on. Why was Rosewood involved?

"Jack, that's a kind thought, what does the colonel think, does he know? I don't mind love, you go. Do you know how long you will be away? We will miss you terribly. What about the children, what do you want me to tell them?" She could feel herself getting upset, she wasn't angry but she did feel a touch left out, but that was a woman's lot. She wasn't for all the women's rights nonsense, she liked things to be simple as they had been before the war. Find a good man and marry him her father had told her, and she had, twice. She trusted Jack with her heart and her life, and this was an unexpected upset but she knew not to interfere with what men did, it just made things worse.

"I should be back in a couple of weeks Alice, you might want to make up the spare room for Albert. Tell the children I'm going to collect Albert, they haven't seen him for ages so I'm sure they will be excited. Yes the colonel knows and says if it's a problem then Albert can stay at the house. Alice, love if its ok with you I'm going to go tonight, General Rosewood has sorted things out for us so it will be nice and simple. I've been given some things, clothes and the like so don't worry and I'm quite looking forward to the trip. The colonel has said it is alright for me to call you on the telephone at the colonel's house tomorrow at 6pm to let you know how I'm getting on. Alice, I love you, it'll be fine, poor Albert must be in a right state and I'll see you in a couple of weeks."

With that he hung up the phone and closed his eyes, he hoped it was all true and that things would indeed turn out alright. He turned to look at the collective of the most senior ranks he had ever kept company with, it felt like the old days and there was a thrill in his stomach. Like it or loath it the war had left a deep scar on his psyche. There was a part of him that missed the danger, of just living day to day in the war, it had been replaced with the certainty that there would be a tomorrow and much as he loved life and all it brought him he did miss the danger.

"Well, it looks like I'm going back to France."

CHAPTER 21
Swift Justice, Swabia, 1924

Everyone had been so nice, the funeral had been well attended but he didn't know many of the people there. He didn't have many friends and Monica had even less. They had always kept themselves to themselves. Most of the people there were either colleagues from the *Stathalle*, showing support for the mayor, or simple woodcutters that Monica had often seen in the woods; she would offer them a touch of kindness by giving them drinks of lemonade or elderflower water.

The police had visited the house and, of course, they were very concerned that such a brutal event could happen here. They promised to be thorough and diligent in their duty, they assured him they would find the culprits and bring them to justice. They wouldn't. Albert had already found them and no one would ever find them again.

Everyone knew the *Brownshirts* had been causing trouble, some might even have known the four men who visited Albert's house to 'pass on a message'. Although, Albert still wasn't sure what the message was.

He had found them within twelve hours of finding

Monica; they were getting drunk in a bar. One of them had blood on his shirt and another had a swollen eye and scratches down his face. Monica had not given in without a fight but ultimately she had lost to these thugs.

Albert had followed them to a guesthouse just outside Tuttlingen, they had no idea the killer they had revived: Albert stalked them like prey.

The first one to die had stepped drunkenly outside to relieve himself, when he died he still had his cock in his hand only now it was separated from the rest of his body. The swiftness of the strike had totally caught him unaware and before he could scream Albert drove the blade of his hunting knife straight through his right eye socket and into his very confused brain. The last thing he ever saw was the cold, dead eyes of Albert Hagerman, and the last thing he felt was the brush of death along his neck as Albert sliced his jugular vein, *the gurgling choking rasp of a dead man* thought Albert. It felt good to feel nothing. It was a familiar feeling from long ago.

He needed to talk to one of them. He needed to know who had sent them, who had given them the right to unravel Albert's life? Number two fell in much the same way as number one, the price he paid for coming to look for his murdering swine of a friend. When he walked outside he could see the body of his colleague lying in the dirt, blood surrounded his body. Albert smashed the butt of his Luger pistol onto the temple of the near vomiting man; he went down as if he had been shot. Albert dragged him over to the scrubland, but didn't speak he just took his knife and sliced the Achilles tendon on both the man's legs. The man screamed, he couldn't run primarily because he was now crippled but also because Albert had tied his hands behind his back and round a tree stump. This man was the bait to get the others outside, he wasn't disappointed as within seconds the other two men came running over to where the now whimpering man was tethered. There was a strong smell of petrol; however, it was very dark so they couldn't see where their moaning friend was until one of them lit a cigarette lighter, then there was a loud whoosh. The petrol ignited and the tethered man became a screaming inferno. Albert had doused him with litres of petrol after cutting his Achilles, the latter was pure spite, revenge at its coldest. The now burning man had given him a name as he was being tied to the tree. This was now about ridding the world of vermin.

The smell of burning flesh made one of the two remaining rapists vomit, both sober now that the screaming had sorted any remaining drunkenness out. The screaming only lasted for a couple of seconds before the shot came out of the darkness and the burning man's head exploded as the pistol bullet smashed into his melting skull.

The next shots were aimed and precise, right into the kneecaps of the two remaining men. Bang, bang. Two shots within a second of each other, both men fell to the ground and cried in pain. Albert walked out of the darkness, he had been standing no more than five feet from the men and they had no idea from where he had appeared. The next two shots were aimed into the groin of each man. A cry became a howling scream as testicles exploded.

"I am going to ask you both a question, how you die depends on the answer you give me." The voice was like ice, it chilled the soul and both men knew they were about to die.

"Why did you kill my wife? She had caused you no hardship, who sent you to kill her? Answer now and I will kill you cleanly."

Both men were furious and raged in agony, one spat at the man stood in front of him. Albert had seen their type before, in the war: storm troopers, vicious and evil, a remnant of a repugnant type of warfare that ultimately had been as futile as it was hateful.

Albert drew his knife and sliced across the stomach of the first man, it was a virtual disembowelment and as the man's intestines flowed out of the near surgical incision he let out a pitiful scream and he grasped at his own guts with both hands, there was no pain but the psychological impact was instantaneous. Albert grabbed the oozing bowels and pulled, now there was pain, like the man had never dreamed there could be. Albert was in a killing frenzy and cut the bowel free from its lifelong host. He threw it onto the still burning body, it landed with a hiss. There was urine flowing down the man's leg as he lost all control.

"A name, that is all I want, then I will finish you quickly." He looked into the eyes of the other terrified victim as he plunged his knife back into the guts of the dying but still very much alive man. This time the blade sliced the main descending aorta and in a gush of bleeding the man bled out and died. Albert was furious that he had been so clumsy and killed the man quicker than he intended but it had the desired effect and the dribbling, blubbering eunuch in front of him gave him the name he needed.

Albert nodded. He felt no pity or shame. He shot the man in the temple and all four were dead.

He walked to the guesthouse and knocked on the door, an elderly gentleman answered.

"Are they gone?" said the old man.

"Yes, they have gone, and won't be bothering you anymore old friend. Thank you for your help. I need to borrow your van, please?" With that Albert went to dispose of the bodies in a place they would never be found.

CHAPTER 22
The Telegram

Albert sat behind his desk in his office. It was only two weeks since the murder of Monica. He was still feeling numb.

He read the telegram from his dear friend Jack; it brought a smile to his heavily lined face. It had arrived only this morning and announced the arrival within the next few days of his old friend. It read:

On my way to visit you at this sad time stop
Pack a bag stop
You're coming home with me stop
Jack stop

Albert knew that Jack would come to see him, he had been a friend for a long time now. He also knew he would be going back with him to England for a short break. What he couldn't possibly know, of course, was why Jack was visiting. Jack wouldn't have known the funeral would have already taken place, things moved fast in Germany and the dead were buried quickly.

All of Albert's senses had become heightened and there was a little voice in the back of his mind that said trouble was on the way, but he wasn't sure for whom.

CHAPTER 23

The Dream

Jack was sitting on his own. *First class no less*, he thought. He lit a cigarette and drew the calming smoke deep into his lungs.

His mind was racing. Germany seemed an awfully long way away and he had never travelled like this before and he did feel very apprehensive. It was true he was looking forward to meeting his very dear friend, and it had been too long since they had been in each other's company. It was also true that he would be a fool to think this was in anyway a natural meeting, it had been choreographed like a dance and he felt slightly manipulated.

It was going to be a long journey and there were several stops and changes of train along the way, but this leg from Calais to Paris left him time to rest his eyes. From Paris he would board the Orient Express direct to Munich but for now he was at the liberty of the national railway company.

Sleep didn't come easy. Every time the train stopped Jack would look out of the window to see where he was. The names of the towns all seemed so familiar. Bethune came first, it had been a hive of activity during the war and all around in the countryside there was still plenty of evidence of that conflict. There were hundreds of new cemeteries being built by the newly formed Imperial War Graves Commission. Their work of collecting the fallen and relocating them in large purpose built military cemeteries was a sight to behold. Not many people from home had ever had the chance to come and see where their loved ones had fallen and now laid, finally to rest. For Jack it was a poignant and painful reminder that dragged up the long since dead faces of those men he had known and those he had killed. It wasn't long before Arras came into view, and still the rebuilding of a city smashed to the ground in the war, was taking place. It had been flattened to rubble the last time he saw it in 1917; the work that had taken place astounded him.

He could feel himself relax with the soporific movement of the train, and slowly he drifted off to sleep. He heard the shells screaming in over his head. The constant *crump, crump, crump* was mixed with screams from the men under the exploding ordinance. He crawled on his belly and as he did he could smell the shit in his nostrils, his face covered in the stuff but on no account would he lift his head. He pushed past a body, recently departed from life, the remains oozed entrails and blood onto his hands, the warm sticky blood covering his fingers and the guts of the man still in spasm as if trying to stay alive and avoid the cloak of darkness. The head of the man had been separated from the body and rolled towards him and despite his efforts to move the spherical orb it kept rolling back in front of him. With a huge effort he picked the decapitated head to throw it away and in doing so he looked at the face, it was Jim. His eyes were open and he looked straight into Jack's eyes almost accusingly and then the mouth moved as if trying to talk. Jack was desperately trying to move away but couldn't, he was trapped by the weight of the dead piling on top of his crawling body, very soon he was stuck and his breathing became more and more laboured. He was struggling to catch his breath and clawed at his throat to unfasten his tunic and shirt but his ghillie suit was caught in the button and he couldn't move it. He could feel himself starting to lose control and consciousness and with a last effort he pushed himself into a shell hole. Down and down he fell in a spiral death spin. When he looked back all he could see were the bodies of his friends and his victims following him down to eternal darkness. With a sickening thud as he landed, he awoke.

"Monsieur, Monsieur, réveillez-vous?" There was a guard stood next to him, he had a soft touch and held Jack by the shoulders.

"What? Oh sweet Jesus, I'm sorry. Please forgive me I was having a dream. I'm fine, really, I'm sorry." Jack was soaking he was covered in sweat, his shirt clung to him and was stuck to his back.

"Ah, vous êtes Anglais?" The guard had a kind smile and produced a hip flask of cognac. He offered it to Jack.

"I am English, and I'm sorry to have frightened you, Monsieur. It was a bad dream about the war, *La Grande Guerre.*" Jack took the offered flask and sipped the warming brandy.

The guard pointed to himself and said "Je suis un *poilus*". Jack knew he too had seen the things he saw in his dreams, and the shaking in his hands started to subside. He was with friends.

It was only a short time to Paris and an opportunity for Jack to clean himself and have a wash and shave in the men's room. It had been two days since he had shaved and it felt dirty and alien for him to have stubble on his chin. He changed his shirt and suddenly and without warning he started to feel quite homesick. Although it wasn't a good feeling it made him smile. He needed to phone home, so he went to the telegraphic office and placed a call to Colonel Alcot's number. It cost him five franks but was worth it just to hear his wife. Dear Alice, he loved her so. Then he sent a telegram to Albert and told him where he was and what time he could be expected in Munich.

On the platform stood a magnificent engine coupled up to a luxurious line of carriages. The Orient Express was indeed a name associated with all things luxurious and Jack looked at his first-class ticket and thanked General Rosewood for the kind thought of making sure Jack only travelled first class.

He didn't much want to go back to sleep, so he had some dinner and a glass of red wine, it was a deep red and tasted smooth, after three glasses sleep wasn't an option, it was inevitable. The dream never returned and he slept deeply as the Orient Express carried him deeper in to a foreign land and further away from home.

CHAPTER 24
Time to Leave

Albert looked at the house, he knew it would be the last time he ever saw it. The police had visited yesterday and said that the men they had been looking for in connection with his late wife's murder had disappeared. Obviously it was a suspicious event, but no one had yet connected the disappearances with Albert.

The police commissionaire had taken Albert to a quiet corner in the mayor's office and simply asked: "Albert, these four men, you wouldn't happen to know where they ended up, would you? Only with your history it would be easy to think that maybe you had a hand in their disappearance. Just as a warning, I heard the secret police are looking into it personally and your name has been mentioned a number of times. Be careful old friend, we have been friends for all our lives and nobody cared for you and your family more than I. It might be for the best if you considered 'disappearing' yourself for some time. The tide of Communism has turned and the Nazi party are growing in power and strength. I suspect that they have plans for you to disappear."

Albert knew it was true, he had been careful not to leave any trail back to either himself or anyone he knew, but deep down inside he knew he would have to leave sooner or later. Knowing Jack was on his way to Munich gave him an escape and a reason to leave. He would go back to England and who knew, he might never come back.

*

He had recovered one of the bodies and dressed him in some of his clothes then he sat him in Albert's rocking chair. He left a Luger pistol in the dead man's right hand with the finger jammed into the trigger guard. When they found the body it would look as though Albert had shot himself in the head. Obviously there was the wound to the dead man's knee where Albert had initially shot him, but with luck no one would look that hard at the remains of a burned out woodman's hut.

The house had been doused in petrol and the weather had been dry, all the timber in the house was dry and would burn easily. He lit a long match, felt it strike along the sandpaper of the striker as it flared into life, the flame was yellow and long and he let it burn for a few seconds before he dropped it onto the patch of porch soaked in the remains of the petrol. There was a malicious almost whispered whoosh as the fumes and petrol embraced the tinder dry timber. Within a minute the flames were roaring. No longer a whisper; now a roar of defiance as Albert walked back to the van.

He started the engine and with one last look at the past over his shoulder and with a tear in his eye, Albert Hagerman left his home and past life behind him.

CHAPTER 25
Hello Old Friend

The drive from Tuttlingen to Munich had been quiet. Lake Constance glistened in the moonlight and Albert thought what a beautiful place he had lived in; five hours later he was sat in a café near Munich's magnificent *Hauptbahnhof.*

He would meet Jack from the train although Jack didn't yet know this was the plan. How did the old saying go, 'No battle plan ever survived the first shot?' It was something along those lines and Albert had made a slight change to the initial plan by ensuring that no one was looking for him back home. By now the fire would have burned itself out, leaving a charred body that he hoped would be mistaken as Albert, he wouldn't know it but back at the house his plan had been a complete success. All the rescue service had found was the ashes of a house with the incinerated remains of what they assumed had been their mayor. There was nothing left, the body was virtually ash and there was no way that anyone would be able to distinguish who it had been other than Albert Hagerman. Albert wouldn't see the obituary his friend the police commissioner had prepared for release. That was a shame because it was a wonderful piece of writing, heartfelt and full of sadness. It was also a chance to say goodbye to an old friend, wherever he was.

★

Jack felt the train slow; the guard came along the corridor and told everyone that they were approaching Munich.

"Munich, the next stop is Munich. Passengers, who are continuing the journey onto Wein please, stay in your carriages. No new passengers are boarding at this stop. Munich is only for passengers who are leaving the train."

Jack collected his case from the service guard and shook hands with the guard as the train came into the station. As the station emerged from a cloud of steam, Jack was pleased that he had, at last arrived. Tired and stiff through lack of movement and the fact he wasn't used to the soft furnishings he had been in for the past couple of days. The doors opened and a step appeared as if from nowhere for Jack to step down onto the platform. As he looked along the length of the train he noticed that only three people had disembarked, and with a smart nod of his head as if in salute the guard replaced the step and closed the door, before blowing his whistle long and hard to let the driver know that all was clear for the journey to resume. With a long toot the engine let out a massive sigh of steam and the brakes allowed the big wheels of the engine to turn and take the strain. It all looked so effortless to Jack, the massive train smoothly gained momentum and before Jack had turned to face the station the guard had passed him and as he saluted Jack he closed the last window.

Jack bent to pick up his case, but as his hand clasped the handle another hand engulfed his, Jack looked up in surprise and once again found those familiar blue eyes of his old adversary, who it appeared still had the ability to creep up totally unnoticed. "Hello Albert, I wondered how long it would take." Jack smiled and offered his hand in eternal friendship, the kind forged in the furnaces of hell that were the battlefields of Flanders.

Albert took Jack's hand and held it, he didn't just shake it as you might expect but held it. He looked into Jack's eyes as though he was looking into his soul.

"My dear friend, thank you for coming, you can have no idea how much this means to me, an old enemy, that you care enough to come when I need you most. I have a story to tell you Jack and I think it might be better if we move from here. There are people spying on everyone in Germany and the things we fought for are not any longer important to the leaders."

Albert led the two of them to a waiting cab, horse drawn as most were here in the south of Germany. They were booked into a guesthouse not far away, a safe place recommended by the commissioner of police back in Tuttlingen, just for one night. Tomorrow they would be on the move again, not by the magnificent train Jack had arrived on but an altogether less salubrious train. Albert would need to explain to his tired and now confused comrade, but he felt safe in the knowledge that Jack would understand and support him.

In a quiet corner of the bar, the two men sat full of *bon ami,* comfortable in each other's company. There was much shoulder slapping and several beers later Jack had to ask for water, he wasn't used to the strong German beer and the effects had started to slow his already tired brain. It wasn't really Albert's plan to get Jack drunk, it was intended to let the bar empty so he could tell Jack what had happened over the past few weeks since his beloved Monica had been murdered.

In time, the bar emptied and Albert told Jack about the four men he had killed and the warning that he was a suspect and how he had taken steps to throw the hounds off the scent. Albert was calm whilst he told his tale and Jack was now very sober, his instincts were screaming and his thinking was crystal clear. Albert had an escape plan, it was perfect but Jack would expect nothing less, once again Jack marvelled at the ingenuity of Albert Hagerman.

It was time to get some rest, tomorrow was going to be a long day, but the thought that Jack would be back in England earlier than expected was all the motivation he needed. It was obvious that this country was in turmoil and the sooner they could get away the better for everyone.

CHAPTER 26

Homeward Bound

The next morning came very early and the knock at the door arrived just as Jack opened his still sleepy eyes. It was as Jack expected, Albert's smiling face greeted him at the door.

"Good morning, has the sleep been good?"

Jack smiled at the still imperfect English his friend spoke, it was much better than his German, and he rebuked himself for even thinking it.

"Morning Albert, come in."

Albert entered the room and took a seat at the window. Jack dressed and sat on the edge of the bed, he needed to ask Albert a few questions about the things said last evening.

"So, Albert can we just go through what we discussed last night, just so I am clear in my mind. Monica was murdered by members of the Nazi party who came to pass on a message that they knew about you from the war. What did they want to tell you, have you any idea? Anyway, you have sorted that out and you dispatched them and disposed of the bodies. You then received a warning from your friend the police commissioner that the secret police were looking for you, and you burned your house down with a body inside so that if they found anything they would think it was you inside the house. You then came here to meet me and today we are going back to England?"

Albert sat and listened. He nodded at each salient point, he was pleased that he could still understand Jack's English despite it being some time since he had either spoken it or listened to it.

"Yes, Jack, that is what happened, and today we need to keep moving because if my plan has not worked, they will be looking for me even more. We need to get a train from here before my papers are checked, it will be very fast that the secret police pass on my picture at the *bahnhofs* and borders. So my friend we need to start."

Jack was up and ready to leave before Albert had finished. He had packed his small things away and they left.

At the station, Jack was busy looking around at everyone and it struck him that Albert was doing the same subconscious checks to see if anyone was looking for them. Of course, it was easier because anyone looking for them would really be looking for one man not two, but better to be safe than sorry, it had kept both men alive many times back in the battle torn fields of France.

They boarded a train bound for Stuttgart, from there they would connect with another train for Saarbrucken and from there to Verdun, Reims and finally onto Paris. This train was busy, and although the two men were sitting together talking became awkward as Jack didn't speak German, and he felt very conspicuous. Funnily enough the fact the train was busy gave Albert a feeling of security, hiding in a crowd was still hiding and as the ticket conductor checked his ticket he didn't look the man in the eye, he just handed his ticket over with a nod, his hat hid most of his facial features.

The further away from Munich the train got the more relaxed Albert became and at Saarbrucken the train almost emptied, enough so that Jack felt able to talk. He had much to tell Albert, all of which had been pushed to the back of his mind with the urgency of their departure and the reasoning why. Now Jack started to tell Albert that Alice and the children were looking forward to their arrival and that they should be home within the next couple of days. He didn't mention that there was an ulterior motive for his visit, but then that could wait, with a bit of luck it needn't ever be mentioned. Conversation on the train was confined to niceties and so it stood out when a large gentleman sat opposite and started talking to Albert about the political situation in Germany. This man had noticed that Jack was English, and he asked Albert how he knew the Englishman, Albert spun a yarn about him being his brother-in-law, married to his eldest sister who lived in the north of England. The big German nodded and said "Hello", but then went straight back into his native tongue and spoke to Albert direct. Presently he left the carriage to visit the men's room. Albert quickly took the opportunity to say to Jack that he mustn't say anything in front of this fellow, as he was sure he could speak English and was just listening to what Jack said without showing any sign of understanding. Jack agreed to say nothing further, but sighed that it was going to be a long way home. Was Albert being paranoid or just careful? Either way Jack knew that it was best to take Albert's lead. The large German returned and took his seat, within a few minutes he was talking to Albert, his voice was deep and authoritative, it turned out he had also fought in the last years of the war and he felt very let down at the slowness of the German recovery, this new chap, Hitler, would show the world how Germans could fight. The French and British had asked for too much and the Americans were spiteful and greedy. The German nation would rise again, in time, but for now it was the duty of every German to try and do their best. The economy in Germany was in a shambles and inflation was out of control, the price of everyday things was astonishing, how could it cost millions of *Deutschemark* for a loaf of bread? He had, only the other morning, seen a woman with a wheelbarrow full of money going to the bakery only to be robbed in the street by a communist who left the money and stole the wheelbarrow. The country needed a strong leader, he said, and Herr Hitler seemed to be saying the sort of things he wanted to hear.

Albert just listened and nodded, Jack couldn't understand a word of what was said so just looked out at the beautiful countryside, *not so different than home* he thought.

In what seemed a lifetime the guard approached with an official who looked at the travel documents of everyone on the train. Although they were still officially in Germany, this part of the industrial heartlands was being governed by the French and Belgians. This was proving to be a very painful time for the German people who just couldn't pay the debts that the French and others had laid at their feet for starting the war in the first place. The guard announced that the train was about to approach the ancient town of Verdun.

Jack had never been here, but the French had lost hundreds of thousands of men here prior to 1916, and the Germans had lost nearly if not as many men here. As Jack looked out there were yet more huge military graveyards being dug, regiments laid line after line, thousand upon thousand. The sheer scale and size reflected the true loss of one battlefield. Albert said there were no German graves and Jack looked at him incredulously, "What, you mean that's just the French? dear God it must have been horrendous. Where are the German graves, do you know?"

"There are none yet, well not like that. The French don't think we should, ah in German it is *bedecken*. You call it putting people in the ground, but I don't have the word."

"Bury, we bury our dead," said Jack.

"Ya, bury, the French think we should just leave our dead here or take them home. We were not welcome guests here Jack, we were an invading army."

"But surely, there must be somewhere that your dead are buried Albert?"

Jack was truly shaken by the sheer size of the graveyard.

"Yes Jack, we are buried in large holes in the ground, as they died; together."

Jack held out his right hand, he offered his hand in friendship. Albert gratefully received it.

"I'm so sorry, Albert. It must be as difficult for you as it is shocking for me, all those lads and for what? For nothing that's what."

They changed trains here in Verdun, the next stop would see them in Reims and the further into France they travelled the calmer and increasingly happier Albert became. For the first time in a fortnight, he felt safe.

CHAPTER 27

Home Office, 1994

Andrew Phillips looked very smart in his suit, cut by *Austin Reed* and made to measure. He definitely had style: a pink shirt and baby blue silk tie finished with bulled toe caps on his *Oxford* shoes; his father had shown him how to bull shoes when he was a small boy and he had never forgotten. He looked every bit the diplomat and today all his powers of management and diplomacy would be needed. He was meeting the Permanent Undersecretary of the Diplomatic Service and the German Ambassador to the United Kingdom, as well as a representative of the intelligence service MI6. What the hell had he got involved in? His boss at the Commonwealth War Graves Commission, the Director General, was away on compassionate leave otherwise he would have been here as well, but for today he was flying solo with a remit to take notes and report back at the end of the week.

The door opened and a very smart, attractive and, obviously used to the looks, lady smiled and invited him into the Permanent Undersecretary's office.

"Andrew, welcome. Please come and take a seat. Let me introduce you to Peter Hartmann, The German

Ambassador and Andrew Carnegie from MI6. We are all friends here so you have no need to be nervous, no one will bite." Permanent Undersecretary Leslie Smyth was old school Diplomatic Service and Phillips felt instantly intimidated and yet strangely comfortable. Smyth's suit was *Savile Row* and fitted him like a second skin. His aftershave was musky and masculine and Phillips knew instinctively that the man in front of him was a political predator. His guard was up, he knew he needed to say things very carefully in this room because if he didn't they would bury him and his team in an instant.

Hartmann was nearly seventy years old but looked much younger. He had a warm handshake, firm and dependable, with a kind smile and a face you felt comfortable with; Phillips liked him instantly.

Carnegie was a different kettle of fish, he looked like he could smile and stab you at the same time.

"Come, take a seat, I am very interested in what you are going to tell us Mr. Phillips." Hartmann gestured towards a chair.

"Thank you, sir." Phillips shook hands with the other men and took a seat at the table.

"Do you mind if I call you Andrew, it makes it much less formal, and after all you are the one we wanted to meet." Hartmann did seem like a gentleman and Phillips felt himself calming after the initial flush of fear and anguish when he first came in.

"Thank you. Yes please call me Andrew, and thank you for giving me the opportunity to show you our findings."

Phillips had all the information pre-printed in folders and handed them round, one to each man. He also had it on a compact disc in the form of a presentation but for now, in this small forum, he decided a folder would be sufficient.

He let everyone have a quick look at the folders in front of them. They read them very quickly and looked up at him. It caught him a little by surprise, how quickly they had scanned the pages; now they needed him to tell them what on earth had happened.

"As you can see, following a grave site collapse we were presented with a number of skeletons or remains as we prefer to call them. There were sixteen bodies found in the bunker, ten British, four French and two German. Or so we thought, it turned out that one of the British bodies was in fact German, well Austrian to be precise. The British bodies were numbered 01 to 10, the French remains were labelled 11 through to 14, and the German remains, 15 and 16.

We had names for all the German and French remains as identified by individual ID tags found on the bodies at the time. In accordance with our procedures now, we took and sent DNA samples of all the bodies found. We confirmed the identity of the remains labelled at the time simply as number 08, with the Interpol DNA database, as indeed we did with all the other specimens. However, only number 08 came back with a marker. This one was flagged as 'Of International Importance.' This individual has since been identified as one Adolf Hitler.

We have since informed and worked closely with the German embassy in London and France to try to ascertain if there is any possible explanation as to how and why this has happened."

Phillips was really getting into his flow now and as he relaxed his voice became more excited and he became more animated. Hartmann smiled reassuringly, he thought *he could get to like this young man given a chance*. Andrew Carnegie sat and had what he termed as his 'poker face' on. He showed no emotion or even interest in what was being said. He flicked through the pages of the report in front of him and only occasionally looked up at the narrator sat opposite him.

"We were able to compare the sample from remains number 08 with a tooth that had been removed from Adolf Hitler in the early 1920's by a dentist in Berlin. We understand he was a stand in for Hitler's regular dentist who was on leave at the time. His name was Abraham Meir, who along with his wife was executed in the Dachau Concentration Camp near Munich in 1935. We have found records with the help of the German embassy that confirms that he and his wife Eliana were taken as political prisoners the year before.

Abraham Meir left behind a number of medical exhibits or samples in the clinic where he had been working. One of these samples was the tooth he extracted from Hitler. This had been moved to the archive within the hospital because it wasn't thought of as significant, how it survived without being thrown away is a miracle. We were able to compare DNA from both the tooth in the jaw of the skeletal remains and the sample tooth from Vienna, they were a hundred percent match. In fact Doctor Robert Deville has even been able to match them with a notch that fits between both teeth and again they fit perfectly. There is absolutely no doubt that the tooth we found in Vienna and the skeleton we found in France belongs to the same person. We just have no idea why he would be in a commonwealth war grave in France."

Lesley Smyth spoke first, breaking an almost magical spell.

"Thank you, Andrew, fascinating, absolutely fascinating. What do you think, Peter, it's all a bit farfetched isn't it?"

The German Ambassador tapped his pen on the table; it was an old habit that was normal when he was in deep thought.

"Do you know how he died, the man you think is Adolf Hitler?"

Phillips had expected this; he could see that his story was as farfetched to this gathering as it had seemed to him the first time he heard it.

"We have had various tests done, Ambassador and although the bones were definitely pre-World War Two we have found traces of potassium cyanide from a bone sample. It has a very similar fingerprint to that used by senior members of the Nazi party much later as a suicide pill. I have had a full post mortem report done by our forensic pathologist, Doctor Robert Deville." Phillips handed a copy of the post mortem to the Ambassador.

He took it with a smile and opened the file as he moved his reading glasses from the top of his head.

Phillips continued, "As you can see there were no obvious signs of injury to the skeleton, but of particular interest to me and my team was the lack of a head wound. We were all led to believe that Hitler had committed suicide by shooting himself in the head in the *Führerbunker* in Berlin in April 1945. This is clearly now in question. The evidence my team has collected, and I have presented to you today, tells a very different story. That in itself presents us with a problem, because it challenges what everybody perceives to be historical fact. However, historical facts don't change what we found. To answer your question Ambassador, we don't really know how he died, the cyanide could be from his surroundings but it would be remarkable if he had absorbed such a large amount from the ground to affect a bone sample, but it's not an impossibility. Doctor Deville thinks it is more likely to have been ingested. That would suggest he either swallowed it himself or was forced to swallow it. We have never had a situation like this in any of our departments at the Commonwealth War Graves Commission. My biggest problem is what to do next with this information, sir."

Phillips looked up. It was only when he had finished he felt unsure. He and his team had been through this a hundred times, he knew it was all fact but it all sounded so improbable even more so at that precise moment as he looked at the other three men, who were all looking right back at him. The silence was very disturbing.

It was Andrew Carnegie who broke the silence.

"What an interesting story Mr. Phillips. Would you kindly pass on our congratulations to your team, they have done a wonderful job. However, clearly there is a mistake somewhere along the line. I would appreciate some more time to consider all the information you have presented to us today. Given that it is widely known how Adolf Hitler met his end I can see no benefit in changing the course of history. I along with my colleagues at the ministry will review this information. In the meantime, I think we have covered all the ground we need to cover today." He stood and offered Andrew his outstretched hand. Phillips was so taken aback he stood and shook hands. Obviously the meeting was at an end. He shook hands with the Permanent Undersecretary and the German Ambassador, and before he could react he was leaving the office. Phillips heard the door close behind him: he was sure he heard his career coming to an end.

Back in the room Lesley Smyth looked directly at Carnegie and with his coldest stare he said, "What information do you have Carnegie, what are you not telling us?"

The information Andrew Carnegie had in his briefcase he had hoped to keep there, but now knew he had to submit it, or at least some of it.

He didn't necessarily have to give them all the information. If he could just miss out one or two of the more sensitive points it might help save some embarrassment in the highest office in his department, damage limitation they called it, but he knew he was up against it. If he told the German Ambassador all the information that he had, well, the consequences might be seismic. The fall out of the truth could be as influential on Germany's current relationship with the United Kingdom as the last conflict that ended in 1945 had been, only this time the result might be significantly different. He drew a deep breath and sighed, this was going to hurt.

"Well gentlemen, it would appear that there was some kind of mission in the early 1920's that was headed by my department. The lead in this mission was Major General Julian Rosewood, he was department head of MI6." With that he handed over a buff coloured envelope to the two men. On top was marked 'MOST SECRET' in bold letters. He couldn't help but feel that this meeting was about to uncover a skeleton of its own and the ramifications would more than bite his arse.

CHAPTER 28

Home at Last, 1924

The journey through France had been as uneventful as it had been slow. It took a further two days before the boat docked alongside in Southampton. Both men were tired but had managed to sleep on the boat, each with their own thoughts. Albert, full of grief and anger and Jack who was full of anticipation and excitement. They knew they had to catch a train to London and from there onward home to Langwith, all in all another ten hours. By the same time the following night they would be enjoying dinner with Alice, the children would be over tired and over excited and Jack couldn't wait.

The first surprise was to see Jim Cunningham sat smoking a cigarette at the side of the car. Jack knew instantly that the train ticket he had bought only two hours previously from the purser on the ship was now redundant. The second and by far bigger surprise was to see General Julian Rosewood standing in his army greatcoat talking to the colonel by the passport control. He waved and Jack acknowledged with a nod and wide smile, maybe Alice would be with them.

"Hello Jack, welcome home." General Rosewood

shook Jack's hand warmly and then, with a beaming smile, he greeted Albert as if he had missed him for years. Albert was totally shocked at the greeting but felt it as warmly as it was offered.

"Herr General, how nice to see you again, and Colonel Alcot, what a wonderful surprise. I wasn't expecting to meet you again until tomorrow." Jack was aware that Albert was trying his very best with his English. He sounded quite posh. It made Jack laugh and shake his head as he walked over to the passport desk to present his 'Old Blue' as his passport had become affectionately known. It was at this stage that things became 'out of the ordinary': Albert reached inside his coat for his passport, similar to the British one but on this occasion equally unwarranted or required. Both men were shown to a gate where there was no passport control and as Jack went to ask what was going on, the general said it had been "taken care of, old chap". Then like royalty they were shown to their car.

Jim hugged both men, as he would a brother, he quite forgot he was on 'official business' and it was only when the colonel coughed politely that Jim realised he should open the back door of the car for the four men to get in.

Jack was a little confused and said, "Why are we going by car, colonel, is anything wrong?"

It was General Rosewood, who answered.

"We are going to London, Jack, just overnight if you don't mind. I have taken the liberty of booking you both into a hotel tonight. I rather need to talk to Albert and we thought it might be better if we did that here rather than Langwith. All things being equal you should be able to get back home tomorrow evening."

For the first time Jack felt there was something underhand about this trip. He started to realise there were things he hadn't been made aware of about the trip he had just undertaken. The gamekeeper's instinct had returned, all his senses became heightened and from here on in his guard would stay up.

The journey to London would take them until lunchtime and initially the conversation was careful and cautious, but within an hour the driver's dividing window was open and Jim was chatting like a London cabbie, the mood lightened significantly and the talk became much more convivial. Memories of battles long since passed were relived, sometimes the ending had changed and the detail was somewhat sketchy in other parts, but the four men in the back and the driver in the front had all become as one in the condemnation of war. Its futility and pointlessness wasn't lost on these old warriors, all had been touched by tragedy and the grim reaper had left his hollow sadness with those who survived his visit. Jim had lost so very much but nothing compared to Albert and the colonel who had both given a son to the conflict. Jack had been left with both physical and mental scars, well-hidden but omnipresent and in a subtle but no less damaging way General Rosewood had to live with the scars of knowing he had condemned so many young men to death. His orders had been as deadly to many as the machine gun bullets or artillery shells. It was a private burden, as so many were, but he was acutely aware of the cost, it was a heavy cross he had to bear.

Eventually the topic of conversation turned to Jack and Albert's last mission together, and once again it was Jim who asked them to regale them with the tale. It was an old story that had been told many times but interestingly none of the facts ever varied, not with this story. The memory of it was as fresh as if it had been only last week: the time Albert and Jack had spent together planning and then actually carrying out the mission had been fairly short, but the consequences of their success had been far reaching.

*

If the Bolsheviks had been successful in the attempt to kill the kaiser, who knew what might have happened? Many thought it might have been a good thing, and that in actual fact Jack and Albert had saved the mad kaiser from death only to let him carry on until the end came over a year later. The revolution in Russia had shaken everyone, and the Bolsheviks had taken a huge amount of support back to Germany following the German defeat. Lenin's message of 'Peace, bread and land' had found widespread acceptance, and Germany was no exception. People were starving in Germany: a direct result of the British blockades; with the war ended the burden on an already over loaded food chain had snapped and civil unrest was rife. The doorway to the far right and the emergence of the Nazi party were perhaps a consequence of the whole event; a politically shrewd National Socialist German Workers' Party had nevertheless choreographed it. The flames fanned ever so slightly and at just the right time to have maximum effect and impact. Germany needed to have belief in itself and the Nazi's were not lacking in belief in themselves.

Initially well received in the south of the country, the Nazi party were now feeling the effects of a violent past and support for them had dwindled, but the underlying feeling amongst Germans and indeed many people in high office in England, were that changes to the old regime in Germany were as inevitable as they were going to be welcome. All that was needed to spark this new rise in Nazi popularity was a smooth orator, and Hitler was fast becoming this man. Hermann Goring, his right hand man was quickly becoming a drug-addled nuisance, but the flame of a new Germany had flickered and in time with a gentle hand to guide it, it would grow like a fire to be a blazing furnace.

*

By the time the car arrived in London the occupants needed a drink, the office was the best place to meet but not drink, so after dropping Jack and Albert at the main door of the hotel and dismissing Jim for the night, Rosewood and the colonel retired to the club for drinks before meeting the two men at a swanky restaurant in Piccadilly at 20.00 hours. This had all the hallmarks of being a long night.

The seeds of the meeting had already been sewn, but had slipped the attention of all the protagonists involved. General Julian Rosewood had truly become a master at chess, and all the pieces were falling into place nicely.

CHAPTER 29

Drinks and a Stranger, London

Jim had been able to spend a little time with his old foe and now, somewhat confused, friend Albert. The two of them chatted easily, as old soldiers tended to do. The conversation eventually came round to what had happened in Germany, to Albert and his wife Monica. Monica's death had shaken everyone and the horror had been personal; Jim had never met Monica but knew of her only by name and reputation. Albert's past life with Jim had been at a time of conflict when relationships could be built on trust, and a man's word was his bond. Jim trusted Albert because he had never been given reason not to. Jim knew that Jack and Albert had made a frightening team, efficient and deadly to their enemy. He knew of no man who had come away from that war the same as he left for it. Jim had knackered lungs, Tim now dead bless him, and Jack, well Jack had changed but not in a way that many would notice. Jack was careful, not quite the happy go lucky lad he had always been before the war but he was not bitter or twisted. In Jack's world there had been huge change, marriage, children and a responsible job had all come since he returned wounded and broken back in 1917. A hero albeit a reluctant one, but that was Jack Adams' way, never one for fuss or bother and always a word of encouragement for the people that worked for him. Jack was not just liked he was loved and Jim was very worried about what the next chapter in Jack's life would hold.

Clearly there were plans made because standing in front of Jim was the one man who had ever bettered Jack in the field, and although Jim could be a bit slow, he was way ahead on this one. Trouble was looming for someone. Jim shook hands with Albert and left for his room in the hotel, tonight he would be alone and if he was honest he was sad to be left out. Jim knew he was crippled as a soldier and although not a charity case he was dependent on the job he had from the colonel. His days of fieldwork were behind him. True, he still had a great eye for detail but he struggled to get into the field these days let alone work there. Today there were better men to do that kind of work but there was none better than Albert and Jack, of that he was certain.

*

Albert met Jack and together they left to walk the short distance to the Criterion restaurant where a table had been reserved for the four men. There would obviously be drinks ahead of dinner so the two had set off a bit early, time to share a cigarette and sit and look at the sights. They sat on a bench and lit a cigarette each; the flame from the match flickered bright, and by the time both men had lit up, the flame had burned down to Jack's fingertip, he blew it out and looked through the smoke, out towards the rest of the world. His blue eyes had turned ever greyer over the years but they were still sharp and bright. Those eyes had kept him alive so many times over the years and as the smoke made them water slightly, he blinked away the sting and turned to Albert.

"What do you think this is all about then, Albert? I was asked, to come and make sure you didn't do anything daft. I was going to come over and see you anyway but once 'old Rosewood' said he would pick up the bill it made sense to come straight away. I never even got chance to say goodbye to Alice. I knew then that something was afoot, but I'll be honest I have no idea what."

Albert took a long drag of his fag, he hadn't smoked a cigarette for years he had always been a pipe man, and back home he would smoke the occasional cigar. The strong English tobacco tasted rough but hit the spot like no pipe ever could.

"I think they want us to kill somebody Jack, like the old days, and I think I have an idea who it might be. I was so pleased when I got your telegram telling me you were on the way. As you now know I am a troubled man and I have committed murder, I am a criminal in my own country, Jack. I am sure Rosewood wants you and me to kill someone important, but the questions are who, why and where? Rosewood has gone to a lot of trouble to make sure we are together again. Think carefully Jack, who would they want a German and an Englishman to kill? The only one I can think of that might need that, as far as I can think, is Adolf Hitler, and I would dearly love to put a bullet into his cold, evil heart."

With that he dropped the remains of his cigarette and ground it into the street. The hustle and bustle of the West End was in full flow and as the two men walked they looked around with an equal amount of disgust and bewilderment: was this why they had spent all those murderous days and nights in the trenches, so that the upper classes could live like kings. The truth was more upper class officers had perished than working class soldiers; it was just that there were more working class soldiers than upper class officers to be killed. Both men knew they had ended more officer's lives than ordinary men.

When the two men arrived at the Criterion they were met at the door by a very smart doorman, he showed them in and as the door closed behind them another man dressed much the same as the doorman asked their names and if they had a reservation, and if so what name was it booked under. Jack said he thought it would be booked in the general's name. They were shown through to the lounge, and were met by Colonel Alcot, General Rosewood and another man who neither of them had met before. Lord Curzon was the Secretary of State for foreign affairs, they were none the wiser for being introduced, neither of them had ever heard of him.

"You don't really need to know who or what I am, needless to say I am the one who has and will continue to fund this whole operation. On completion of this task, both of you will receive financial security for the rest of your lives. I understand it might prove difficult for you to return home now, Herr Hagerman, on account the Germans think you're dead. I understand you had quite a leaving party."

Albert looked on in amazement, *how did he, how could he know this?* Lord Curzon smiled as he realised Albert had no idea as to the amount of power and information he held over the two men.

"Now you mustn't worry, Hagerman, we won't let on that you are very much alive, but we would really appreciate you helping us. Along with young Mr. Adams here. You see what we want you to do is pop back over there and escort Herr Hitler back here so we can have a word."

This time it was Jack who looked on with incredulity.

"I'm sorry?" Said Jack, "you want us to go back to Germany, kidnap Adolf Hitler and bring him back to England so you can have a talk to him?" Jack could hear his own voice as it got higher and higher in pitch, not loud but totally disbelieving.

"Quiet now, Adams, we don't want the world to know now do we?" Said Lord Curzon.

"But that's madness, how the hell do we do that? And what if he doesn't want to come back with us? That's like asking us to kidnap the Prime Minister here in England, isn't he going to be guarded?" There were a million questions popping into Jack's head.

"Ok, we will do it." The voice was as cold as it was firm. It was Albert.

"What?" Said Jack, "now just wait a minute, I never said I would do it, what the hell are you thinking, Albert? We could be killed. We have done our bit for king and country. I'm married and settled with a good job and a family. I'm in no rush to jeopardise all that. Why the hell would you choose us, we aren't even in the army anymore. For Christ's sake, that's asking too much."

Albert held up his hand as if to quieten Jack from his complaint. Jack stopped talking as if he understood, and looked at Albert sternly.

"Gentlemen, would you kindly excuse us for a minute whilst I have a talk to my old friend here." Albert was as calm as if he had just been told to buy some milk. It was quite disconcerting for Jack.

"Of course, Albert, we will go through to the dining room. Please join us in there when you have finished." General Rosewood was as charming as ever, he knew he had his man; all that was needed now was to convince Jack Adams that this really was a good idea, who better to do that than Albert? Who indeed. The three men stood and left, leaving Jack and Albert sitting in the comfy seats; all of a sudden there seemed to be no one else around and they were quite alone.

Albert held his hands in the air as if in surrender, "Jack, my old friend, do you not see? This is a great chance to rid the world of a devil, a man who will happily take our countries back into a war with each other. Do you think I have any other choice but to do as they wish? We are, how do you say it? Like chess pieces? We have been moved into this. I can see why you might not want to do it, but what about me, I have no choice; I will happily see that rat Hitler on the end of my bayonet, he is mad. If anyone can do this it is us, we should do it. It will be like the old days my friend."

Jack sat back in his chair. He was stunned.

"I'm going to need a lot more convincing than that Albert, and when we get home Alice is going to need more than me. Let's go through and hear what those three have planned for us. I don't like it Albert, I'll tell you for nowt, I feel conned and it doesn't sit easy with me. Still let's go and listen."

With that they went through. All five men knew this mission was going to happen, not all were happy about it and some were happier than others, but they all knew. Jack Adams had taken the *king's shilling* once more and Albert Hagerman was now a British soldier in all but name.

CHAPTER 30
Dinner for Five

As Jack and Albert sat at the table a wine waiter appeared. Jack didn't want wine just water, he needed his head clear and already there were a million different questions and voices running around his fuddled brain.

Albert told the collective what had happened in Tuttlingen, about Monica and his vengeful acts to punish the men who had done it. When he had finished no one spoke. Colonel Alcot who sat next to Albert patted him on the arm as would a father to show support. Rosewood gently shook his head and felt the grief well up inside him. Lord Curzon, sat like a viper and stoked the flames of hatred.

"Do you know who was responsible for the order to do these things Albert? These men didn't do this on their own, they were told to do this by someone, but do you have any idea who?"

Albert sat as if in deep thought.

"I have wondered who would do such a thing. Was it because I was the mayor? I don't know. I do know that before she died in my arms Monica said they had been sent to pass a message. She said that the men that had done this to her had called me a traitor because I had 'worked with the Englishman'. Then before one of the killers died he told me who had sent them. I was shocked to hear his name, but it made sense to me because the only man in Germany who knew of the things I had done in the war was the very man Jack and myself had been sent to shoot in 1917, Erich Ludendorff."

Lord Curzon actually smiled.

"Yes, Albert, we had heard the same here in England. I have some more information for you and when we have finished eating dinner I want you both to come back to Rosewood's office. We have some information you might find very helpful, and Jack, you might find some answers that you need to convince you that it has to be the pair of you that go and bring Herr Hitler back to England."

Albert spluttered, "You want us to bring him back here, not kill him? I want to kill him."

Lord Curzon looked very hard into Albert's cold eyes. "I want you and Adams, here, to bring that bastard Hitler back alive, if possible. However, should that be too difficult then you have my blessing to do whatever you like to him. It would be easier if he chose to work with us here in London. It's my understanding that he is getting up a head of steam and support. He will take our two countries back to war if given half a chance. The situation in Germany is inflammatory, the people are the kindling and the Nazi party are the spark. We must do all we can to avoid the two ever coming into contact with each other, it would mean another catastrophic conflict.

By removing Herr Hitler, I think we might remove the head of the serpent I see as the Nazi party.

I want to tell him that I think the Treaty of Versailles went too far, that was the French and the Americans, Lloyd George was too weak. Well now, we have to try to ease the situation in Germany, but that can only work if we avoid the threat of another conflict in the near future. Maybe by doing it quietly he will see our point of view, but if we did this through the official channels we would look as if we are undermining the French and Americans and we can't afford to let that happen either. Bring him to me and let me talk to him."

At that moment, the first course arrived. Jack didn't feel very hungry; he was confused and angry that Albert was so unconcerned that the two of them had been tricked and manipulated into something they didn't understand or know about until ten minutes ago. He played with his food, it was noticed by Colonel Alcot who like the champion he was spoke quietly to Jack.

"You don't have to do this Jack, I'll support you if you say you don't want to go and I'll understand why."

Jack smiled at the kindly old man. He had real feelings for Gerald Alcot, he was the father he lost in that tragic house fire. No replacement, but a man he could trust and put all his faith in knowing he would never be let down.

"Thanks colonel, I don't know how I feel about this really. I'm a bit confused and in my game that's not a healthy thing to be." Jack spent the rest of dinner in a moody silence.

CHAPTER 31

A Plan, but not for Jack

After dinner the group reconvened in General Rosewood's office. It was getting late, but the momentum had started and all apart from Jack seemed very keen to get on with a plan.

Jack needed to talk to Alice and the children, he missed her and now that he was back in England he felt tortured by not being able to see them. *He wasn't a prisoner, why couldn't he just go home?* It was Rosewood who noticed more than most; he pulled Jack to one side, it was time for a man to man chat.

"Now listen here Adams, this is a job of such importance that I had to get clearances from the very top to get your old chum in there back to England. I accept you feel slighted by not knowing all the details, but if I'm honest things have been very sloppy in the planning and much as it's a tragic event, Hagermans wife being murdered has helped matters significantly. Why, he is prepared to take the whole bally lot of them on, and on his own if needs be. What I don't need now is you spoiling the pot by sulking. When I spoke to Gerald about this in the first place he said he had reservations about you going, I told him I thought it was nonsense, that you would love another pop at Jerry. Now pull yourself together man. You're being well paid and most men would jump at the chance to help king and country."

Jack snapped.

Rosewood was a big man, but he flew through the door like a rag doll. As the door crashed open the people inside jumped up in shock; it was the sight of this large, rotund man tumbling head over heels and in close pursuit was a rage, a fury, like none without active service had ever seen. It was Albert who rugby tackled Jack and dropped him like a stone. As quick as it had started it was over. Jack was held on the floor with Albert laughing, sat on his chest. The colonel, initially shocked, rushed to help Rosewood back to his feet and sat him in a chair. Lord Curzon looked on in disgust, a puller of strings but never a man to get stuck in. He couldn't comprehend violence he abhorred it, and yet ironically he liked to watch boxing. This was different.

Jack said in a voice that would freeze gin, "You can take your job, and shove it, you can't speak to me like that. I'm not one of your soldiers any more, I did my bit and now I'm done. Colonel, I will hand my notice into you at the house when I get back home, which is where I'm going now." With that he rolled away from Albert and walked out of the office.

Jack walked the streets in London for hours that night, he had no idea what he was going to do. He had lost his temper and with it the job he loved, a house and a good wage. By telling them to stuff their job he had lost his big pension, probably lost Albert as a friend and once he was on the heap along with the millions of other men he might well lose everything. He found a bench and sat down, dejected.

He didn't know how long he had been sat there, but he was numb with cold when a policeman walked over to him.

"Evening sir, everything alright?" He had seen the type so many times before, down on his luck, ex-soldier probably, nowhere to go. The doss houses would be closed for the night now. This chap would be spending the night in a cell, at least that way he would get a hot drink inside him before a rough night's sleep, but he would be dry and have a blanket which was more than he had now.

"Oh hello officer, didn't see you sneaking up. Yes everything is fine, well no actually it isn't but you wouldn't understand. Am I doing anything wrong? I just want to sit here and think if that's alright." There was something about this policeman that was kind, he did at least seem interested.

"Have you got somewhere to stay tonight, sir? If you don't mind me saying you look like you lost a fiver and found a bob. You're not the only one you know, I see men like you every night here on the streets, given your best in that war and now cast aside. I can offer you a hot drink and a warm cell but you shouldn't sit here, it's not safe. Come on, I'll speak to my sergeant and get you a hot brew. I'm just heading back to the station, now."

Jack looked at the policeman. The realisation that he

really didn't have anything hit him hard. Tomorrow he would somehow get home, but for tonight a police cell seemed better than sitting on a bench, freezing.

"Thank you officer, I won't be any trouble. I just lost my job tonight along with my temper, but tomorrow is another day and I'll get back to my life up north, back with my family. I'll take you up on your offer of a brew though." He stood and the two of them set off.

"Jack, Jack." He could hear the call coming from behind him. The policeman looked round and there was a huge Rolls Royce with a madman shouting.

"Friend of yours is he?" The policeman was smiling, this had to be one for the bar and a beer: he lifts a down and out only to find he has a Rolls Royce motorcar and a chauffeur.

Jim could see the two men up ahead. Jack was obvious but why was he with the police, *had he been arrested, was he in trouble?*

Jack felt the relief flood over him as Jim pulled up alongside.

"Evening officer, has my friend done something wrong, is he in trouble?"

Jim was leaning out of the window of the car like a farmer, it looked odd.

"Trouble? No we were just going to the station to get a cup of tea, but now you're here maybe you can do us both a favour and take him home."

Jack looked into the eyes of the copper, there he saw an honest man, with compassion and kindness. Jack had always prided himself on being able to judge a person's character quickly. He held out his hand to shake the policeman's gloved mitt.

"Thank you, you have no idea how much your kindness has meant to me tonight. I'll go with this chap here, he will look after me. He always has."

It seemed quite a statement of thanks for just offering a cell, but he was glad things were looking better for this strangely, likeable man he had just met. They shook hands and Jack got into the back of the car. There in the back sat the colonel with a huge beaming smile. For the first time in years Jack felt like crying.

"Hello Jack, come on let's get you home. Back to those you love, shall we?"

On the way back Jack felt as though he had been released from his fate: a future of homelessness, unemployment and poverty had seemed unavoidable after his outburst with General Rosewood, but Colonel Alcot was a bigger and better man. There was no such vindictiveness or even a hidden agenda with Gerald Alcot. Jack had felt bad about the whole business right from the start and if it hadn't been for a series of spectacular coincidences he would never have agreed to let Jack go in the first place. Now sat quietly in the car with Jim and the colonel, Jack felt relaxed.

"By the left you caught old Rosewood a corker when you clouted him, he'll have a shiner tomorrow I'm sure of it." Alcot chuckled out loud, and Jack feeling better than he had for days, laughed.

"I didn't mean to push him colonel, he just made me so angry, he called me a coward and although I'm sorry I struck him, he should choose his words more carefully. I'm very sorry colonel, I didn't mean to cause you any embarrassment."

"Embarrassment? Good God, not a bit of it Jack, the blighter deserved it and after you left, he sat in his chair and toasted you. He thinks as much of you as I do Jack. Said you 'had spirit' and old Albert said if you didn't go and do it he wouldn't either. So you see the ball is very much in your court now, but have a couple of days at home first. Spend some time with Alice and the children. I know you'll do the right thing. This madman Hitler needs sorting out, Jack. There's people being murdered by him and his henchmen and if you don't go then someone else will have to, but if you go there isn't a better man to do the job. Think hard Jack, there's a lot at stake here."

Jack sank back into the sumptuous seat in the back of the car, the gentle motion of the car journey and soporific murmur of the engine soon had him in her grasp, and he fell asleep and did not move until they stopped at Langwith.

CHAPTER 32

No place like home, Langwith

The journey north took nearly all night. The roads were clear but there was no direct route and given that Jim had been in bed when the colonel called, it seemed like a sensible idea to allow Jim an hour's rest half way. Once rested they had pressed on and arrived at Langwith at 5am. There were a surprising number of people up and around. The day started early in Langwith.

David Symes was the 'knocker-up' and he had done his rounds. Symes, like most men folk in the area had returned from the war a different man, preyed on with nightmares of his time as a tunneller he found sleep, at best, a fitful event. Night time held so many fears for so many men that sleep didn't come easy and often needed strong beer to help. The downside of intoxicated sleep was a full bladder and although most men in these parts had a potty under the bed, once you were awake you tended to stay awake.

Symes had a job and he was grateful for it. The local pit had taken all the men back on once they had returned, but conditions were as bad if not worse than the trenches; although they all had work it was done both begrudgingly and with nearly as many risks as at the front. Nearly all the men from the pit had gone as tunnellers, it was what they were good at, and now they were back and in harness the mine owners wanted productivity beyond what they were capable of. No one could ever do quite enough to please the boss.

Symes couldn't go back underground, he could hear the screams, always the same screams of men trapped by a German *camouflet*; he knew what those poor devils went through as they died deep in the bowels of the earth, he knew them all by name. They were his friends and he had been one of them, trapped. Only by snapping his own fingers and breaking his own arm had he managed to escape. Now he didn't go underground, he stayed up top and woke miners up before they went off to the pit.

On the main street, Harry Barber's shop was being set up for the day, fresh game was being hung outside by one of the shop assistants; Harry would be out back finishing the butchering for the day. The first customers would be at the shop within a couple of hours, and the busy bustle of daily life would continue as it had for a hundred years. Further on up the road came the gates to the big house, Jim swung the car round the corner and just up the lane was the row of houses that Jack and Jim lived in with their families. Alice would be getting up soon, she was always an early riser and liked to get on with her housework before either Jack or the children got under her feet; today would be a nice surprise as Jack would set the fire and get the water on before she got up.

"Jack, come and see me at the house tomorrow, once

you have had a while with the family." The colonel spoke quietly as Jack got out of the car.

"I will colonel, and thank you for being so kind, and once again I am sorry about the commotion I caused."

With that he winked at Jim who said he would come round in the afternoon with Edith for a brew. He closed the door and walked up the path to everything he loved in life, he put his stuff down on the mat and walked in. Alice was already up and a pot was on the stove boiling some water for a cup of tea. She jumped when Jack came into the room, then she squealed with delight as he came and hugged her as though his life depended on it.

Over the next couple of days Jack was very quiet, deep in thought and Alice knew there was something troubling him. She never asked, working on the premise that if he wanted to tell her, he would.

It was after Sunday dinner that he said he had to talk to her. The children were outside playing and as Alice sat at the table she reached out and took his hand.

"Jack love, what is it? You've been distracted since you came home. Nothing wrong is there?"

Jack looked at her, her eyes were the most beautiful eyes in the world, she had her mother's eyes and Elizabeth had Alice's eyes.

"It's difficult Alice because I don't want to upset you lass, I'm not sure how to tell you what's happened. It starts with Albert in Germany and finishes with me thinking I might have lost my job here at the estate."

This was Jack's way, he stumbled through the story going off at tangents and then coming back to the story of how Monica had been murdered by the Nazis, that Albert had reaped his revenge on the men who had carried out the despicable crime and had faked his own death. He didn't mention that the powers that be wanted him and Albert to go back and bring Hitler to England until right at the end; he was dreading her response, surely she had been through enough in their time together and before. By the time he had finished his tale he was shaking with emotion, although not sure what emotions they were, anger, sadness or shame because he didn't want to go and leave his family again. His place was here by Alice and their children.

He was completely shaken by her answer.

"Jack Adams, I love you, now pull yourself together, what has got into you? Why on earth haven't you told me all this before, it must have been a terrible burden for you to bear. I'm your wife Jack, you should have told me, not try to protect my feelings. Didn't we have enough killing and sadness in that last stupid, blasted war? If you have a chance, even if it's just a small chance to prevent any kind of madness and fighting then why on God's earth wouldn't you take it?"

She got up from the table and walked round to him and put her arms around his neck. As he turned to look at her, she smiled and kissed him on the nose.

"I know you think you have done enough Jack, this is our world here in Langwith, but how can we ever live in peace if we know what's going on in other parts of the world. From what you have told me you have little choice but to go and bring this Hitler back, it might be the bravest thing you have ever done, and if there's a chance you can prevent another war, you have to go. Don't worry about us here love, we are fine and the colonel looks after us as does Jim. You shouldn't be gone for long and besides, Albert needs you more than ever now. When do you have to go?"

Jack shook his head, he was in absolute awe of his wife: she had just put it all into perspective in just two minutes. It looked like Jack was going back after all. After lunch he would walk up to the big house and talk to the colonel. He needed to wash his face so went into the new parlour to the large sink that had a new tap, all fitted whilst he had been away. He ran the cold water over his hands and then washed his face and hair, it felt fresh and clean. He shook his head again as he dressed, looked at Alice who was just going about her day, lifting a fresh loaf from the oven, it smelled wonderful, and Jack knew why he had to go, this life needed defending but none of the answers were here they were hundreds of miles away in Germany.

Later he went to the house and was greeted by the colonel.

"Fancy a ride out Jack, you can take Tim's old mare." Together they rode through the countryside and Jack told the colonel he would need some time off. The colonel just nodded.

CHAPTER 33

We Need a Plan, London

It only took a phone call to a Whitehall number for the ball to start rolling. Albert was as excited as he was expectant; he knew that Jack would agree, it had only ever been a matter of time.

The next day a ministry car collected Jack and after a tearful goodbye with Alice, he shook hands with both Jim and the colonel. He had been back just three days and now it was time to leave again. He assured everyone he would be careful and also that he should be back within a fortnight, depending on transport over the channel being available both ways at short notice. In actual fact, he thought he would be in London within the week but that it might take a little while longer to sort out the details. He wasn't sure whether he would be expected to escort Herr Hitler back to Germany once the planned meetings were finished. He was sure there would already have been some planning meetings held in London. Albert had been there all the time Jack had been home, so he was sure that some initial plans would have been made.

The ride to London seemed to take an age, plenty of

time for Jack to think. The quiet calm of solitude was a very dangerous time for people like Jack and Albert, it always had been, but the discipline in the field was different to the quiet of night time at home, or like today on long journeys with little to distract one's thoughts. It was easy to let your mind drift and without the steely determination of a strong mind, weakness played like a morbid seductress on the darkest and most painful memories that were best tucked away in the box marked 'never open again': a Pandora's box of nightmares. Jack had entered the dark zone in the darkest recesses of his memories. The faces of the men he had killed, never in full focus and just slightly blurred, still ghastly and tortured and all with the accusing eyes of the dead. Every day Jack carried with him, and lived with a huge burden: it was guilt.

He knew he had been exceptional at what he had done during the war, bettered by very few, if any, his only peer in the field had been Albert Hagerman. The truth was they were both angels of death, the reapers right hand men, call it what you wanted it made no difference to the mothers of the dead or the wives or orphaned children. The simple fact was they were murderers by any other name. Only the situation had legitimised the killing to an almost acceptable form of sport. The price men like Jack had to pay was the constant guilt. Those men who had survived the carnage of war carried scars either physical, or like Jack's in their mind.

War was indeed hell, and anything Jack could do to avert another one would be worth any effort. They had said there would never be another war, they had promised. But then again they had said the last one would be over by Christmas and that those that went would be covered in glory, *glory* thought Jack, *unless it smelled like shit and blood there wasn't any such thing.*

The battles that the men who had returned from the hell of France were still being fought daily, and little in the world had changed for the better; however, from what Jack had already seen over the channel things were in a much worse state there than in good old Blighty. If Jack had any doubts before, he certainly didn't have any now. This man Hitler was taking the two countries slowly back to the battlefields of France, it became very clear now and if he had any chance to prevent that, then he had to commit to it, and commit he had.

It wasn't long before they reached the great sprawling metropolis that was London, and within no time they were at the offices of Julian Rosewood. If Jack had anything to say he had better think of it quickly because within a few minutes he would be standing in front of the man he had cuffed round the ear, he didn't feel angry now he felt ashamed and felt he owed Rosewood an apology.

Major General Rosewood opened the office door with a huge disarming grin. He rubbed his chin in a mocking but gentile way and Jack couldn't help but smile then laugh out loud. Rosewood held out an outstretched hand, it was taken in gratitude.

"Jack, glad you came." Rosewood stood aside to allow him entry to his office and showed him to a chair.

Jack started to speak.

"Sir, I just wanted to apologise for my outburst, I hope you will forgive me and accept my apologies." He felt better just saying it; it was like a doorway back to something comfortable.

Rosewood held up a hand to stop him speaking.

"Jack, it is I who should be apologising not you, I was a fool and spoke like one. It's behind us both and I would take it as a great honour if you would forget the whole sorry event, and let's move on as friends. Please take a seat. Would you care for some refreshments? Tea, coffee or perhaps something a little stronger?"

Jack asked for a cup of tea, he was parched. Both nerves and a long uninterrupted journey had left him with a keen thirst. What happened next made Jack howl with laughter as an outpouring of nervous energy and emotional relief welled up and then came flowing out. There was a knock at the door and in walked Albert Hagerman wearing a waitress's pinny carrying a tray with tea and biscuits.

All frivolity petered out with the realisation that the mission to abduct Adolf Hitler really was about to unfold. Albert set the tray of refreshments down on the table and undid his pinny.

He nodded his head as he grasped Jack by the shoulders and in an unusual show of affection hugged his friend and patted his back, "Welcome back, Jack. I knew you would return, we are a team once more."

Jack looked at Albert and for the hundredth time the memory that this man had once been his mortal enemy, to be killed without any remorse or compassion wormed its painful way into Jack's heart, he would have regretted it forever, and was eternally glad he had failed so miserably in his given task. He had indeed become a wonderful friend. Once more they would take on the might of the Germans together. Only this time it wasn't to kill anyone. It was, in effect, supposed to save millions from an inevitable conflict that once again would quickly become a world war. There were many who thought the Germans should have been crushed after the last war to ensure that this situation would never arise again, and yet here it was staring them right in the face. Jack thought this was the result of the Versailles treaty, which was a huge kick in the teeth for a failed war effort by the German nations. In a way both Jack and Albert sympathised with Germany, they had seen first-hand the destruction that the war had brought. On paper it seemed that the politicians had done a good deal at Versailles and indeed they had for France, America and England, but no one could agree with what the consequences of the treaty had done to the ordinary German people. What the Germans thought of as a despicable act of revenge was certainly not the pacifying politics of a compassionate victor.

Germany was in turmoil and it was the people who once again, just as in the war, stood out as the real victims. Fought less than five years ago, there surely couldn't be another, there just mustn't be. Everyone in this room wished for that; peace in our time. If this war was to be avoided then the time for action had arrived. Jack and Albert would leave tomorrow.

Before they left they would have to take care of some administration.

Albert Hagerman was dead to the German authorities but there was no point in taking chances. There would need to be a new passport, and although France and Germany didn't really use them much since the war, Rosewood said, "… it would be better and more realistic if Albert had one". Despite Albert's rapid grasp of the English language it would be best if they, perhaps, made Albert either Swiss or French, his English was after all quite accented; after some discussion it was decided that Albert would be French, Albert Hagerman was dead, Albert Faire had just been born. To go with the new passport there had to be a history: the new Albert would be born in Alsace, which would explain his German as opposed to French mother tongue, in truth Albert didn't speak any French; they hoped it wouldn't be a problem.

All this had been prepared whilst Jack was at home pondering his future, there was no point in procrastinating and at some stage Albert was going to go and do the job with or without Jack.

Both men were issued with identity cards and new clothes. Jack felt chuffed that his wardrobe was being filled with good quality clothes at the government's expense. This was the second new set of clothes he had received in the past three months, at home he would have worn one lot until they were beyond repair then he would have bought some new ones. Both men were given cash, French francs and German *Reichsmarks*; the new currency now being introduced and used in

143

Germany since the massive inflation in the country had totally devalued the *Papiermark*.

They also had a letter of introduction for the British embassy should either man find himself in need of a safe haven.

CHAPTER 34

The Long Road to Glory

The weather was hot, summer had been wet in England but over in France it was hot and dry. The ferry to Le Havre had been quiet. This was mainly due to the very rough and quite unseasonal weather in the channel, most people stayed in their cabins or inside on the benches that made up second-class passenger travel. The majority of passengers were soldiers going back to France to join their regiments in the new army of occupation, as well as old soldiers and families going to look for loved ones who had fallen and were now being placed in regimented lines in the new cemeteries all along the Western Front.

Sir Fabian Ware had formed the nobly named Imperial War Graves Commission at the end of 1917, its role was to try to identify the fallen and give them a formal grave, somewhere that could be the last resting place amongst friends and in some cases foes, together. Every soldier Jack had ever talked too had agreed this was a splendid idea, it was universally well received. Even now new memorials were being planned and in some cases work had already started in building them. Huge cathedral sized memorials to the lost and fallen.

Jack found he was nodding approval as he was thinking about their grandeur. The dead were well looked after; however, the dead of the war had been reinforced by the numerous dead from the flu that had taken so many more than it ever should, just a year after the fighting had stopped. Alice had lost her mother to the flu, and much as it was a tragic event it felt somehow worse that so many men who had survived the fighting should ultimately succumb to illness. So close to home, but still so far. Death knew no borders and cared less for circumstance, millions had died at a time when no more deaths were needed. Families were in the process of being reunited after years of separations and the insatiable appetite of the Grim Reaper.

As he stood outside, Jack was enjoying the blowing wind and sea spray splashing on his worried brow. He had decided to take in the fresh air to help clear his mind, deep inside there was a nagging, a lingering doubt that he couldn't quite put his finger on. He had been a God fearing man all his life and on many occasions had offered up prayer for guidance and indeed forgiveness for what he had done and what he had to continue to do. He was reminded of the Four Horsemen of the Apocalypse and remembered their description in his bible, *Book of Revelation*, chapter 6, verses 1–8. The first Horseman of the Apocalypse:

> *I looked, and there before me was a white horse, Its rider held a bow, and he was given a crown, and he rode out as a conqueror bent on conquest.*

The first Horseman Jack thought of as the Germans who he felt in his mind represented the Antichrist.

The second Horseman of the Apocalypse appears in *Book of Revelation*, 6:4:

> *Then another horse came out, a fiery red one. Its rider was given power to take peace from the earth and to make men slay each other. To him was given a large sword.*

The second Horseman refers to terrible warfare that will break out in the end times. A war to end all wars they said, how could anyone not see the connection?

The third Horseman is described:

> *and there before me was a black horse, Its rider was holding a pair of scales in his hand. Then I heard what sounded like a voice among the four living creatures, saying, 'A quart of wheat for a day's wages, and three quarts of barley for a day's wages, and do not damage the oil and the wine!'*

The third Horseman of the Apocalypse refers to a great famine that would take place, likely as a result of the war from the second Horseman. Jack nodded, were not the people of Germany subjected to great suffering and hunger following the pathetic war? Were people in England, France and Belgium not suffering the same fate? It all made perfect sense to Jack.

Then the fourth Horseman as he recalled was symbolic of death and devastation:

I looked, and there before me was a pale horse, Its rider was named Death, and Hades was following close behind him. They were given power over a fourth of the earth to kill by sword, famine and plague, and by the wild beasts of the earth.

The fourth Horseman of the Apocalypse would bring further warfare and terrible famines along with awful plagues and diseases. *Could anyone deny this had been the case for the past years?* Once more Jack bowed his head to pray, silent and private, he asked *that there should be no return to the killing or suffering and begged for the strength to make this mission a success.* He didn't hear Albert approach, his gentle touch on Jack's arm made him jump.

"Amen." Said Albert, "I have no idea what you were asking but I am sure it was very important."

It was only then that Jack realised he had been mumbling the Lord's Prayer.

"We are going to need all the help we can get old chum, I just have a feeling that this could all go wrong so easily. I just have a nagging doubt, it all seemed so straightforward back in London, but I'm not so sure now. Let's go back to our cabin and look at the plans again, just go through them once more, eh?"

Back in the first-class cabin, Jack took off his sodden coat, his hair was thick with salt from the spray and he could taste the sea on his lips. He wasn't cold though and within a few seconds he was dry, his hair combed back and his parting was all in order. His coat hung on the back of the door dripping onto the carpet, so Jack put the towel he had dried his hair with under it to catch the drips. Albert had rung the steward and fresh hot coffee and a plate of sandwiches were on the way. He dipped his hand into his bag and pulled out a hip flask of the sweet kirsch and the two men took a deep slug of the warming nectar.

"Tell me about your worries Jack, what do you think is going to happen?"

There was a knock at the door and Albert moved the towel and opened it, the sandwiches and coffee were being offered by a smart looking lad who didn't look old enough to have left school, it was a sign they were getting old. Once the coffee had been poured the two men sat opposite each other with a map spread out on the table before them, coffee cups on two corners and a salt and pepper cruet set on the opposite diagonals.

On the map was planned a route. Route A, was marked in red wax crayon and this was the way into Germany. They would travel by train through Rouen, Reims, Verdun, Metz and Strasborg, all in French hands still, and then into Germany itself via Stuttgart, Ulm and, finally, Munich.

From Munich they had a car arranged. This car would take them the final hundred miles to Berchtesgaden and Hitler's home. They would have to stop at Rosenheim to collect a cache of supplies that had been left for them. In this cache there would be weapons and spare ammunition, not that they planned on either needing or using them. Along with the weapons there was extra money in the form of cash and a gold ingot that could be converted into any currency they may require.

The plan was a basic one really, the best they could hope was that Hitler, once found, would just agree to come with them. They did after all have an invitation from the head of MI6 for him to attend lunch, albeit only a verbal invitation.

The big worry was that Herr Hitler would say no. If that happened they would have to become a little more persuasive, and should that persuasion be met with reluctance they would have to be forceful and make him come whatever. It was this last option that bothered Jack so much, how on God's earth would they manage to drag a screaming and kicking Hitler across Germany, France and God knew where back to a ferry for England. Even if they did manage that, there was a very good chance they would be arrested on the English side because no one would believe them if they told the truth.

It was Albert who came up with the idea; Jack sat and listened, speechless. If nothing else it was audacious, no, it was madness. He knew it would work because nobody would credit any chance of any success. There was an irony that wasn't lost on Jack, but sailed over Albert's head like the many aeroplanes that flew above them as they crossed the channel.

"Just tell me again Albert, how the hell are we to make this work?"

Albert was a very patient man, he knew that Jack was anxious and if he was honest his plan was *"Verrücktheit"*, he asked Jack what the right word was. He mimed his impersonation of a lunatic, he crossed his eyes and grinned inanely then rotated his finger round his right temple; Jack just started to laugh.

"You mean 'mad' Albert, and that's just what this daft plan is, madness," he shook his head. "But tell me again, anyway."

Albert continued, "We kill him Jack. For me I don't really mind if we really do kill him, but to get him back home…" he realised that for the first time he referred to England as home, Jack noticed and smiled a grin of reassurance. Albert continued, "We drug him Jack and put him in a coffin, we become *leichenbestatter* , er," he paused, "undertakers."

"Where do we get all the equipment to do this Albert? We need a hearse, some kind of uniform, it's impossible to arrange all that without making a fuss." It was at this precise moment Jack saw how this plan could work.

It was well into the evening, the ferry wasn't due to dock until the morning, the crossing had taken much longer than planned and the weather near the coast was much rougher than out in the channel, so it had been decided to sit it out till morning. Outside the cabin there was a flurry of activity as stewards collected blankets for the second-class passengers. Inside the first-class cabins, each seat folded into a snug but perfectly acceptable sleeping cot. Pillows were supplied and each had two blankets. The captain made his apologies but hoped the passengers would understand the need to run at slow, drinks and light refreshments would be made available for the ladies and any children, but unfortunately there wasn't any stock or supply of food on board.

Jack told Albert his adapted plan, now it seemed feasible. One way they could make this work is if they were dressed in uniform, how about military uniform? Returning a dead soldier to his hometown. Who would notice another returning hero? But instead of bringing a body back from the front they would be taking one away! For transport all they needed was an old army truck and some soldiers' uniforms, surely that must be a lot easier to obtain than a hearse.

Albert agreed instantly, this was a much better and safer plan. It would only need to be for a short time, until they got away from the area where Hitler might be recognised easily. Once they had cleared the border they could use the rail system again before catching a ferry and a quick escape back to England. It would also give them a simple base to sleep in on the journey.

All in all a triumphant mission, Albert slapped Jack on the back and congratulated him on finding a solution. They pulled up the collars on their greatcoats, heavy and thick, not dissimilar to the military ones they had worn yesteryear. It was easy to forget that Albert was so much older than Jack, seventeen years to be precise, Albert was already nearing fifty and Jack had just turned thirty-one, in the very prime of his life. Both men had far too many miles on their body clocks for their age but then so did so many others who had lived through the traumas that had been ever present in the last twenty years. Life was hard but at least they were alive to find it so.

CHAPTER 35

France Remembers

At first light the Captain eased his battered ferry into Le Havre harbour, it had been a long night.

The smell of vomit and seasickness pervaded the air and passengers were both irritable and tired, all in all it had been a thoroughly rotten night and everyone was ready to disembark, even the crew. Jack and Albert on the other hand, had rested and for the first time, felt sure of what lay ahead.

First they had to get to the main station ready to embark on part two of their journey. It didn't take long; there were only the most cursory of checks, instead people were let through to be on their way, it was felt these poor wretches had endured enough for one trip.

The railways had adopted the old military railheads that had been left by the army in 1919 and maintained them with the hundreds of miles of spare track and all the paraphernalia that went with it. Some of the rail stock had been left over as well, so it wasn't really a huge surprise when they boarded an old but luxurious first-class carriage. It was still in the brown paint livery of the Great Western Railway from before its loan here at the outbreak of the war. Jack and Albert were delighted when they came aboard to find they were alone in a sumptuous compartment. They opened the sliding window that was within the door and as the train puffed steam and smoke there was a comforting aroma and atmosphere that reminded both men of happy days long since passed. Albert got out his pipe and rolled some tobacco in his palm, Jack tapped his pipe clean on his heel making room for a fresh rub. He had taken to the pipe after he came back from the war, he found it didn't make him cough quite so much as cigarettes and was easier to keep clean and dry when out in the woods back on the estate. Both men filled their pipes, Albert had a large *Meerschaum* made in Tuttlingen with a large bowl that held a good amount of rub, Jack on the other hand found that his smaller half bent *Billiard* fitted into his coat pocket easier and stayed alight for a surprisingly long time without any attention. Within minutes there was as much smoke billowing around the carriage as there was outside, only this smell was much more agreeable to most people. The two men sat back and for the first time in an age enjoyed the company of another similarly minded man doing the same thing; just sat thinking their own thoughts punctuated with the occasional nod to no one in particular. It would be at least a couple of hours to Reims, plenty of time to think and consider their next moves, the secret from here on in was to be adaptable, nothing was more certain than it would all go belly up at some stage and it was always better to plan for the worst; anything better than that was a bonus.

As they chugged their way towards Rouen it was surprising how quickly the world was recovering from the past. Everywhere there were signs of recovery, be it buildings being knocked down and rebuilt or repaired. The land was showing signs of healing with farmers returning the land back to fields of crop. The story wouldn't be the same further north where the ground had been pummelled into muddy holes by a vicious and hideous constant bombardment of ordnance much of which was still there, waiting to be found either by deadly accident or collected and stored ready for disposal.

Rouen came and went with hardly a stop, some families disembarked to go and visit the new graves of their loved ones. There had been some big military base hospitals in Rouen, and the death rate was constantly mounting with more and more seriously injured soldiers waiting to be transported back to England. There would be some very large graveyards here.

The next stop would be Reims. It was whilst here that Jack and Albert would see how their plan could work. At the rail head waiting for a train in the opposite direction stood a motor truck with two coffins in the back ready for a private repatriation to some country graveyard back home in Blighty. Stood alongside it were two soldiers from a regiment Jack couldn't quite recognise having a cigarette, escorts thought Jack, both men looked too old to be serving so Jack assumed they had to be Territorials, old sweats who couldn't, or wouldn't, let go. Maybe they were family, but either way it comforted both of them to see that old soldiers were doing the job, but would it be the same in Germany? It must be.

Jack noticed that it wasn't the only military truck, there were many that were sat, waiting for the train to take the remains of men back home. These men had been dug up or found recently in fields up and down the length of the battlefields of France and although repatriation wasn't encouraged, it wasn't discouraged either. If a family was able to pay for the cost of repatriation and reburial, then the government wouldn't get in the way of the process, and if it gave a family some kind of comfort to have their loved one back home in a local cemetery, then Jack was all in favour of it. Both men nodded their final respect. Despite no one being able to see them, it was their way.

CHAPTER 36

Landslip

Verdun was just about coming into view when the train started to slow. It had been a long five hour journey and both men were looking forward to a good leg stretch and an overnight stay in Verdun.

Albert pulled down the window to look out as the train finally came to a standstill, there was a commotion outside and there was clearly something wrong. Suddenly and without warning there was a huge explosion, the whole train rocked sideways and there was a low groaning as slowly the tracks buckled under the weight of the engine and coal truck behind. The driver was urgently trying to relieve the engine of its built-up steam and the whistle screamed a mournful bellow as if it knew it was dying. There was another quieter familiar *crump* and both Jack and Albert ducked instinctively. If they had been able to see the other passengers along the length of the carriages they would see a similar picture, every soldier and ex-soldier on the train recognised the dreadful *crump*, it was a shell going off.

The first huge bang was the instigator of a course of events that would last only a few minutes, but would bring death and destruction to a now quiet city that had known such destruction and grief in 1916.

It was a huge mortar shell that had lain in the ground since the siege of Verdun, probably German but who knew it could just as easily been French. It had waited long enough to do its ghastly work and as it exploded it took with it, in turn, a number of smaller but just as deadly shells that had been put aside prior to their disposal. The first explosion had ripped to pieces five farm workers who had stopped their daily toil of tilling the land to wave to the train driver and his engineer a cheery "*bon voyage*". It was the last thing they would do.

The vibrations from the train had been the cause of the detonation, and the disposal team who had been tasked with the shells safe removal had also paid the ultimate price for any complacency. They had set up a slowdown signal to the train driver who had done exactly as ordered but this time their luck had run out, it was a complete shock to everyone. The track had been smashed apart and the train now finally gave up its balance and slumped over onto its side, with a gush of steam and a scream of its whistle the train broke away from the carriages and lay on its side, dead.

Quickly there was the sound of doors opening. The deafening boom of the shell exploding had, for the main, gone and was replaced with an eerie quiet, the soldiers knew that this wouldn't last long and that within seconds the peace and calm would be replaced with screams and anguish. Chaos and carnage are comfortable and familiar friends of the devil and in this moment of calm things moved very slowly. Then the first cries for help started and the doors continued to clatter as men jumped down onto the trackside and ran to the engine. The driver was injured but the fireman was in a bad way. He had been trying to close the firebox doors before the engine fell on its side, in doing so he had somehow dislodged a live steam pipe to the whistle and scalded his chest badly with steam, his leather jerkin had saved his legs but burning coal had hit his shins and set alight his trousers. The driver had burnt his hands quite badly putting the fire out on his pal and workmate, after all they were a team and had been together for quite a few years since they had returned to work following their own demobilisation from the French army in 1919.

By the time Jack and Albert reached the front there was a line of men offering to help but they needed direction, someone to take charge. Albert shouted for everyone to be quiet, they all instantly fell silent. The guard was dispatched to fetch help, it made sense for him to go as he was French and would be able to communicate what had happened quickly.

"Listen to me, we need to find the injured and take them somewhere safe, I need six men to set up a clear area over there by those wooden huts." He pointed to a row of rail track workers' shelters, each one empty with the glass windows now blown in, the train engine had taken most of the blast so the huts had survived.

Jack noticed that some of the men were shaking quite badly, *shell shock* he thought. He gathered them together and spoke to each one asking them if they were ok, each one nodded back despite fighting their demons, they were fighting fear and Jack was a reassuring hand.

"We'll go," said Jack, he knew the best thing to do with these fellows was to get them busy and clearing out a few wooden huts would be perfect. Albert could see what Jack was doing. He admired him for his compassion.

"Ok", said Albert, "next we need to find anyone injured and get them away from this train engine, it's full of steam and might go boom." He struggled with the correct English but got his message across quickly enough.

There were four coaches in second class plus two first class at the front, "All the women and families should go and sit in the last three coaches." He shouted, "I need two men to organise that, empty the first-class dining bar of brandy and make sure the ladies are ok. The rest of you look for anyone that might be injured and take them to the huts."

Jack and his team of jolly shakers had the huts cleared in no time, truth was there wasn't much in them to clear out but the water butts were full and Jack asked one of the men to go and ask the ladies if there were any nurses amongst them, if not could they make some form of bandages for the injured.

There was a large amount of people cut from flying glass, some were nasty but in the main they were only grazes, most people had been seated when the explosion happened and many of the ladies were wearing hats which offered them some further protection. The main body of the train was undamaged, only the coal tender and engine had actually toppled over. The train had been slowing and had almost come to a standstill when the shell went off, but there was no hope for the bomb team and the farmer's labourers, they had all died instantly with the explosion. Albert tasked a couple of the more sensible men to collect and cover the body parts. It was a macabre jigsaw with an arm here and a dismembered leg there. There wasn't much more left, but a quick look wouldn't do any harm and the different limbs were collected and placed in a tarpaulin that Jack had found in the huts.

There was an air of calm returning and cigarettes were being lit all around, the injured had been collected and their wounds dressed with makeshift bandages. The rest had been given drinks from the first-class bar and were sat chattering like canaries as the shock finally settled. Jack had poured gallons of cold water straight from the water butt onto the scalded engineer's chest, initially it had been too strong a current so Jack had used an old riddle that looked clean and covered it in some petticoat cloth torn from a slightly bemused young lady to stem the flow of water from a cascade to a trickle. Its cooling effect on his burned chest was soothing and helped him, he was French and spoke no English but one of the ladies who had been a VAD in the war spoke the lingo well enough to communicate what was needed. Help was already nearing and the men now started to reflect on what might have happened. Some were shaking now the action was over, one chap's hand was shaking uncontrollably as the man tried to light his cigarette, Jack reached out and took his shaking hand holding it steady whilst the poor chap lit up. A deep drag from the calming smoke helped settle his nerves.

"Who were you with?" asked Jack.

"The Rifles," said the now calm man. "I was a sergeant with them, started in 1915 and nearly got through unscathed apart from these damned shakes when I gets a fright."

Jack's six men had gathered together in a collective group, each giving the others support in a quiet way. They had stopped looking terrified now and most had stopped shaking all apart from one who was sat on the bank sobbing whilst his wife held him in her loving arms. All the others were humbled and none spoke ill of him, there but for the grace of God they thought.

A doctor arrived to tend to the injured, trucks and horse drawn carts turned up and the passengers were loaded onto buses and taken into Verdun. Jack thought how kind people were, coffee had arrived even before the main body of helpers turned up, and small cakes and sandwiches were offered to everyone very quickly.

Albert walked over to Jack, he had a huge grin on his face, "Just like the old days, eh, my friend? I admit, I do miss it sometimes."

Truth be known most men did, in the pubs and bars all over the country they would chat about the war. There wasn't much need to talk about it at home, as long as they could in the company of men who understood the fear in the other's eyes.

"Aye, Albert you looked like you knew what to do These poor blighters, digging up these damned bombs and shells, that's not a job I'd relish and no mistake. We need to be getting on one of those buses and getting a move on."

The two men walked over to the train carriage and collected their belongings, not that they amounted to much, just a couple of old military holdalls with their clothes, they hadn't seen any need to bring a lot, they weren't planning on being here long. As they walked over to a bus, a lady stopped them to thank them for the things they had done, Jack said, it was nothing that anybody on the train wouldn't have done, to which she said "yes that's true but they didn't do it, you did." It made Jack feel good and Albert was sure he could see Jack Adams blush.

CHAPTER 37

Verdun

The ancient city of Verdun, is situated on the river Meuse in the north-eastern area of France, and over its bloody and long history it had been the site of many battles and sieges but none that compared to the battle in 1916.

The city was blessed with many forts built for a war a hundred years before and war between the Germans and French was nothing new. This time, however, General Erich von Falkenhayn had barbaric plans that would cost the lives of nearly a million men. His plan was to attack Verdun and knowing the strategic importance of the place he also knew the French would fight to the last to keep it in their hands. Falkenhayn's plan was to bleed the French army white by continually reinforcing the French *poilu* the Germans could tie down and, ultimately, defeat the French. Once the French had capitulated it would be easy to blockade the English ports with the German 'U' boats and in a very short time starve the British to the negotiating table.

Jack remembered how this dreadful war of attrition had so nearly worked and, if it had not been for the British and French sacrificing thousands on the Somme in July of 1916 Falkenhyne's plan would have had severe implications on the war. As it was it caused enough problems, Joffre had been removed by the French, who like their allies the British, were always looking for a scapegoat. This upheaval had caused severe problems in the French ranks and the British had to toe the line once more to save the day. The Somme offensive had been thrown together with the underlying aim of drawing the Germans away from Verdun to repulse the British attack.

Jack shivered at the memory of the battle, he had felt useless in the past, and unable to do what he had been so good at, but on that hot morning on the 1st July only eight years ago he had been stunned into inertia. So many of his friends had fallen that day, it was a futile attempt and ultimately took until November to finally win the battle. But with that sacrifice came reprieve; reprieve for the French army here in Verdun. The price the allies had paid in those five months was less than a quarter of the fallen French in defending this sacred city. The Germans had paid a heavy price for the audacious plan. Jack had heard that the Germans had lost over 300,000 men in this city and the French even more. This was bloodletting on a scale the author HG Wells couldn't even imagine and the landscape was more akin to Dante's Inferno than the ancient Gaul city Verdun once was.

★

Albert looked out as the bus drove along the roughly repaired roads. Nearly everywhere you looked there were graveyards for the fallen, collected together and reburied here as a band of brothers in death, thousands and thousands of crosses in regimental lines seemed to run for ever one after the other.

"These were just the French." Said Albert and Jack looked over the saddest vista he had ever witnessed.

"What happened to the Germans?" He asked.

Albert shrugged, "somewhere else I hope."

It was the first time since their trip from Germany that Jack had seen a thoughtful Albert, and for the second time he offered his German friend the hand of friendship, Albert took it and the horror of the day caught up with them both. Albert nodded and when Jack looked closely at his friend he noticed a wetness around his eyes.

Verdun does that to you.

CHAPTER 38

Moving On

It was whilst the two men enjoyed a day off from travelling that they finalised plan B, the one where they might need to subdue Hitler to bring him back. Jack had laid the bones of the plan out for Albert to cogitate over, but now after the previous day's drama it seemed like a good time to actually look at the things they might need.

Both were surprised how much military equipment was around, it would be easy to borrow a truck for a few days and the chances were no one would miss it if they took it at the weekend. After all they would return it by Sunday night. As for uniforms, Jack felt sure they could either buy some or get General Rosewood to get some issued. Albert mentioned that Rosewood might disapprove of being involved so maybe it would be better if they could buy them. Jack nodded his agreement, he hadn't thought about Rosewood for a couple of days, but Albert had spent a lot of time with him whilst Jack was thinking the mission through at home in Langwith. Funnily enough, Jack wasn't homesick at all. He put it down to having a busy mind and after yesterday a very busy time of it altogether.

The police wanted to take statements from the two of them at some stage today and it served their purpose to spend some time thinking what happened next. In actual fact, they needn't rush anything for a couple of days, up to now they had made excellent time and were ahead of any loose schedule they had.

Tomorrow, they would have to move on with things. One thing was certain the uniforms would be easier to obtain here rather than further up the line; however people were already far too interested in who these two men were and why they were here. Not exactly keeping a low profile as they had been told to do.

Jack let a long plume of smoke drift out and rise towards the ceiling, and as he did this he noticed a tough, thick skin had developed over the pad on his right middle finger where he held his pipe. He often found he played with this skin and his thumb nail when he was deep in thought. Albert noticed the habit as well and said, "Jack, what are you thinking?" it snapped Jack back into the moment.

"Are we sure Hitler will resist? Surely it's in his best interest to be friends with the English isn't it? I can't believe he'll want to see our countries at loggerheads with each other again. I'm no politician, Albert, but I would have thought those men with schooling above ours would be of a mind to make sure this never happens, ever." Jack felt quite aggravated, almost aggrieved, that some upstart might have eyes on a second Great War. "This bugger isn't even German is he? Who is listening to his rhetoric and bile, I just don't understand."

Albert nodded; he had a much better understanding of the situation in Germany. "Jack things are really terrible in Germany, but they have been very much worse in the not so distant past. We had hardly anything to eat, the French stole everything we made, food, industry, railways, factories, everything. The treaty that was signed was very harsh on the Germans, not on the upper classes but the poor working class. The Communists have seen that there is a great opportunity to thrive in the sickness that is a depression. Hitler hates the Communists as much as he hates the Jews, he blames them for losing the war in the first place. Losing the war was everyone's fault but not the German soldiers'. For them there can only be praise. This is not what I think, but what Hitler says, and the Germans want to believe they never lost the war but were betrayed. The price we have had placed on us is very high, Jack. Most Germans are like you and me, we just want to look after our families and live in peace, but the French and the Americans and sad as it makes me feel, the English, are asking for everything and not leaving much for people to live with."

Jack really had no idea it was as bad as that, but this was the truth and maybe it was even worse.

Albert continued: "This man Hitler, people want to listen to him, he tells them the things they want to hear. That Germany will once again be a great country, not like before all fat and rich but a shared wealth with our traditions being respected it's our way of life that he appeals to. When you have nothing Jack and someone comes and offers you the world, it is very hard not to listen, but I know it's a dream Jack, a nightmare, and so do many Germans. They are rounded up and silenced, they disappear. Hitler isn't the nice man he pretends to be. I agree with a lot of the things he says but I don't believe him. He is a dangerous man Jack and the world doesn't need more dangerous men. The likes of you and I have seen what the dangerous men can cause and do. Hitler is scared, Jack, he is scared that the Communists will make Germany like Russia and if he can scare the rest of the German people he will raise another mighty army. If he can control the political system in Germany, Jack, there will be another war. We have to stop him and his friends in the Nazi party, they are evil. It was the Nazis who killed my Monica and why did they do that? I have no idea other than they think honest men like me, will stop him because we have seen war Jack and we don't want to see it again. That is why they killed Monica to make sure I did as I was beckoned, to keep me in line and not cause any trouble. All across Germany, Jack, men like me are being forced to do as the Nazis say or we have to pay or worse. I know of good men who have been found dead, always looking like a suicide, an accident or just disappearing and never heard of again. The one thing all these men have in common with me is they are my age, Jack. Too old to fight but have seen enough fighting to know we don't want to see anymore and we have a voice. That is until it is silenced by the Nazi scum who work for this madman, Hitler."

Jack took in everything Albert said, he hadn't either believed or understood how bad it was in Germany.

He had a clearer understanding now. The situation was indeed urgent and, more than that, he understood why it had to be Albert who he supported. Albert knew there was no going back to Germany, there was no happy ever after for his trip, when this was over he would have to settle in England and Jack felt sure there would be a place for him at the colonel's. It was true that employment was hard to find and houses were in short supply but the colonel had always been good to Jack, and for that matter Albert, when he was a prisoner. Albert had worked hard and was popular with the staff, his jovial sense of humour and ability to think for himself made him a useful asset to the farm.

Jack said, "We leave tomorrow Albert, we need to get this done. I have a doctor to see this afternoon as do you, the people from the hospital said they wanted to see us to say thank you for trying to save the engine driver." They had learned that despite their best efforts he had died that night. The medical team had given him plenty of morphine to kill the pain and he died in his sleep.

Later that afternoon there was a knock at the door at their hotel, as good as his word, it was the doctor from the hospital.

Jack had said he was fine but Albert had told the doctor he was struggling to sleep. The events of the previous day had disturbed memories of his time at the front and he would wake terrified and screaming. The doctor told him he had some sleeping tablets, they were very strong but he felt sure that if Albert could get a few nights' sleep the nightmares would subside.

It was normal these days to hear of such problems, the men of France weren't immune to the nightmares of a war that had taken so many of their friends, and he could see no reason why the Germans would be any different or indeed anyone else that had lived through that disaster. He told a story of the men in his wards that were totally normal until a sudden noise, then they turned into shaking wrecks, many unable to stand upright. The disfigured men had a sign for people to see and warn them. The men who had lost limbs wore their disability as a medal should be worn. The physical injuries were now easy to treat but those poor men with mental disfigurement, for them the war was still happening every day. Some men could cope with it better than others but he was no stranger to home visits to sign death certificates for those who couldn't cope and ended it with a shot to the head, self-inflicted mainly, but not always, sometimes they were a mercy, a blessed relief. No man could punish these people and the law was never involved other than to cursorily investigate. Accidental death, it was always that. The country owed them a small pension and at least let their families keep that. God knows they have given their men.

The doctor spoke perfect English and Jack appreciated him looking out for his friend. At last the doctor left once more thanking them for their efforts with the engine driver and his mate. It was a miracle more hadn't died.

CHAPTER 39
Gathering Gear

When they were alone Jack said, "I didn't know you had problems sleeping Albert, are the dreams bad?"

Albert tapped the side of his nose, "I sleep with a clear conscience my friend, we did what we had to do to live ourselves. There are no dreams. I needed the tablets for later, just in case we need to make our man sleep."

Jack laughed, he said Albert was a crafty old fox and then set about writing a list of kit he thought they might need. From walking around the area of the cemeteries he knew it wouldn't be hard to gather some of their effects.

The easiest thing to get was a truck, initially they were going to steal one, or at least borrow it, but when they discussed it they thought it would just be easier and more sensible to buy one. They were not a lot of money and truth be told money wasn't a problem, they had plenty.

Uniforms might prove more difficult, but Jack was fairly sure they would be able to get some if they went to the local bar and asked quietly around.

Later that evening they did frequent a bar that had all the noises they searched for, soldiers singing. Inside it was smoky, and dark; there was a man on a piano hammering for all he was worth on the keys, the jolly tinkling was being roundly supported by a small choir of men half filled with drink, of all nations, trying to both keep up and keep a tune. Unfortunately for most people's ears they were failing in both. At the bar sat the sergeant in charge of the British labour platoon here in Verdun, here to help with the grisly task of recovering the dead from as long ago as ten years in some cases. Buried in haste in either mass pits or the single graves marked at the time with a wooden cross and a map grid reference for future use. Initially buried by their friends with all the dignity that the men who had laid them to rest could muster and in a time of great tragedy and danger; it was time to give these lads a proper burial.

It was no wonder the lads took to drink thought Jack, *no one would enjoy the task at hand, and these lads would be back in the fields around Verdun and the forts helping their comrades the French first thing in the morning.*

As Jack got to the bar he motioned to the barmaid, a bonny lass in her twenties, a cigarette on the go and her hair tied on top with a hair band, she was in great demand. He asked in his best French, which was nearly worse than useless, to buy a round of drinks for all the soldiers regardless of nationality. In the end it was the sergeant who came to his rescue.

"Are you struggling with the lingo, mister? Can I help? I speak it fairly well. Did you want a beer for you and your friend?"

Jack thanked him and said, he wanted to buy a beer

174

for all the men in uniform and the sergeant stood up from his bar stool to shake Jack's hand. He ordered the drinks to be served in jugs and he ordered six jugs, he could count about fifteen men and thought that amount of beer might just cover it. The men all cheered and waved as the jugs were passed around, most were nearly drunk anyway and another pint or so would help nicely. The sergeant asked for Jack's name.

"Adams, Sarge. I'm an old soldier come over to help find some lads of my regiment who are further north." Jack knew that the same gruesome task of finding and burying the long since dead was taking place all up and down the Western Front. "My friend here is from Alsace. We became good mates back then and he is on a mission to find his son – German army – it's been difficult so far but we have found him. All we need to do now is take the poor bugger home." Jack could see he had him, he was listening intently and nodding in the right places to show he sympathised with the two men.

"Mates eh, and him a Jerry, well we are all in it together now, Mr. Adams."

Jack said he needed to purchase some equipment to help get the lad back to his homeland for a Christian burial, but was at a loss as to where to buy such equipment. As he watched the cogs of capitalism whirl in the sergeant's head he asked if he could buy another round, again there was a cheer.

"What equipment are you looking for Mr. Adams? Maybe I can point you in the right direction, I've been

175

here a while now and I might know a few people who can help."

Jack had recognised a poacher the second he walked into the bar, men like this were always on the take and would steal supplies at the drop of a hat. Jack had been taught by the best to recognise poachers and thieves, his mate Jim Cunningham could spot them a mile off and he had passed that on, almost like a sixth sense.

"Really, that would be very much appreciated, I can't help but notice that just about everything we need is all around here, we could do with a truck for a few days to carry the coffin in. In fact, a coffin would make his family very proud and if we could perhaps borrow a couple of uniforms to dress in, so that we can carry the remains into church?"

He looked at the sergeant who said without batting an eye, "Oh, I'm sure we can manage that, how do you want to pay? Do you have cash?"

Jack smiled, greed was an easy tool to manipulate a crooked man.

"Francs or pounds, Sarge? I have both." It took no time at all to agree a price, after all it was really only a loan, they would be back in a couple of days and the sergeant could have the stuff back then. So the price was set and agreed on a handshake and another beer. It was arranged that they would pick up the truck and uniforms the next afternoon and meet at the café again at 3pm to exchange cash and keys.

Albert hadn't said a word, not one. He sat and drank beer, tapping his foot to the tune on the piano. When

Jack tapped him on the shoulder he turned to see the big sergeant and Jack eyeing him up. They mumbled something that he didn't catch and the sergeant wandered off again. Albert had just been measured for his uniform, not exactly Savile Row.

CHAPTER 40

On Our Way

The next day was bright and sunny, unlike the mood or the slightly sore head from drinking too much beer. The mood was soured because Jack hated thieves and scoundrels and today he was to buy goods from just such a man. Corruption wasn't new to the army supplies department, quartermaster's stores, like everywhere else had good and bad, but Jack had seen in the last bash, how much difference a good quartermaster could make.

When he had first started his job all those years ago in France at the number one Sniping School, he had been dismayed at the fact that sniper scopes were just handed out from the stores because they didn't want to have to account for them. Good men had died trying to get those sights working and they had done so because they should never have had them in the first place. At least not until their training in using them had been completed. He didn't often think about things like that because he couldn't turn the clock back and it did no good to let bad memories fester in the brain. Today he had remembered that and consequently, he was grumpy.

Albert on the other hand was in fine spirits; he was looking forward to getting on with the mission at hand. By tonight they should be in Strasbourg, a long drive but the roads were very quiet and it promised to be a nice day. They should be there in six or seven hours.

As they approached the café, the truck was parked on the side of the road. The sergeant and a couple of men were sat at a table outside, when Jack and Albert appeared the men stood to greet them. The truck was fully fuelled and in the back were a stash of blankets, two full uniforms complete with black armbands in the pockets, and red crosses sewn on the right arm. Medical Corps insignia was on the cap and shoulder tabs. Also in the back was a service coffin and lid, as an extra treat two thermos flasks full of hot sweet coffee and a couple of loaves of bread with some dried meat. A large can of water was strapped into the holder on one side and three full fuel cans were strapped onto the other side in the back. The truck was nearly new and started first time. Once Jack was satisfied everything was in order he wandered off with the sergeant to give him his money. Surprisingly, it wasn't expensive, just a few francs really. Jack did say he thought it would cost more, but the sergeant just said there were plenty around where that came from. Further to that, he thought, the job Albert and Jack were doing in taking Albert's dead son home, was a Christian thing to do.

Jack felt quite guilty.

The two men climbed aboard the truck and with

a map and a 'cheerio' they set off on the second, and hopefully less eventful leg of their journey.

As they wound their way out of the city and along the riverbank, the sheer size of the task that the burial crews were taking on became apparent. Huge cemeteries were being prepared and continually added to daily. The reburial of the war dead was a honourable quest, and the knowledge that it was countrywide, all up and down the old front, was both humbling and yet a strangely proud experience. The dead deserved nothing less, they had given their all, in most cases willingly. To see this work being done today made Jack feel maybe it hadn't just been a waste. It helped focus the mind of both men that from now on they needed to keep their wits about them.

The road to Strasbourg was tidy and easy, they stopped a couple of times to allow the engine a chance to rest and drink the coffee and eat. By 6pm they were at the next crossroads, with a decision to be made. Did they press on to Offenburg where there was a place Albert knew or should they hide in the woods for the night? Obviously they would need to sleep in the truck but they had plenty of blankets and room wasn't a problem, both men had slept in much worse than this in the past and it really wasn't a hardship. They agreed that they would press on, it would make the journey tomorrow that much shorter. Tomorrow they would reach Augsburg, this was important because General Rosewood had arranged a meeting with a local agent who would brief the two men on Hitler's whereabouts and his programme for the next week or so. It was from this meeting that the final plan would be made. It really was a bit fly by night as far as planning went.

*

Gustav Rolf was the man Rosewood had contacted via the embassy and he was heading off to his parents' house away in the woods just outside Augsburg. They had a hunter and woodcutter's hut there and he knew the ground like no one else alive, he had been born and brought up in those woods. His father was a forester before the war and when he came back, although he was scarred by the events of the last five years he was in general the same man, unlike so many others from the area who didn't come back at all. All the local men were members of the Bavarian Regiments, they had been a keen regiment and had paid a heavy price for their loyalty to the Kaiser. Gustav Rolf had played no part in the war, he had been conscripted but hadn't even finished his basic training before the war ended, much to his relief, but that was nothing compared to the relief of his parents. No one wanted his or her son to fight in that stupid stubborn war.

Augsburg was the third largest city in Germany and buried deep in its Swabian roots. It was in many ways still a beautiful place, but for Gustav, nowhere compared to these woods. He was to stay there every night until the meeting.

No one suspected him from the town hall where

he was employed as a senior clerk, a position he had been offered after the war when the British were administrating some of the Stadt's recovery. He had been educated in the city and although his father was a simple man, Gustav certainly was not. He was educated on a scholarship and attended the city university. A career in the political sector was planned for him. That was until the National Socialist German Workers' Party reared its ugly head. Ironically this was when the British had approached him, they sold him the concept of the middle conservative model; a model he was very pleased to be associated with prior to the war and one that was desperately trying to stand up to the communist revolutionary bile that most people were happy to look towards for their survival. It was quite simple then, you were either a communist or not, now there was a third way, a way just as evil as the communist diatribe but poles apart. From extreme left to extreme right, both were filled with hatred at their roots and both looking for a scapegoat for the defeat of Germany's mighty army.

Gustav was an easy target for the men who worked in the shadows; with a helping hand up here and a door closed there, he was soon installed into a position where he could prove useful, providing information that might help avoid the inevitable conflict that was surely coming their way in the future.

CHAPTER 41

A Hunter Returns

Jack held the map in one hand, his pipe in the other. He used the mouth piece as a pointer as he followed what looked like a road on the map but was in actual fact just a dusty rough track.

"Albert, we have gone wrong somewhere old chum, this road isn't even marked on the map." Albert just smiled.

"Relax Jack, this is my homeland. I know exactly where we are going and you don't need a map, you need to hang on."

Albert drew a long lungful of smoke from his pipe and blew out a never-ending plume: a blue cloud. He was enjoying being back, but it was hugely tinged with sadness. He had lost everything here; all the things he loved had been stolen from him, violated and murdered which in turn had made him into a murderer, not that it was buried too deep. He hated the Nazis and he could see they were as much trouble as the older and wiser people thought they might prove to be.

Presently, the truck turned up an even smaller track, barely wide enough to allow passage. At the top of this lane sat an old wood cutter's cottage; Albert had a pang of pain in his heart, it was so very similar to the one he had made his home and had to burn back in Tuttlingen. Everything he had owned had gone up in smoke, including him, according to the German police.

When they arrived at the lone house, it was empty, so Jack wandered off to have a look around. He could *feel* someone looking rather than see anyone. He knew he was right, Albert felt it too, and he just nodded an understanding nod, almost indefinable if you hadn't seen it before. Jack had, and he knew now that Albert's senses were alive as well. They were being watched and neither man liked it at all.

Gustav had heard the truck start the climb on the gravel roadway, he thought it might be best if he wasn't there and he slunk away to a hide he had made in a tree, almost like a flat tree house with ferns as a roof. Unless you knew what you were looking for, you wouldn't see this. He pulled up the small makeshift ladder he used to climb and looked down on the house below about fifty yards down the hill. He used his father's binoculars, they were superb, and he had a clear view of the truck well before it had stopped. The two men inside fitted the description he had been given but he thought it prudent to wait a while to see if anyone else had followed them.

Albert suddenly disappeared from view. It happened in the blink of an eye, one second he was there, and as Gustav moved his binoculars to see that Jack stood at the back of the truck, he was gone. He scanned round to see if he could see the missing Albert and by the time he realised he couldn't, Jack had disappeared also. He knew instantly he was in trouble, these two were way too skilful for a simple woodman's son to find. Like a couple of deer in the woods, they had been spooked and gone to ground. Much as he tried, he couldn't see either of them. He realised he felt quite terrified and as he frantically moved his binoculars left to right he gave away where he was hiding. Both men saw the movement and made their way round the back. It was comforting to know that neither had lost any of their skills that had ensured they remained above the ground and not buried, dead beneath it. They didn't need to look for each other, they would not be able to see, but they knew where the other was just by feeling and a hidden sense.

It took them precisely nine minutes to circle round to the back of the tree where they had seen Gustav move. His hide, although good, wasn't anywhere near good enough, he knew they were somewhere out there but had no idea where they were, he decided it best to just give himself up.

He called out, "I am Gustav Rolf, who are you, and what do you want?" Albert answered because he knew Jack wouldn't have understood a word, it being in heavily accented Swabian. "Come down Gustav, we mean you no harm. We have travelled a long road to see you. I knew your father, I'm surprised he isn't here to meet us." Albert had seen the house was empty when they arrived.

Gustav stood up, he still couldn't see either man. Jack had a shovel, it was the only thing he could lay his hands on in a hurry, but he knew how to make a simple shovel a deadly weapon should it be needed. Albert came out of the woods as though taking a Sunday afternoon stroll, there was no indication of the menace he was capable of, and as he walked to the tree Gustav climbed down.

"Hello Gustav, I'm Albert Hagerman, I understand you are here to meet us, by us I mean Jack and I." As if by magic Jack was stood there next to the tree.

"How did you do that?" Asked a still worried but more startled Gustav.

Jack said, "Do you speak English? It would make it a lot easier if you do."

Gustav noticed the Englishman had a kind face, the sort of face a man could trust in a crisis.

"I do speak English, are you Jack Adams?" Jack nodded he was. "And then you must be Albert Hagerman, my father speaks of you still." He offered his hand in friendship. "Come lets go inside the house, it is safer there."

The group retired into the wooden building, its layout so familiar to Albert, they were all the same, these woodman's houses. He turned left into the parlour where a kitchen table and chairs filled the room nicely. There was no fire in the hearth.

It had been a pleasant day and although the nights were chilling, the autumn sun still had warmth to it. The trees shielded the cabin from the sun's direct brightness and cast a dappled shadow, constantly dancing in the breeze, it made for a very pleasing ambiance.

"Where is your father Gustav? I thought he would be here somewhere."

"My father is in the hospital, he has kidney problems, but he asks for little, which is all he gets. He deserves better but there is no money or help really, just the basic doctors in the clinic. He has stones in his kidneys so it isn't unusual for him to be there. My mother spends most days with him, and at night she sleeps in my apartment in the town. I come here at weekends normally to ensure things are in order. Did you know my father from before the war?"

Albert said he had known Gerhard Rolf since before Gustav was born, "We ran around the woods before you were ever thought of. When Gerhard met your mother we were just young men. It was then he moved here from Tuttlingen, she was a life changer, your mother."

"My father was very upset when he heard you had been killed in the fire Herr Hagerman. I have to confess I am surprised to see you are indeed not dead. There was talk of you being hunted by the police for a murder, but when they found your body in the burned out house well, obviously they stopped looking."

"As you can see I'm very much alive Gustav, but for all our sakes it might be better if I remain dead. General Rosewood tells us you might be able to help."

The kettle on the stove was shrilling an ear piercing whistle, and it wasn't long before the fresh smell of ground coffee was permeating the room, it was wonderfully comforting. Neither Albert nor Jack had enjoyed the stewed thermos coffee they had left Verdun with two days ago.

The truck needed oil and water as well, and it just so happened there was both in the shed.

Dinner was a veritable feast, a smorgasbord of meats and potatoes, wild mushrooms and garlic all mixed and truly wonderful. The conversation was a mixture between business and pleasure, old war stories combined with tales of Gerhard's young days thrown in. With almost a verbal full stop, the atmosphere changed and then they spoke about Adolf Hitler. It was obvious from the onset Gustav wasn't a supporter or fan.

The best news was that Hitler was working in Munich.

Gustav had the address and better than that he knew the area and who else would be there. That was the end of the good news, the bad news was that his security secondment was made up of old soldiers and party faithful, nasty vicious men and at any one time there would be as many as ten guards in the house. Hitler tended to stay in his office upstairs with his mentor learning and perfecting his performance for the meetings and public rallies he was planning to attend to spread his venom.

It was decided that the next day they would drive to Munich, park up and walk around the area to carry out a recce. If all went well then they could lift their target the day after that, but before that they would rest properly.

Gustav insisted they slept in the house, there were beds enough and the two men would be fresh for the next day. With that Gustav produced a jug of local *dunklebeir* or dark beer for Jack, similar to a mild stout; for Albert it was like nectar, and even Jack who didn't partake often, enjoyed the dark bitter brew. Later they retired to sleep, it was a deep sleep restful and undisturbed. There were no recurrent dreams or nightmares, just darkness. It was good that they slept so well, they were going to need their energy tomorrow.

CHAPTER 42

Let's Go Look See

It was a sound, almost alien but reassuringly familiar that woke Albert, it was the *craw* of a Jay, he hadn't heard that birdsong since he left his woodland weeks ago. As he cleared his head the thoughts of what he had to do today started to form in his mind. He always liked doing reconnaissance, he liked looking and seeing things other people missed, the way the sun threw light on a tree at a certain time, spoil created by animals that was fresh and undisturbed, the calls of birds when danger presented still singing, but to a different tune once predators had been sighted. These were the ways of a countryman, a man brought up in the woods, before he had become inflated and important. First and foremost, Albert was a country boy as was his close friend Jack.

He could hear the noises of a breakfast being produced, but more prevailing than noise was the smell of the coffee, strong and black, it would give him a mental lift and further heighten his already superb skills as an observer. It was these skills that had made him a famous hunter and later a feared sniper. Albert washed his face in the cold fresh water from the hand pump that sucked clean and almost freezing water from deep underground. He washed and shaved before discarding the contents of the bowl into the soil. Jack came out to see him, and as Jack pumped more gushing water from the pump Albert plunged his head under and washed his hair, he had never felt so alive. The favour was returned. Both men came into the house, towels over a shoulder feeling invigorated, and said their greetings to Gustav who was head cook and coffee maker.

At the table they sat around and discussed Munich. The streets were unfamiliar to Jack and Albert, so they marked the roads on the handmade map Gustav had provided; clearly they would see and understand the layout better once they had visited the city.

When they had formulated a route they wished to walk then drive then maybe walk again, they were ready. They went back to their rooms and dressed. Albert asked Jack if he thought it might be possible to visit the hospital to see his old friend, it seemed like a good reason to be in Munich and what harm could it do, Jack tended to agree.

Gustav, set off on his bike, he wanted to meet the two men in the city and the best way was to take the train from Augsburg to the Hauptbahnof in the centre of Munich. From there he would board a tram to his apartment, this was his normal routine and it had been agreed that it was best to stick to that. Jack asked Albert to drive, should they be stopped it would be the driver that was spoken to and if necessary Jack could just play dumb: another casualty of war, deaf and dumb wasn't uncommon these days. Albert almost hoped to be stopped, he had come to realise how much he missed speaking his mother tongue and the thick Swabian accent was as a reassuring hug to his ears.

Once down from the track, the road was smooth and it didn't take them long to cover the thirty miles to the outskirts of the city. Here it was planned to leave the truck and jump on a tram to the city centre, once in the city they would first walk, then ride on a tram or bus around the same route or as best they could. The plan was to see how different the roads were to the streets.

The address Gustav had given them for the headquarters of the National Socialist German Workers' Party was on a street that connected with a wider road at a junction, but critically for the two would be kidnappers it was quiet. It was, however, overlooked and it didn't take long for Jack to see that the house opposite was watching the front of the house, not all the time, but periodically there would be a movement as the curtains were eased aside to take a peek. It wasn't difficult to see the watchers but then it wasn't anticipated that anyone would be calling unexpectedly.

There had been an assassination attempt on Hitler as early as 1921, right here in Munich, shots were fired at him from the crowd he was addressing and since then two more unsuccessful attempts had been tried only last year in 1923. They were right to be concerned about his personal safety and it was clear to see why he was guarded, but no one would ever expect anybody to come and get him, surprise was a huge benefit for Albert and Jack.

The two men had split up, each approaching the

house from opposite directions, in fact they had crossed each other as they walked past the front door, one looking left one looking right almost as if greeting each other. In fact they were looking, analysing, observing movements and times; there was a huge amount of information to be gleaned just by taking an innocent walk. No one suspected anything, it was all part of a normal day. Tomorrow night would be different, then the fury of hell would be released on anyone who got in the way of either of these two polite gentlemen greeting each other with a courteous nod as they passed each other in the street. It took them the best part of four hours to walk and then ride the route, it was getting late in the afternoon when they met Gustav at the tram station.

They had decided against visiting Gerhard, it might cause problems for the mission and for everyone concerned if Albert, who was supposed to be dead suddenly appeared like the prodigal son, reincarnated. Gustav said that once they had left he would tell his father what had happened; he knew his father would understand. Albert had a heavy heart, he so wanted his life to return to the way it had been just a few months before but he knew it had all gone too far, this was indeed the last time he would be here, he closed his eyes and breathed in the city, it was vivid in his mind.

The walk back to the truck was quiet, each man had his own thoughts. It didn't take very long and soon they were back on the road heading away from the urban streets to rural solitude, the place where hunters felt safe and the hunted hid.

Once dinner had been taken the two men sat outside smoking a pipe of tobacco and drinking coffee; sat there in their shirt sleeves and braces holding up their pants, the last days of autumn giving of its best. Jack could understand why Albert loved his home, it made him miss Langwith and his family.

CHAPTER 43
And so it Starts

Before they left there were a couple of things that still needed sorting. It wasn't planned that they would come back here or this way, and Albert was very keen to make sure Gustav was safe and there was no way that anything that was going to happen could be traced back to him. General Rosewood had made it clear that the priority was to extricate their target, but both Albert and Jack were determined that there would be no problems after they had gone, no retributions.

Gustav said he had a gift for them from his father. He would visit the old man tomorrow and explain to him his old friend's arrival and visit. He knew that Albert and Jack would be leaving today and the chance of seeing them again was slim. As they walked round to the wood shed there was an air of tension that hadn't been there last night, more like a winding up of a spring than outright tension, but there none the less. He opened the big doors and as the light invaded the dark dusty hut rodents scurried back into the dark corners. Gustav pulled back an old tarpaulin and under it lay some planks that were moved to the side to reveal a pit snugly holding a long wooden box, old, covered in dust and cobwebs; both men knew instantly what it was and what it held, an armoury.

As they opened it, it was as a perfect gift box for the needy, that is if the needy wanted rifles, grenades, sights and handguns, ammunition enough to start a small battle. Jack thought *he hoped it wasn't a Pandora's box.*

"Where did he get all this?" Asked Albert as he lifted out and caressed his favourite Mauser rifle. This wasn't any rifle, it was the exact same model as the one he had used all through the war, and although it needed a clean it was almost brand new, if there had been ten rounds fired through its pristine barrel there had been no more, better still it had the sight fitting needed for the Ziess sights and there in the bottom of the box in a familiar leather case were the sights to fit.

"Papa, brought them back one day after the war, he knew there were going to be problems with food and buying rifles was both expensive and difficult, so he collected these. He was going to use the rifle you're holding to hunt deer, boar, and wild pigs here in the woods, he just never did. As for the other things, I didn't know he had them. God only knows why he has, but you are welcome to take whatever you need."

There was plenty of ammunition, so Albert said it might just prove wise to go and zero the newly fitted sights to his own eye, there was at least another two rifles for Jack to choose including a shotgun with a big dent in the barrel.

"Have you got any tools, Gustav?" Jack fancied he could saw off the end of the barrel and make this useless shotgun a valuable weapon. Quickly a hacksaw and vice were found and within two minutes the ugly snub nosed sawn-off shotgun was finished. It was cleaned in the expert hands of a seduced lover; for both men weapons were second nature, almost part of their own body. Gustav watched mesmerised, it was that kind of show. The rifle was stripped in seconds, checked, cleaned, oiled and pulled through until it was spotless, even the wooden stock was caressed and oiled, it really was quite sensual. The rear sights were flicked open and slid up and down the corrugated slide, just to make sure they were all in order. The optic Ziess sight was quickly slotted into position and the bolt was worked four or five times with a beautiful *clack*, *click* noise. A full magazine was clipped into place. It was poetry in motion.

It took three of the five rounds available in the magazine for Albert to zero in the rifle, then Jack had a couple of shots, he was just as deadly, amazingly the rifle fitted both marksmen.

There was an old knobbly walking stick in the hut and with a saw and some strips of lead from the store for fixing windows, Jack had fashioned a trench club, similar to a policeman's truncheon but not quite so long, it was, however, far more weighty and much more deadly; a very useful addition to the quickly growing number of weapons available to the two of them.

So with two rifles, a sawn-off shotgun, an ugly, stumpy, trench club, a Luger pistol and three hand grenades plus ammunition for all stored in a box in the back of the truck, they were ready for the mission.

There was handshakes and knowing looks for Gustav.

"Look after your parents Gustav and please give your father my very best wishes. They should be very proud of you, you are a good man. Thank you for all your help and please look after yourself."

They climbed into the truck, looked once more at the house and set off. It really was about to happen.

CHAPTER 44
Time to Go

It was late in the afternoon when they pulled into *Hindenburgplatz Straße.* The street was very quiet, there was no traffic on the road at all. They parked the truck up and walked the fifty yards to the house.

Albert and Jack simply knocked at the door to gain entrance, it had really been far too easy. The first thug, a big blonde with huge shoulders and a neck like a bull had hit the floor at an alarming speed. It was not a surprise to Jack as he had just smashed his chin with the club made of stout wood and wrapped with a sheet of lead; a second blow landed just behind his left ear and he fell like a chopped tree. As he lay on the floor Jack noticed that the blond man had a boxer's face, a broken nose and scars both above and below his eyebrows. He was in the middle of some kind of seizure and Jack knew that the damage he had inflicted on the man's brain would probably kill him.

If he had been a fighter, he had taken some beatings but none as convincing or indeed as devastating as the one he had just received.

Albert had taken care of two more likely lads in a

199

room that served as an office, Jack hadn't seen what happened but it was as brutal as it was swift. Within a couple of minutes all three were bound by both hands and feet and were laid out in the office.

Up the stairs there was another room and inside sat four men, all armed with service weapons and dressed in the uniform of the *Braunhemden* commonly known as *Brownshirts*. These men had each been in the military and had been left with the feelings of failure and inadequacy by the beaten nation. All felt aggrieved by the way their once powerful nation had been left. Downtrodden and bereft of any future, they had been willing volunteers for the newly formed Nazi party, and guarding the new leader of the Fatherland was both an honour and financially rewarding.

They all jumped up when the door opened, Albert stood facing them, shotgun in his hand shortened at the barrels, and each one knew that the cut of weapon would be deadly in such a confined space. In his other hand, a Mills bomb, pin removed and armed ready to blow each one to smithereens.

"Good afternoon gentlemen, please accept my apologies for this intrusion, but I have to ask that you all sit back down on the floor. My friend here will tie your hands but apart from the inconvenience, no one should be hurt." The four men looked at Albert with fury and hate in their eyes, he had seen it a million times before. One man in particular looked at him as if in some way he recognised him.

"Where are you from?" He asked, "Did you fight

200

in the war, you look familiar." Albert ignored him and instead spoke to Jack.

"Once they are sat back to back, tie their hands tightly, Jack." Jack said he understood and the *brownshirt* instantly knew.

"He's English, you called him Jack. I know you, you're Wolfgang!"

At the mention of a name he had long since forgotten, Albert felt the cold fingers of fear caress his guts.

"You're the sniper who saved the emperor. We were in the same regiment you and I, you were a legend to us young soldiers. I heard you were dead. Why are you doing this?" It was the last words he said, as Albert brought a mighty smack down on his head with the butt of the shotgun.

"Drag him over here Jack, tie him to this one with this." He produced a rope, only thin but very strong, and in it was tied a Staffordshire knot: a three looped knot fashioned in such a way that when the ends were pulled all three loops would tighten at exactly the same time. This knot was originally designed to hang three men accused of murder ironically in the English army, none of the accused men would confess or blame any of the other two so the three had to hang together to ensure that justice would be meted out to the rightful murderer. Now with a little thought Albert had a plan to ensure the two men tied together behaved and didn't try to rush their escape. It was impractical to knock the four men unconscious so as Jack tied their hands in the loops of the knot, Albert carefully placed the hand grenade with the sprung arm in the third knot. Should either of the two men try to make good their escape the grenade would explode and certainly kill the men in this room: it was a brilliant idea.

The four men were bound and then gagged, each with their backs against the others and the grenade sat like a deadly egg behind them, primed and ready to explode should anyone move.

Once Jack and Albert had secured the men, they closed and locked the door with the large metal key. The key was then thrown away.

It was only when the building was secure that Jack and Albert went in search of the man they needed to convince that a trip to England was in his best interest. It didn't take long to find him.

CHAPTER 45

The Meeting

Adolf Hitler stood in front of the mirror: it was a full-length theatrical mirror the type with light bulbs all around the outside. Over the past few months it had been used often.

Hitler had been using the services of circus performer and clairvoyant, Erik Jan Hanussen for months. Hanussen had an uncanny knack of being able to predict events and had a very convincing stage presence. He had been coaching Herr Hitler in speech techniques and hand gestures to help soften his violent image. It had been working so well, not least because Hitler was a diligent student who practised endlessly, normally in front of this very mirror.

He heard the creak of a floorboard behind him but was far too engrossed to turn around. He had been rehearsing for a speech he was due to give the next evening to a group of sycophantic party members and had become totally overcome by his performance. There was a trickle of spittle coming from the side of his mouth and his eyes were as wild as fire. His breathing needed more control. It was something he would remember tomorrow night.

The sound of slow handclapping irritated him more than distracted him and as he turned round to see who had disturbed him his blood froze in fear, he was being watched by two men, both strangers and certainly not invited or included on the list of private audience guests. What made him aware that the dread in his heart was well placed was the *click clack* of a cocking pistol, a Luger to be exact and it was pointing right at his chest.

"What is this?" he shouted, hoping that his security men in the next room would be alerted to his predicament.

"Who are you and what are you doing in my rooms? Why are you pointing a gun at me? Do you know who I am?" he was starting to sweat. Where were the men he paid such good wages to, ensuring he was safe from these Bolsheviks?

Neither men spoke, they just let him panic. Jack raised an eyebrow as he looked on and Albert nodded to show he had heard the alarm in Hitler's voice. The agitated and now very intimidated leader of the National Socialist German Workers' Party suddenly darted to the desk, in there he had a weapon himself and he was determined to show these imbeciles that he was superior in every way to them. The explosion that smashed a bullet into his drawer couldn't have been placed there more perfectly. It was such a good shot splinters of wood lanced into his hand, the bullet had missed his fingers by a hairsbreadth.

It was Albert who spoke first, his German clipped and staccato, "When you have quite finished Herr Hitler, sit down. The next shot might not miss. You can shout but there is no one to hear you Your 'men' are incapacitated and won't be awake for some time yet. So please sit and let me explain what is going to happen."

Hitler refused to sit, it was only when Jack pulled the chair away from the desk and pushed him down by his shoulder that he eventually did.

Albert continued. "We have been sent to ask you to meet some people for a conversation that might prove very beneficial to everybody concerned. Please don't be worried, if you agree to cooperate you will be back here in less than a week. However, should you decide that you want to protest, let me assure you that you *will* be coming with us! The choice is yours, Herr Hitler."

Hitler rubbed his face, he knew it was best to think before he answered. Soon his men would notice there was something wrong and they would burst in and kill these Bolshevik swines.

"Why would I agree to your meeting?" He asked, "Who is it that wants to meet me and where are they? Why don't they come here and discuss their demands?" His voice was getting higher and louder as he lost the slight bit of control his temper had allowed him.

"Quiet." Said Albert, "Do not presume to shout at us Herr Hitler, it would not help my mood. I will answer your questions and then you have a decision to make, will you come quietly or not? Believe me it would be far more pleasant if you decide on the former. But before we go any further let me ask you a question, who do you think we are?" There was something in his tone that spoke louder than a claxon, his voice was frightening in its coldness. Hitler looked at Albert, he tried to stare him down but failed and had to bow his head in defeat.

"Are you not the communist scum the Bolsheviks sent? You don't want me to come quietly to my execution, you want to kill me here and hang me out of the window. Well let me tell you, you have tried in the past and failed. You will not succeed this time either." He was the epitome of a beaten man. In his heart he knew he was dead or at least would be very soon. His men had let him down, where were they when he needed them?

"Once more, you have judged the situation incorrectly, Herr Hitler. We are indeed not Bolsheviks, not even Communists, look at us as messengers or perhaps deliverymen. The people who want to talk to you aren't Bolsheviks either but they are powerful leaders. It is the British government who want to talk to you, but they don't want you to be embarrassed and knew that an official meeting would only be seen as a political game of chess. So they have sent my friend and me to escort you to the meeting. As I said it will only be for a very short time. Now, how do you wish to travel, on your feet or in a box?"

Jack didn't understand a word that had been said, he still found German far too quick for him to understand; he had picked out the word, Bolshevik, but had no idea as to what context it was in relation to. He watched as his prey became more and more ashen. He didn't know if Adolf was scared but he certainly looked like it. Albert had a way of doing that, and Jack remembered the first time he had met him in his hide out in the middle of the Somme battlefields all those years ago. He scared the hell out of him then and he was clearly doing the same to Herr Hitler now. At least everybody had stopped shouting and it didn't look like Albert was going to shoot him.

Hitler stood on shaking legs, he wasn't used to feeling this threatened. Hung on the hat stand was his heavy coat, and although it wasn't cold he wore it like a badge of rank. Jack, who hadn't said a word so far, went to lift it for him and Hitler spat venom at him.

"Get off, I can do it myself."

He was as a petulant child and Jack dropped the coat into his grasping hands, he didn't need to understand what the words were, their meaning was obvious. Hitler picked his hat from the stand, turned to look at his office from the doorway then walked towards the top of the stairs. Albert behind with a pistol and Jack in front, they walked past the room full of unconscious men without so much as a cursory glance, that work was done, the next problem was getting him in the truck. As they approached the hall that led directly to the front door, Hitler noticed the blood on the tiles, a smear about five inches wide lead into the room at the side. When this had been a family home this room would have easily been the parlour, now it was a grave for two men who had become casualties of conflict; the irony wasn't lost on Jack who thought *these two died so that we can try to avoid another war*.

As they got near to the front door there was a solid

thunk and as Jack turned in alarm he managed to catch the very unconscious Herr Hitler. One mighty smack with the handle of the Luger had laid him out cold. Albert had administered the sleeping potion in a sweeping clout to the back of Hitler's head, he had gone out like a light.

"What the hell are you doing, Albert," cried Jack as he caught the hapless body. "He was coming quietly, now we have to carry him to the truck."

Albert had a malicious grin on his face. "Jack my friend, trust me, he would have raised the alarm as soon as we got him on the street. He certainly wouldn't have cooperated once we had him in the truck. It only really occurred to me when we were coming down the stairs. He thinks we are taking him to kill him. Did you not notice the way he looked at his office when we left? Like a man who isn't going to see it again. Ask yourself, why would a condemned man just go quietly like that? There are troubles coming our way I can feel it in my gut, it has kept me alive before Jack and I have learned it's best to listen to the feeling and act now rather than later. Quick let's get him on the truck before…"

Just as he was about to finish there was a huge explosion from the top of the stairs, the grenade had gone off. All the glass in the upstairs room windows splintered and tinkled onto the street. Upstairs one of the two men had woken and feeling the rope around his wrist and before his colleague could warn him to stay still he had released the small metal orb, the trigger lever had sprung and the fuse, set to three seconds had done its ghastly work. No one had time to even shout a warning, the two men had died in an instant the third man having thrown himself onto the floor, had survived, but pieces of red hot shrapnel had pierced his legs and back. His ears were bleeding from the concussion but he was alive, briefly. The fourth man was remarkably unhurt apart from his ears bleeding slightly. His unfortunate counterpart who had shielded him from everything and then absorbed most of the blast with his body had saved him. Out of the four men tied together there were two dead, one would be shortly, and one was untouched apart from his ears ringing in his head like the church bells.

Downstairs, Jack and Albert picked up the limp sackcloth that was Hitler, and heaved him over Jack's shoulder. Albert now took the lead to ensure there were no uninvited guards or sympathisers to get in the way of their escape. The path being clear for now, they ran to the truck. Jack dumped the groaning lump onto the tailboard and Albert jumped into the cab. Fortunately it started immediately and as Jack pulled the now prostrate body of their passenger into the back, he pulled the tail cloths together to exclude the rest of the world.

Jack opened the first aid kit and lit the torch that was stored in the back, Hitler had a nasty lump with a small cut on the back of his head, Jack felt it best if he put some kind of bandage on it to stop the bleeding. Whilst in the pack he rummaged around for the sleeping tablets they had collected in case this situation arose. Now it had he was glad of Albert's foresight, it was as if he had done this before, it was uncanny how good Albert was at this sort of thing.

Jack helped sit up a still barely conscious Hitler, he gave him a flask of water to sip. He had already pushed two tablets into the back of his spluttering throat before he had started to come round and the sip of water was only a further precaution to ensure Hitler swallowed them properly. The doctor had said, back in Verdun that these tablets would guarantee at least eight hours sleep if you only took one, Jack felt it best if he took a belt and braces approach to the sleeping pills. Hitler drank greedily before he realised he was a prisoner and not a passenger; he started to shout so Jack offered him a fist or a finger over his lips, the universal sign of *shhh*. Hitler chose the finger, his head hurt like hell and he really didn't fancy another clout. His mood wasn't made any better by the sight of the coffin he was sitting next to, he felt sure it was for him.

He wasn't sure if it was the fumes in the back of the truck with the back curtains drawn across or the soporific effect of the warmth and gentle rocking but he did feel sleepy. Maybe it was adrenaline that had been pumping through his body, and the stress of being abducted but he felt tired, almost unable to keep his eyes open and with a few drunken head nods he fell into a heavily drugged sleep.

Behind they had left chaos and carnage, the security men had gathered their senses and started to form into small groups to find their missing leader. The phone line was busy making calls to other cells and members and, in turn, these members would call to arms more men to stop the truck and rescue their monster leader.

By now the truck had cleared Munich. Jack sat in the

cab alongside Albert who drove steadily north on empty roads. Hitler was in a deep sleep; he would stay that way until they cleared the line that marked the border between Germany and France. They were heading towards Augsburg, it shouldn't take them more than an hour, once there they should be able to relax a bit, but the plan wasn't to stop there it was to carry on back along the road to Verdun and that was a long, long drive away.

★

In Munich things were alive with activity; the telephone lines were singing from Munich to all other towns and cities on an escalating radius outwards. The truck had been spotted leaving the area and a general description had been circulated. Any complacency would and could prove fatal and for both the hunter and the hunted the stakes were high.

From the German point of view the web had been triggered and now that they knew how the getaway was planned it was just a matter of finding where the kidnappers were heading. Once they had been found it would be a simple job to stop them and release their hostage and then the kidnappers would be disposed of in the cruellest way they could have imagined. The point was, who were the kidnappers? Clearly Bolsheviks but who were their masters that had ordered such a stupid thing. Once the truck had been found it wouldn't take long to stop it. Then they could ask, before they killed the men responsible.

211

Rudolph Hess was in the house, walking around picking up on the men who had been so audacious. The bodies of the men killed, six in all, had been collected and taken to a place where they could be quietly buried. Any family member would be well cared for and financially secure, the money would be taken from the swine that had caused this uproar, the Jews. It was always the Jews, only this time they felt sure it was the Jewish Bolsheviks, there would be reprisals and recriminations for this outrage. As he finished searching he went into the office of the great man himself, the lights were still on around the mirror and as Hess walked in he could see himself in full length, he looked vengeful. Sitting at the desk was the man who had been in the other room when the two men burst in. He had been the one who hadn't been injured and although Hess had to raise his voice slightly, this man was very helpful.

"Yes sir, he was a German. Guttes, said he knew him from the war."

Guttes was dead now, blown to pieces by a hand grenade, bits of him were all over the room next door, and bits of him were still on this poor man's face. Hess called for a wet cloth, the least he could do was offer to clean his face. These were good men, made to look incompetent and foolish by just two men, how the hell had it been so easy? Hess wiped the terrified man's face with the damp cloth, washing the blood from his brow. He should feel angry, but what was the point? First they must find their leader and bring him back safely. Then and really only then would they have the facts and the truth.

"Tell me more about this German? Who was he?" said Hess.

The cleaned up and less shaken trooper was more talkative now.

"Guttes said his name was Handleman or something similar, he said they had been in the same regiment in the war but he was supposed to have been killed. Guttes thought he had seen a ghost but he didn't get a chance to say much more before he was smashed on the head and knocked unconscious. It was when he woke up he set the grenade booby trap off, sir. Albert Handleman I think he called him, the other man was an Englishman I think, called Jack, sir, but I don't remember hearing anymore."

★

Later that night Hess had to meet the Deputy Leader Ludendorff. At nearly sixty he was not as physically able as he had been but his mind was as sharp as a razor, he would ask questions and Hess had better have the answers.

Ludendorff did indeed ask questions and it was a good job Hess had the answers because he was furious that incompetence was so close to home.

"Tell me again Hess, what was the name of this Jew who has taken Herr Hitler? And you say there was an Englishman with him, an English Bolshevik?"

"The men think it was Handleman, Albert Handleman. He was in the same regiment as Guttes but was supposedly killed, that's really all we know at the moment. We have road blocks set up on every road, they won't get very far."

CHAPTER 46

The Hunter Becomes the Hunted

It was Ludendorff who used all his experience and his years as a leader of men that first made a connection. He demanded the records of all the men who had served named Handleman, Albert Handleman, there were only three and all of them had been killed early in the war so it wasn't that name but one like it. It didn't take long to arrive at Hagerman, there was only one, and he had been killed in a house fire in Tuttlingen quite recently; although there were suspicious circumstances surrounding the death and the fire. Alarmingly, he had been noted as a troublemaker and men from Ludendorff's party had been tasked with deterring any anti-establishment actions or thoughts he may have. Those men had not been seen or heard of since, it was suspected that they had been killed or perhaps just deserted their posts, but that was highly unlikely.

Of more interest to him was the fact that he was a war hero and had worked on a mission with an English soldier. *The traitor, how could he work with the English?* The next thing to do was find a connection with the events that had happened last evening and the forceful abduction of the head of the party. There were always connections to be found and the men doing the finding had experience in police work so were very efficient, even more so if you allowed them the intimidatory licence they requested. There were no boundaries in this investigation, they were simply ordered to do what had to be done to find answers quickly.

The investigation centred on a connection between Hagerman and Hitler, the only link they could find was the war and regiments closely affiliated with each other during it. It transpired that there were very few people who were either alive or in the area and who had served with Hagerman's regiment, in fact there were only five left. One was in hospital, one was in Munich, the other three were simpletons affected by gas and trauma and living in either long-term institutions or at home with their families, each one would be questioned within the hour.

Gerard Rolf recognised the kind of policeman walking down the ward towards his bed immediately. They were the trouble kind.

"Herr Rolf, good evening. I am sent to ask you some questions of the upmost urgency. I trust you will be able to answer them for me."

So that was it, no introduction, and no names, just business. He asked the nurse to help him sit up and put some extra pillows round his back to support him.

"You are incapacitated here in hospital, how long have you been here?" Clearly he already knew the answer, he would have checked that before he even came onto the ward. It was not a private clinic but a semiprivate clinic and the information this man wanted would be easy to obtain.

"I have been here for two weeks. I have a kidney problem, it recurs from time to time."

"Was it a war injury?" Gerhard knew where this was heading immediately.

"It hasn't been attributed to the war, no."

"Are you a wealthy man, Herr Rolf? I was led to believe you were a huntsman woodcutter? If that is true, how do you afford the clinic costs, they cannot be cheap?"

"My son helps with the cost. My wife and I have been careful with our savings, it is sad that they now pay for my care here instead of a happy retirement."

"Your son, what position does he hold and where does he work?"

Gerhard was wondering what this was about.

"I'm sorry but why are you asking me these questions, what has happened? Is my son in trouble, am I in trouble?"

"Please Herr Rolf, just answer my questions, it is most urgent. Do you know a man named Hagerman, Albert Hagerman? I understand you might have known him in the army."

Of course he knew Albert Hagerman, he was a hero of the regiment as well as a childhood friend. "Yes I know him, or at least knew him, he was killed recently in a tragic event in his home in Tuttlingen. Why do you want to know about Albert Hagerman?"

217

"Can you tell me where your son works, and what he does?"

"My son works for the town office as a clerk. What has he got to do with anything?"

The sinister man, who it turned out later wasn't a policeman after all, cut short the visit. He had all the information he needed.

★

Ludendorff and Hess were sat at the table with maps pinned on the wall. The room in which the grenade had gone off had been cleaned and was now being used as a holding centre for the men involved and coordinating the rescue of Adolf Hitler. There was a sickly smell of cordite, blood and sweat in the air and despite the windows being opened for the last twenty-four hours it was as strong as ever, almost impregnated into the fabric of the room.

Twenty-four hours, that was all it had been, it had taken them really very little time to figure out that the two men they were hunting were Albert Hagermann and Jack Adams. They could, of course, just go to the British and complain, but they knew this attack hadn't been sanctioned by any authority that would care to admit it.

They had called ahead to Verdun, and indeed all the towns and cities going north, they would be stopped in no time; it was then that the truth would be learned. It was a ridiculous notion to believe they might get away with such an outrageous and foolhardy plan.

There was a low groan from the chair, sat slumped and blooded, face pummelled and smashed, fingers broken and barely conscious was Gustav Rolf. He was a broken man, it had taken the thugs less than an hour to get all the information they needed from him, but the next three hours were gratuitous violence. He had told them, despite his best efforts, that he didn't know where the two men who had abducted Hitler, had taken him. They were convinced now that he didn't know where. As they broke first his fingers then his wrists he begged them to stop. They did stop, but not before they broke the fingers on his other hand, and they were convinced he knew no more.

Hess said he had been most helpful, and dismissed him. He was done, two men carried his slumped and wounded body outside. They took him into an outbuilding and there they shot him in the back of the head.

CHAPTER 47

Run Rabbit Run

Hitler was awake; he was shouting but being ignored. In time they would sedate him again but for now the two abductors were sat in the front of the truck. They were heading north and after a very brief telephone conversation with London they thought it prudent to slightly change their plans. It was causing some concern in the offices of Julian Rosewood that there had been no contact with Gustav Rolf despite there being strict protocols for there to be a call to confirm everything was as it should be. Given the nature of the call it was felt that it might be safest if the two men and their load divert around Verdun. As it turned out they were correct in their assumption, there was indeed an unexpected welcoming committee awaiting their arrival. There was another waiting in Stuttgart. The lines of communication were alive with orders; sympathetic ears listened to the demands that the truck be stopped and to make it all the more beneficial a huge ransom was placed on the rescue mission. Like rabbits in the field the hunted were running for their lives.

Jack pulled over, it was time for a plan. Currently

they were heading north towards Nurnburg but at some stage they would need to veer west back towards France. Albert said if he was hunting them he would block the roads at Ulm and Stuttgart, he would also have people watching the roads south back towards Tuttlingen, because if they made the painful assumption that Gustav was being held captive it would only be a matter of time before the Nazi vermin knew who had taken their precious leader. It would be an obvious conclusion that they would run back to where Albert felt safest, back to Tuttlingen. Jack agreed with him, it's what he would have done as well.

"So we head north, then come west, head towards Mannheim and onto Metz. I think it's safe to say they will follow us to the port, so at Metz we head north again towards Calais. I don't think they will have arms that long, but here in Germany they have plenty of support. This is turning into an adventure and that's a fact."

Albert approved of the planned route. The next question was what to do with their passenger? They went round the back of the truck to open the canvas. Hitler was furious, his eyes wild and although he was no match for either Albert or Jack they were glad he was bound, unfortunately he was not gagged.

Albert said they should just shoot him but Jack wasn't sure that was the answer yet, although he didn't mind. Hitler's eyes went wide as he listened to his executioners deciding his fate.

"Don't worry Herr Hitler, we want you to meet our leaders alive, but please be under no illusion we would both happily shoot you should you prove to be troublesome. If you are agreeable you should be back here in less than a week with little or no harm done. However, we have already learned that one of our friends has been taken into the care of your friends. You had better prey that no harm becomes of him."

Jack didn't understand more than a couple of the words spoken but he knew that Albert would be laying the law down, and he could see the fear replace anger in Hitler's eyes. The message had gone in.

From now on they would be on their own, at some stage they would call London again to see if there was an update on Gustav, but for the time being it was a case of running north as fast as they could. The sooner they reached Mannheim the sooner they could head for France. Once in France they would be able to relax a little but until then they had to assume everyone was against them. They had plenty of petrol but didn't know how far it would get them; they would worry about that later, but for now it was a case of getting back on the road. It was about 180 miles to Mannheim and given the state of the truck and roads it should not take them much more than six hours travelling at thirty miles per hour, seven given they might stop for food and a toilet break.

Hitler would have to wait, Albert spoke to him again and although he didn't tell him where they were heading or on which route, he did say it might be a long drive and perhaps he would care to take some more sleeping pills to help him pass the time. Hitler took the tablets, he thought if he was going to die and he was sure he was he might as well be asleep until he did. Besides the smell in the back of the truck was awful with the sheets closed, it was hot and the fumes made him feel sick. He had a good drink and swallowed the pills; in a short while he would be asleep. He laid down on the blankets that Jack and Albert had been using for bedding in the back of the truck. There was no point in trying to escape, his feet had been bound just enough so he wouldn't be able to run, more hobble really. His hands had been tied with a long piece of rope that passed under and beneath his legs so he could move either hand independently but like a string on a child's mittens; he wouldn't be able to do any harm to himself or the truck.

As they travelled along the road between Augsburg and Mannheim, the truck rattled and rolled around, the surface was old and worn but still very serviceable. They didn't see the car behind them in the distance, the one with four men all armed and with deadly intent. This car had been one of dozens alerted and on watch for an old army truck heading away from Munich. The occupants had been friends for years all ex-army, bitter and vengeful with an ideological bent. They had been instructed to stop the truck only when it was isolated and the altercation wouldn't draw any attention to the authorities. The road to Mannheim was isolated, and here there were no authorities but plenty of woodland to bury the kidnappers should the need arise; all they needed was to follow it for another twenty or thirty minutes and the truck would be in forests thick with foliage, something else to dull the sound of gunfire. For now they must keep back, the dust from the truck was hiding them well enough, or so they thought.

In front, Albert had seen the dust from another vehicle behind them in the distance. Initially he thought little of it but when after fifteen minutes it hadn't overtaken them, he had another look. There behind at the same distance it had been for a while was the whirlwind of a dust cloud. His heightened senses gave him a familiar warmth, trusted implicitly and with good reason, he had learned never to ignore the slight tightening in his gut. He warned Jack.

"There's something not quite right Jack, find somewhere to pull over off the road."

About a quarter of a mile up there was a cutting into the woods, Jack pulled in and turned the truck around to face down onto the road again. Albert explained his concerns, Jack had learned never to doubt Albert's intuition it was as keenly sharpened as his own. He reached back under the seat, pulled out the shotgun and checked that it was loaded. Albert got out of the truck to look at the situation from ground level.

About two minutes later a large black car passed them, Albert noted the occupants and came over to Jack who was sat in the driver's seat.

"Now that car could and should have overtaken us miles back. He should be able to go much faster than us, so the question is are they following us and why? If we wait here they are going to come back looking for us, why don't we ask them?"

Jack was in full agreement, it would be good to know who and why they were being tracked albeit very badly. Albert took his scoped rifle and handed it to Jack.

"It might be better if you take this, especially seeing as you don't understand what they are saying. I will ask them the questions if you will cover me. I know I don't need to tell you Jack, these are not good men, don't hesitate to shoot anyone you feel is going to be trouble. I will keep the stubby gun with me."

It was only a few minutes before they heard the roar of the powerful engine, and it confirmed everything Albert had predicted. Once more there was going to be conflict, and as ever the combatants opposite Jack and Albert were going to pay a huge price.

CHAPTER 48

A Shot from the Shadows

Jack had climbed a small hill about 150 yards out, he was nestled under a large tree that had a huge canopy and was still mainly in leaf. It threw a shadow in a large circle just like an umbrella would; dappled sunlight mixed with a hundred different shades of green. Within five seconds Jack was invisible, he had a perfect view from where he was laid and with the expert hands of a sniper there was a swift *click, clack* as he worked a round into the breech. He started to slow his breathing to a steady speed, slow and deep: the breaths helped him slow his heart rate. From now on he was totally focused on the shot, not that he had a target yet, but he could see Albert walking down towards the road, their truck parked out of sight, its passenger asleep and oblivious apparently.

The noise of the car engine grew louder until it rounded the bend and the driver saw Albert stood in the middle of the road. Stubby tucked into the back of his pants and out of sight, he had on a shirt without the collar which would be worn with it if the dress code was anything other than slovenly, slovenly fitted perfectly when driving for eight hours a day.

The car stopped with a short skid and two of the four men jumped out quickly, one reached behind the driver's seat and retrieved a MP18, a handheld machine gun from the latter years of World War One, it was deadly in a confined space and had more range than Albert's sawn off shotgun. The man gesticulated that Albert should raise his hands; Albert looked puzzled and did as ordered. It was obvious that any conversation was going to end badly but Jack let the other two men collect their weapons and approach Albert, he could hear them shouting at his mate and as he took aim he thought *you probably don't want to shout at him, he definitely has anger issues and a short fuse.*

Jack was just waiting for the driver to start to get out of the car and as the driver's door opened he saw the driver with a Luger pistol start to get out. He took aim at the driver's head; this was going to be over in the blink of an eye. He squeezed the trigger and with an almost hushed crack the driver fell dead. Before the other three could react Jack had reloaded and shot the one with the MP18 and Albert had pulled his sawn-off shotgun from his back and with a mighty *boom, boom* the other two fell down, one shot in the chest the other in the legs. It had taken less than three seconds to kill three men and disable another. Albert moved fast now, he kicked the wounded man in the face and as he dropped his weapon Albert kicked it out of reach and placed his foot on the throat of the now groaning and bleeding quite badly peppered casualty. He hissed, "Stay there you pig or I'll gut you like the swine you are."

Jack walked down from his vantage point having unclipped the magazine and leaving a round in the spout casually wandered over to the prone man pinned down by Albert's booted foot.

"Nice shooting Jack, I counted less than two seconds, you have kept all your skill." Albert managed to make the compliment sound sinister. Jack walked over to the two bodies: one with a neat hole above his nose and slightly to the right, almost over his eyebrow, the back of his head had crumpled and he had died instantly; the other he had hit in the chest just about level with his heart but again slightly to the right and over his sternum, it would have felt as if he had been hit with a sledge hammer and he was dead in less time than his colleague, the one that Albert had shot from close range.

Albert looked down at the agonised face of his victim, the look in his eyes spoke more than he ever could, it was pure hatred.

"Do you know who I am? I have to assume you do because you were quite keen to try to kill me but that was the only advantage you had in that. I don't know who you are, so enlighten me, who are you?"

The bleeding man spat venom at Albert, spittle sprayed from his vile lips. "Hagerman, you traitor, you will die along with your English dog of a friend. Killing our leader was your last mistake, we will hunt you down like the dogs you are. We will kill you as we killed your treacherous spy, Rolf. His family will die as he died slowly and in great pain, but it will be a blessing compared to how we plan to kill you."

Albert punctuated his speech with a kick to the mouth, it was a full stop. "You murdering bastard, who ordered the killing? Are you that paranoid that you believe we have killed Herr Hitler? It might surprise you to learn we haven't, he is in the truck, quite well. Unfortunately you won't be seeing him anymore."

Albert was livid. The Nazis had taken no time to find Gustav and even less to torture him and get the information they needed before killing him. He had a mind to just go and shoot their catch, make him a victim as they had Gustav Rolf. Albert knew the family would also pay a heavy price for being on the wrong side of the Nazi party.

The man wiped his mouth, what he said next was his own death sentence. "It was my friends that visited you and your wife, they raped her before they killed her, the only good thing inside that woman was some good German meat. You Swabians think you are so much better than everybody else. When Gobbels sent us with the blessing of Ludendorff it was to teach you a lesson. She screamed your name as they raped her."

Jack didn't understand anything that had been said but he physically felt the air chill. Albert looked like the angel of death, his face was expressionless and as his breath steamed in the autumn chill of the woods, he looked like a demon from hell.

Albert stood on the wounded man's leg, he screamed in pain. Very slowly Albert said, "You are going to die very shortly, you have no time to repent. I am going to kill you, slowly and with as much malice as I can manage before my friend here stops me, because he will, he is a good man unlike me. I am the deliverer of evil. I am 'Wolfgang'." Albert put two more cartridges into his shotgun and asked Jack to walk away. Jack knew it was better if he did, so he turned and walked back to the truck about thirty yards away.

Albert looked into the eyes of the terrified man, he put the barrel onto the man's ankle and pulled the trigger, there was a hideous scream, primal and pained. The foot of the now screaming man had disappeared in a mush of red spray. Albert had four more cartridges and he made sure the dying man could see them. The next shot was to the other foot, the results were the same. Albert did not flinch, all he could see was his beloved wife Monica trying to fight off the men who would rape and kill her.

Jack could barely contain himself. He did not always agree with Albert's methods but he had to admit he would have felt the same, and Albert always seemed to come back with the information he set out to get. Jack went to the back of the truck, Hitler was sound asleep, perhaps it was a cumulative effect of so many drugs; he had taken far more than he really should, but he was grunting so Jack knew he was ok. There was another shot, and another howling scream, it must end soon, no one could take that kind of punishment for long.

Albert loaded yet another cartridge into the hot barrel of the gun. He leaned near the pale and shocked man. He was without any compassion whatsoever but he did admire the resilience of this thug laying before him.

"How many more are trying to find us, tell me this and I will end it quickly. You are going to hell so maybe you're not in a hurry to leave this earth just yet. I have two more shots before you die, you have no feet and after I let this shot off you will have no knees. You are bleeding very badly and although you will bleed to death it will take a while longer yet. He pulled back the hammer of the shotgun and the dying man looked up into his cold dead eyes, he was in agony and was terrified about his fate after he died so he spoke as best he could.

"They will hunt you to the end of the world, the end will be as painful for you as you have made it for me. Killing Hitler was a big mistake, he was the future of Germany. I don't believe he is alive, you are a murderer so kill me and be done with it, I'll meet you again Hagerman, in hell."

Albert knew he had all the information he was going to get, he put the stubby barrel between his man's eyes and looked one last time into the depths of the pit of hell, he pulled the trigger. As he walked back to the truck, Albert shouted to Jack to get the gear from the cab and he would collect Hitler, from now on they would use the car. People were looking for the truck.

It didn't take long for them to pack the car. Hitler groggy and, for once, quite compliant was laid in the boot of the car; it was a huge space, he didn't need any restrictions because he would be totally enclosed so they removed his shackles. He was pleased he was able to take a pee before they helped him settle in the boot, blankets were laid round him so he was quite comfortable. It wouldn't be for long they told him, just until they reached France. From there he could sit in the back until they reached their destination.

The four bodies were loaded into the back of the truck and petrol splashed all over it before it became a funeral pyre. People wouldn't be alarmed at the smoke, it was common at this time of year for woodcutters to burn large amounts of wood to keep the pathways and roads clear up into the forests.

Once the truck was fully alight they climbed back into the car and without looking back, set off on the remainder of their journey, it would be much quicker now in a big saloon car, and much more comfortable to boot.

★

Ludendorff had ordered Monica's killing, the scum that they had set out to shoot in 1917 had survived only to condemn Albert's wife to death. There was no way for Albert to repay the treachery of the man he had gone to war for.

CHAPTER 49

Back to the Old Front Line

Given the information Albert had managed to glean from his dead shotgun victim, it made sense that the Verdun route would be compromised. They looked at the maps they had but they didn't have the right maps for France, the only route they knew at all was the one back to Verdun, and they weren't even sure of that given they were a hundred miles north of where they should be. They were of the opinion that the last car full of Nazis wouldn't be the only one looking for them. They had no idea if the occupants had contacted Munich to tell them they had found the truck, if they had then reinforcements would be on the way and it would be foolish to continue on this road. One thing was for sure, the route to Verdun would be being watched, and they couldn't go back that way.

If they headed north back up through the old front they would be safe. There was a high contingent of British there still doing work on graves and cemeteries. Not really knowing where they were was a hindrance, but they knew they were west of Mannheim about 250 miles from Reims, and maybe a hundred miles from the French border. Between them it didn't take long to work out which way was north and which was west and it wouldn't be long if they stuck to the road before they would see a sign to Saarbrucken. Once there they were nearly in France, both men would breathe easier once they were there.

It was about two hours before they picked up the first sign for Saarbrucken, but they needed petrol urgently. The gauge was showing that they were very low and as luck would have it there was a small garage and petrol station coming up. It was a perfect place to stop and get their passenger out to walk around, he had been very quiet throughout. They pulled into the garage and an elderly gentleman wandered over to them. Albert asked if they had a telephone he could use, there were lines that led to the house behind the garage. The old man looked on suspiciously, he had them weighed up in no time: they were obviously smugglers moving contraband between France and Germany, he saw the rifle on the floor of the back seat and knew it would be trouble if he didn't allow them to use the telephone and facilities. He filled up the car with petrol and walked back to the office for Albert to make his call.

Jack moved the car to a shaded spot at the side of the building and went to open the boot. As soon as he did he knew there was a problem, the boot was full of exhaust fumes and Hitler was lying there as still as a rock. His face was bright red and he was warm to touch, but he wasn't breathing and Jack could not find a pulse. Jack slapped his face and washed it with water from a bucket sat at the side of the building, still nothing. He shook his floppy body and slapped him again but it was no good, Hitler was dead.

CHAPTER 50
Oh, What to Do

Jack closed the boot and ran round to find Albert. Albert was on the phone going through some exchange or other in Paris before being connected to London and then on to General Rosewood's office. Jack placed his fingers on the telephone button and cut him off. Albert could see there was something badly wrong, he had never seen Jack panic but this was as close as he had ever seen. Jack pulled him by the arm outside.

"He's dead Albert, in the boot, he's dead." Jack pulled Albert towards the car and opened the boot again. There he lay, he looked very healthy for a dead man, the colour in his cheeks was better than it had been and he just looked asleep. Albert checked for a pulse, then checked a different place, he slapped his face but there was no response.

"How has he died Jack, has he had a heart attack?" Jack said he thought it was the fumes from the car engine but there was none to smell now. There had been when he opened the boot for the first time but now he couldn't smell anything.

"We need to tell Rosewood, and then we need to get

back. What do we do with him?" He jabbed a thumb towards the lifeless body in the boot.

The old man came round the corner just as they closed the boot, they didn't think he had seen anything but it made them acutely aware that there was now a body in a car they had stolen from Germany. If they were stopped for any reason, they wouldn't be able to explain any of it because this was an unofficial operation. They needed to get rid of it and ask Rosewood what to do next.

It was Jack who spoke to Rosewood; he explained what had happened back in the woods near Mannheim. He also told Rosewood that Gustav Rolf was dead, tortured and killed by the Nazis. They didn't understand why Hitler had died, he was awake when they had told him he needed to travel in the boot of the car until they got to France. When Jack opened the boot he was just dead. Rosewood knew why, he mentioned the gas from the exhaust, it couldn't be helped, if they could they needed to dispose of the body so it wouldn't ever be found and then make their way back to England as quickly as possible.

Jack had calmed down now, he wasn't used to feeling flummoxed like this, there was no real rush now, and they needed a coffee and something to eat before they carried on but before all that they needed a plan. Albert was already ordering coffee and food, the old man's daughter was happy for the cash and in no time at all there was wine, coffee and food on the table. The lady was a widow from the war, she didn't have much but a photo on the wall of her dead husband, a *Polus*; he looked proud and defiant in his military uniform. Like him she had a look of pride, there was no hatred for anyone, what was the point, it was done now and the money this German had would be useful.

Jack and Albert ate quickly and downed coffee to help keep them awake. There was no urgency any longer, they didn't feel the need to rush but they did know that they needed to find a way to dispose of the body. The city was close, but there were no woods to bury him in.

They paid their bill and with a full tank of petrol, full bellies and the body of a Nazi in the boot they set off. The plan was, at best, sketchy and certainly not properly worked out.

They planned to stop further up the road, somewhere quiet and talk it through. Jack thought he might have an idea but it was just that, an idea, he needed to run it past Albert. It was dusk and getting dark quickly, the night was drawing in and the evening was cool. In another few miles they would be in France, there they could park up for the night and maybe find a hotel to sleep. Both men agreed that would be the best idea, a good night's sleep in a proper bed. What they hadn't realised was the call had been heard by more than one pair of ears on both the English side and on the German side, the line initially went to the local post office in Saarbrucken then on to Paris before going on to London. The call had been reported back to Munich and the hunt was back on, only now the hunters knew the car the hunted were in and their route.

CHAPTER 51

The Hunter and the Prey

Up the road from Saarbrucken lies the ancient city of Metz. Until recently it had been an important German military garrison and although it was now back in French hands there were many who felt they were still German, certainly there were many sympathisers to the German cause still resident in this ancient garrison.

Jack and Albert had decided it would be a good place to find lodgings overnight. They needed to remain invisible and anonymous to the outside world for the next few days until they reached the shores of good old England, only then would they both feel completely safe. Just when they both needed to keep their guards up they had let it slip slightly, this had given the hunters the advantage and of all the guesthouses in Metz they could choose they chose the one they shouldn't.

The guesthouse belonged to Heinrich Obart and his wife Freda, both disillusioned and both moved on by the French after the war. Heinrich had been a soldier in the German army. He had been a prisoner of war and was roughly handled by his captors, he had no home in Germany because his home had always been here in Metz and now the city he had always known as German was French, and it didn't sit well with him at all. He did, however, have faith in the new political party that was proving to be quite radical back in the south of Germany. Its leaders had spoken of the need for Germany to reunite and to grow together after the betrayal of the great German army at Versailles. Heinrich and Freda had both joined immediately and were keen for the party to do well, if they had known what their two new guests had in the boot of their car they would have slit their throats whilst they slept. As it was, when the telephone rang it didn't take them long to realise that the two men who had booked in overnight had said they were on a pilgrimage to visit graves of men they had known in the war; one a mute the other a German, neither speaking French were of interest to the party member who was calling them. They had caused the faintest whiff of suspicion, but money was money and the season had just about finished so this was a bonus, cash as well, it may well be nothing but it also cost nothing to report things that seemed slightly out of the ordinary.

In Munich, alarm bells rang aloud. Men in the district of Metz were alerted and a rescue mission was already being planned even before Albert and Jack had fallen into their comfortable beds in separate rooms.

This time tomorrow they would be nearly home, maybe one more night's sleep in France before a boat

Within half an hour they were on the main road to Charleville. The sun was shining and despite the body in the boot, all in all both men felt good about the day ahead. With luck and a fair wind behind them they would be back on mainland Britain by tomorrow night, no doubt then on to London to explain what had happened. For Jack it would mean his pay increase and a far more comfortable life, for Albert it would be a new beginning. A house would be ready for him on the estate and he would start as a forest manager on the Alcot estate within the week. Jack joked there would be plenty for him to do with the autumn winds knocking the tops of the trees, it was always a busy time of year just after harvest with ploughing for the farmers and cutting back for the woodmen. It all had a place in time and Jack liked the order, he would be looking to providing some quality shooting this year and the promise of young Albert along to help his dad filled him with joy. This would be the lad's first year and he had a shotgun ready for him albeit a small bore twenty gauge; however, it was still a lethal weapon and he was looking forward to teaching him how to use it, that is unless Jim Cunningham had beaten him too it whilst he was away. As they chatted about the future the miles simply slipped away, neither really taking any notice of the car overtaking them, no one looked at them and they didn't look back and within the hour they were on the outskirts of Charleville bearing left to head towards the Somme.

As they drove they became mindful of the place names they had seen all those years ago, they had been deadly enemies then – it was a lifetime ago – first they saw signs for Saint Quentin, then Le Cateau and further north, Cambrai: all names synonymous with long and bloody battles.

As they continued towards Albert it was only just after lunch. Most of the work parties had either just started on their way back to the cemeteries or were already there and just about to start the grizzly tasks they had taken on. Albert parked the car on a hillside about a quarter of a mile from a small cemetery, and looking through binoculars he could see the men preparing a row of newly dug graves. This was Jack's plan. He planned to put Adolf Hitler in a new grave, that way once it was covered it would never again be disturbed, no one would ever know where he was and Jack felt some kind of spiritual pull back to the northern battlefields as opposed to the Verdun area. Besides, there was much more activity here, which they saw as they scanned around with the unmounted sight from the Mauser and the powerful binoculars they had with them, they could see groundwork happening everywhere. Within just a few hundred yards or maybe a mile there were ten different graveyards. As an opportunist Jack was the master, they could have just dumped the body in a French grave somewhere but they never knew when it would be disturbed again, here he knew categorically they wouldn't ever be moved. For now they just had to wait until the afternoon shift had finished and packed up to go back to their barracks and tented villages, away from the fields.

The autumn breeze carried the faintest smell of creosote on the air, its peculiar odour made it distinctive as the last of the sun's warmth gave way to the evening chill. The smell of creosote came from the canvas bags the burial parties placed the remains in prior to placing the bodies into the ground with all the respect and understanding only a soldier could provide.

Long shadows cast along the floor from the tree-lined hill and grassy bank that they sat on overlooking the vista in front. All along the view there were the final resting places for so many, some known to each other, others known only to God.

Jack was waiting until the sun dipped finally away, and only then could he place the body, in the boot of the car, in the ground. He had mixed emotions as he drove the car towards the groundworks before him. In his mind this was a sacred place for soldiers that had fallen in the fight and he was about to desecrate it with an interloper. On the other hand, the man in the back had been a soldier as well, he was decorated for bravery and had survived being wounded and gassed. It seemed ironic that he hadn't survived the most innocent gas attack in the back of a saloon car, on his way to be persuaded to follow the path of peace and not war and destruction. The one man who could sway a potentially warring nation had died in a simple accident. He would be forever sharing a grave with someone he hadn't known. In life they had been enemies but in death they would be comrades for eternity.

Albert opened the boot and tucked the two blankets

around the now stiff body, he was in a slightly curved position almost foetal but not too severe and he fitted beautifully over Albert's shoulder as he carried him into the graveyard. This area had been in German hands for most of the war and only in the last few weeks had the lines been overrun as the German army disintegrated into chaos before surrender. Jack found a couple of freshly filled-in graves from that day's work and he started to dig away the loose soil that covered the creosote soaked bag used in place of a coffin for the long since dead occupant. It didn't take long to find the bag and within a few minutes the sacred remains of some lost son, father, brother or husband was sitting on the surface. Jack and Albert laid the body of Hitler on the soil floor, he fitted perfectly, and then they covered his body with a layer of spoil and placed the canvas bag back on top of the 'packed in' new body. It only took half an hour to tidy everything away and once the two had finished they stepped back to admire their work, it was as perfect as before and as tidy as it had ever been.

Albert said they should say some words, some prayer for the dead, but he didn't know the right words in English so they agreed to each say a few words in their mother tongue, especially as they had imposed the original occupant with a new partner.

Jack said the Lord's Prayer and Albert mouthed a similar one in German. Both men were sincere with their wishes and as they wiped the dirt from their hands they reaffirmed their friendship with a handshake, it was time to go home.

CHAPTER 53

Death, the Vengeful Master

Neither man heard the shot. Albert just crumpled and slumped to his knees, then a loud retort from the woods a couple of hundred yards away echoed along the valley. Jack threw himself onto the ground, in front of him lay Albert blood pouring from a large wound to his neck. There was another crack and Albert jumped as another bullet hit his wounded body. Jack jumped to his feet and grabbing Albert's shirt dragged him bodily towards the hut that served as a tool shed for the work parties each day. Albert was groaning in a way Jack had heard more times than he cared to remember, it had never ended well and as he looked at his long-time friend he knew it wouldn't this time either. Jack pulled off his shirt and plugged it into the fresh wound on his friend's neck. Within a couple of seconds it was sopping and soaked in blood. There was another shot but this one just hit the top of the shed, it made Jack stay low though and as he did he saw his dear Albert's eyes shed a tear. He lifted him into his arms.

"Jack, my dear friend, it is my time to die. Where did that come from?"

Jack knew it was over, Albert was mortally wounded and was breathing his last; he had little time to tell him.

"Albert, it's a sniper, he is up in the tree line behind me. If I leave you you're going to die, if I stay here we are both trapped and will probably die together. Hang on and I'll try to get us to the car and maybe get you to a hospital. It's going to be fine, I just need to get you out of here." Jack knew it was a fatal shot.

Albert gasped, the blood in his throat made him cough and the wound in his back sprayed out fresh bright red blood, he was shot twice and both were wounds that he couldn't survive. As Jack held him he looked deep into those blue eyes, there wasn't anything to say. Another bullet cracked into the shed again, above where they were lying.

"Thank you Jack, you have been a great friend to me, we have seen life but now I have to go. You get back to Alice and live a happy life. For me, I have to meet my maker and explain myself. I know we will meet again my friend, thank you." With a tear in his eye Jack watched as the last seconds of his friend's life passed him by. There was no deep sighing breath; he just stopped breathing and was dead.

Jack felt the emotions well up inside him, everything became clear and time moved by very slowly. He wouldn't leave Albert here he would get back to the car and pick up his weapon, then he would slaughter the sniper who dared to shoot at Albert Hagerman, he would kill him and slaughter him like a farmyard animal.

Jack stood and lifted his friend's body onto his

shoulder; he had found a strength he hadn't had for twenty years. The car was only a few yards away and the light was failing fast, but if he went out of the door he knew he would meet the same fate as Albert so he kicked out the back wall like a demented vandal. He kicked so hard his whole foot went through and then the panel fell out and the whole shed rocked as if to fall down. Like an escaping convict he set off running with Albert over his shoulder, the car was there just in front and as he reached it another bullet ripped into his dead friend's body, he had saved Jack even though he was no longer alive.

Jack opened the back door and crawled through to open the other passenger side rear door, he reached down to his limp colleague and grabbing his shoulders he dragged him up onto the back seat. It was getting quite dark now and Jack couldn't see much in the gloom. He had a decision to make but he needed to make it quickly, he could hunt the scum that had taken Albert's life or he could run. Run like he had never run before. Jack Adams had never run from a fight in his life and he had been involved in quite a few scraps over the years. There on the back seat was the Mauser rifle, it was loaded and the sight would be fitted in seconds. The blood from Albert's neck wound was dripping off the seat and onto the floor of the car and as he pushed himself back from the seat Jack put his hand firmly into a growing puddle. It was time to run. There had been enough blood spilt and the enemy sniper had all the advantage, he knew where Jack was for a start and if he was any good whatsoever, he would have moved from his initial shooting place. Jack opened the driver's door, it was now pitch black.

As he started the car he realised he had no idea where the switch was to turn on the lights, he fumbled around and as he pulled the light switch the car threw a bright beam of light outwards. There right in front of the car headlights fully illuminated stood three men with handguns ready to do their nasty work. They were blinded by the brilliance of the huge headlights and as Jack pushed his foot hard on the accelerator the big heavy car lunged forward and hit all three like skittles. One man was bounced on to the bonnet of the car and hit his head solidly on the front of the windscreen, his head exploded as it split with a huge gash and his eyes rolled back inside his head. He fell off the bonnet and Jack felt his rear wheel run over the man's head with an alarming bump.

Jack kept his foot hard down and changed gears as quickly as he could. The car was travelling at quite a speed now and he thought he heard shots coming from behind him, but there were no bullet holes in the window and he did not feel any hit the car. He just accelerated away down the track and within a couple of minutes he was on the tarmac road heading towards Calais. The clock on the dashboard told him it was 7pm. All the events that had just happened had taken over an hour and it had gone dark very quickly, but now he was on the road it seemed somehow lighter, either way he was not planning on stopping again for a while. He could smell the fresh blood from his friend on the back seat. It made him feel terribly sad to know he had lost Albert. He just knew now he had to take him back to England, he couldn't leave him here in France. He just didn't know how.

As he drove, tears filled his eyes; he knew it was a mixture of shock, adrenaline and grief. He wiped them with the back of his sleeve and saw a road sign to Paris. Paris, he thought that's the perfect place, anyone following me will naturally assume I'm going north to Calais and a boat back to England, but I'm safer going to Paris. As he turned south onto the Paris road he seemed to remember it was only about three hours away, he would be there by midnight. He could go to the British embassy and call General Rosewood, maybe he could pull some strings to help get Albert home. He heard himself talking to Albert, telling him his plans.

Jack checked the mirrors in the car, there was nothing, blackness was his only view and at this time it felt like his only friend.

He reached Paris by 10.30pm. He had been racing and as he reached the outskirts of Paris he slowed and wracked his brain to remember where the embassy was based. The grandiose Hotel de Charost in Paris, had been where Jack had received his Distinguished Conduct Medal back in the day and it was then the British embassy. He seemed to remember it was a few doors down from the Elysee palace; if he could find the palace he would easily remember the way to the embassy. Fortunately for Jack the Elysee palace was well signposted and by 11pm he was inside and talking to

General Julian Rosewood who was as ever a calming influence and a reassuring counsel. By the time Jack had hung up, the undersecretary to the Ambassador was arranging tea and sandwiches from the kitchen. Jack sat and cried with grief, relief and as his hands shook he was reminded of that dreadful day in Verdun and the men who lived with this every day. It quickly sobered him up.

★

The next day travel arrangements were made to put Jack on a train and boat back to England that afternoon. Albert would be following the next day and his body would be delivered to The Old House in Langwith in a few days' time. Colonel Alcot had been contacted by General Rosewood and arrangements had been set in place already. Albert would be cremated in Hull, the nearest crematorium and General Rosewood would pick up the bill, it was the least he could do he said.

CHAPTER 54

Home Sweet Home

Jack was never as relieved as when he sighted the docks at Southampton. His steamer had only taken a few hours from France and even from the bow of the boat he could see the Rolls Royce flashing its huge headlights from the dockside. The ever reliable Jim Cunningham was there with Alice as was General Rosewood and the colonel. A full greeting party, but with one obvious exception. He knew there would be tears but he hoped this time he might hold his back.

There was work to be done, and meetings to attend with an explanation to be had. Maybe it was best to get those things over with before he went home but for now he realised he was waving, waving like he had never waved before.

CHAPTER 55

Retribution and Reward, 1994

Andrew Carnegie knew he was in trouble; he just wasn't sure how much. It was a good job really because if he had known, he wouldn't have gone to the meeting, that's why he had juniors. He certainly wouldn't have handed the folder on the abduction over.

He had given the dossier to Smyth and was promptly asked to leave it with them. He was left in no uncertainty when he was told that he could return in four hours; he was far from comfortable but the Permanent Undersecretary made it very clear it was time for him to leave. As he closed the door, he was sure he heard his career running ahead never to be seen again.

Peter Hartmann looked at the manila folder sat on the table in front of him. He wasn't sure quite how he felt, he knew he was angry, shocked, and incredulous even. He was stunned that this folder could even exist. Either it was total nonsense in which case he had every right to be very angry, or should it be true, then everything he had ever believed in and been taught throughout his young life at home, school, university was a lie. In fact everything he had believed to be true about his country's recent history could well be laid to waste in the turning of a beige cover. Interestingly, out of the two, it was Hartmann who appreciated the fantastic detective work that had lead them to this point.

Lesley Smyth looked pensive, he was long passed being embarrassed. He could only hope that MI6 had not done anything so stupid as to keep a copy of a document such as this. How in God's name could they ever get caught with their pants down on this, pensive best described his mood. Furious might best describe his state of mind.

Smyth said quietly, "How the hell did this happen? If this ever got out the repercussions would be seismic. I'm not sure how I feel, should I be apologising or applauding? I tend to lean towards apologetic, Peter, please you must understand we knew nothing of this until now."

Hartmann, smiled a disarming smile, he had the face of a diplomat and the warmth of a sixteen tog quilt, but he was not a man to be trifled with because when it necessitated, ice ran through his veins.

"Lesley, of course it isn't your fault and we all have, if you'll excuse the pun, 'a skeleton or two in our closets'. This is an amazing revelation don't you think? That Adolf Hitler was abducted and killed before anyone really knew of his infamy. I have to confess, my initial thoughts are that it is better for everyone that this information never leaves this room, no good can become of it. That history is so ridiculously wrong raises more questions than I care to imagine, but I have to wonder, who was the maniac that took our countries to the brink of total destruction? Who was behind the deception? It could explain why there was no conclusive evidence as to the last remains of Adolf Hitler in Berlin. I have to admit personally I always believed the Russians had stolen the body to keep as a grisly memento of their barbaric act during the final days of that particularly depraved war.

Do I want to investigate the truth or is it just better to let sleeping dogs lie? The team that has made this unfortunate discovery has done amazing work. I think we owe them an explanation; you certainly don't owe it to me. I understand the sensitive nature of this matter completely, but I suspect Mr. Phillips and his team might need a little persuasion before allowing this to go back to sleep. How we deal with this now is, in my opinion more important. How you deal with Mr. Carnegie, I think it is best for you to decide. The *Bundesnachrichtendienst,* our MI6 cousins, are a troublesome throwback to a time when secrets were a form of currency and like MI6 they have a nasty habit of causing embarrassment. If we can agree a way around this, then maybe it is best we don't take this to our superiors, but only if you think this a wise and agreeable course of action."

In truth, Lesley Smyth was a relieved man. He couldn't really have wished for a better outcome. Obviously there would need to be some house cleaning to do in relation to the Commonwealth War Graves Commission team but that could easily be sorted. He looked down at the file in front of him once more and read the report from Andrew Phillips, there was no doubt in his mind, it was an excellent piece of work, totally compelling and very comprehensive. The body they had found was, without doubt that of Adolf Hitler and the manner in which they had factually arrived at that conclusion was genius. No one could deny the results if they ever got to read this report; the key word in his thoughts of course was *if*, his job was to ensure no one else ever got to read the report to arrive at that conclusion.

He shook his head, composed himself, and looked straight into Peter Hartmann's eyes and offered a hand to shake. "I totally agree with you Peter, we should bury this as deep as we can. This needs to go down not up and from where I'm sitting I think I should say we owe you one. This could have easily become a much bigger problem but with you agreeing and indeed offering such sound counsel, how could anyone disagree. I will deal with Carnegie and his head of department, at best this was careless and at worst it could have escalated into a major diplomatic issue. Leave that one with me. As for Mr. Phillips and his team I think some kind of reward is in order, maybe a promotion or some sound funding for his department, might I suggest a joint venture with Germany?"

Hartmann nodded his approval and said, "I can't help but feel we need to ensure that Mr. Phillips understands that his work wasn't in vain, and I absolutely agree with your suggestions of both a promotion and funding. Do you have the means to arrange that? As for how and who they found in the ground, might I suggest that Adolf Hitler had a brother, a bastard perhaps, or better still didn't he have a real brother that was supposed to have died from diphtheria as a baby? I am sure he could be raised from the dead and that would account for the DNA being the same wouldn't it?

Let me entertain Mr. Phillips and his team at the embassy, I can be quite resourceful when it's needed Lesley. Let me persuade them they have found the answer to a long held mystery. I will arrange a small private reception and explain to them how they have uncovered Otto Hitler, Adolf's older brother by a couple of years, I believe. I will explain that it is best that the information we give them is kept out of the public eye. There is no point in going over old ground, especially as there is a groundswell of pro neo-Nazi sentiment currently spreading across the south of Germany. I am sure he will understand the need to keep it quiet, don't you agree?"

Lesley Smyth rang the intercom to his secretary, a curt but super-efficient voice answered. "Yes Permanent Undersecretary, how can I help?"

He smiled, he liked Kathleen Doyle, she was very efficient, and discreet. "Could you arrange a car to pick me up in ten minutes, I shall be lunching at the club with the German Ambassador." He clicked off. "I think a small drink might be in order Ambassador and this round is on me."

Later he would be speaking with Carnegie, there was no point in getting hot under the collar now. He felt he had just dodged a bullet but the guy who had loaded the gun would be enjoying nothing for the next few years that is, of course, unless there is joy sitting in a radio station in the middle of the Arctic for the next three years. Time for him to reflect about the way he communicated bad news to his superiors and even more time for Lesley Smyth to retire, uninjured. It was a knighthood and a healthy pension he was waiting for, and that was only two years away. That sycophantic buffoon Carnegie had very nearly caused a political earthquake with his smug incompetence. Peter Hartmann could so easily have caused a scene but good common sense had been the order of the day. Who knows he might get that pension after all.

Before he left for the day he arranged with Herr Hartmann to meet at the embassy with the intention of handing over the files on the Hitler case for the German Ambassador to dispose of as he saw fit. Either way he would get all the original files and ensure they were destroyed. General Rosewood had created a bit of a problem. No doubt if he hadn't been killed during the blitz it would have been disposed of after the war, but 'if's and buts' never worked and at least he would now ensure that the files ended up in the right hands.

The Germans'.

CHAPTER 56

Ice Cream and Polar Bears

Admittedly the two bottles of *Pol Roger, Sir Winston Churchill* champagne had helped his mood but he was quite looking forward to roasting Andrew Carnegie's chestnuts, there was always a sense of joy when one managed to rollock a spy, not his words, but for the life of him he couldn't remember who had said it. The knock at the door was almost timid, a knock of impending doom.

"Come in Andrew, take a seat," there was no offer of coffee or any other refreshment. "I thought the show this morning went very well, didn't you? Mr. Phillips certainly gave a good account of himself. I think I can speak for the German Ambassador when I say we were very disappointed that you and your department put us in a very uncomfortable position." He could feel himself getting hotter by the second, his voice was just slightly louder than it had been a second ago. Carnegie went to speak but was stopped in his tracks by a crashing palm on the desk. "I don't remember asking for your opinion Carnegie, damn well wait until I tell you to speak before I have you thrown out of here." He was in full flight now.

"How dare you put me in that position, to produce a secret document in front of the German Ambassador and try to make me look an arse. I should have you fired. I have, however, spoken to Peter Hartmann and we think that there may be a way we can rescue the situation. How the hell did you think you might get away with a stunt like that? Right, here is what you will do, you will hand over to me now every document, original, copies, everything to do with this. I assure you I will be speaking to Sir Colin and I can assure you I won't be sparing you any blushes. He will reassign you and if you know what's good for you I would seriously consider accepting whatever he thinks might be a suitable post for you." Sir Colin McColl had been head of MI6 for the last six years and his tenure was about to end but he owed a couple of favours to Smyth, this could be one of them.

Carnegie was stunned, he had thought he was beyond reproach, after all it wasn't his operation, he had to admit he had been a tad dismissive of Phillips perhaps it was the heady company but this all seemed a bit of a hard pill to swallow. Maybe when Sir Colin heard his side of the story he might be better received, and he was sure there was a slur in Lesley Smyth's speech.

CHAPTER 57
Summoned for Dinner

Andrew Phillips was back in France, he felt at home here. His office was almost like a second home and although he would rather be in the fields working with his teams, if he had to be office bound then this office was the best one he could have.

He had planned a meeting with Robert, Magnus and Carrie scheduled for this afternoon, but the morning was to be spent sorting the mountain of mail that had amassed and was totally filling his in tray: some he would deal with today but most would be directed either into the tray marked 'too hard' or put into an internal envelope addressed to himself and reposted. It really only gave him a day or so but it would massively cut his workload today and he felt less guilty if he received a call asking if he had actioned the urgent request for softer toilet paper or some other crushingly important demand. He would just say it was in the post. The mail was sectioned off into the appropriate piles: 'bin', 'busy', 'repost', 'do now or else'.

Once that was done he would take a terrified peek into his email box. One look confirmed his worst nightmare 1689 emails in his inbox and a veritable forest of flagged ones. He heard himself groan, "oh arse". This was the very reason he didn't like office work or accepting the curse of promotion and the life sentence of paperwork that entailed, with little or no hope of parole. He would have a coffee first.

There was a knock at the door. He rarely closed the door, he was a strong advocate of the open door policy; his only concession to modern thinking was he moved his desk out of eyesight. It was after all a known fact that if people could see you when they walked past your open door they were more inclined to stop and chat, not that Andrew minded the chat, but he would never get anything done if everyone stopped.

"Hello, come in." He looked up to see Lisa his secretary and most often used confidante. She held a mug of steaming coffee in each hand and kicked the door open with her foot. In her mouth was an embossed envelope, it was made of a thick paper almost card and was cream; it looked very classy and when she dropped it on to his desk he saw it even had a wax seal. His heart nearly stopped.

"That arrived about ten minutes ago. I had to sign for it, so thought you might like a cup of coffee whilst you opened it. It's from Germany, by the way."

Andrew needed Lisa, she kept him grounded. If truth be known, she fended off a lot of mundane crap that would have ended up on his desk if she hadn't been there. She was also incredibly nosey and loved to gossip. She spoke French as if she was a native but she wasn't really, her mother was French and French had been Lisa's first language. She had lived in England for fifteen years as a schoolchild whilst her father was in the RAF and was the beneficiary of a great education in private schools in England. Her parents were now retired and living in the south of France enjoying the warmer climate and generally dryer weather than the United Kingdom.

"German eh?" He sipped his coffee as he spoke and fingered the envelope's seal. He examined the beautifully written address box and then turned it to look at the red wax seal, *immaculate*, he thought. He was almost scared to open it, he had no idea what it was or what information it held. In fact he wasn't even sure *how* to open it, did you break the seal and open it that way or was it best to slit the top and leave the seal intact, it would after all, make a great memento. He decided on the latter, he unclipped the *Leatherman* from his belt, yet another throw back to his days in the field, and pulled out the blade. He carefully slipped the tip into the corner having tapped the envelope on his desk to ensure the contents were sat at the bottom and he wouldn't accidently cut through them with his knife. There was a satisfying noise as the blade cut along the thick paper. Once opened he removed the letter and a card, *almost like a postcard*, he thought to himself. It wasn't from Germany at all, it was from London although technically the German embassy is Germany. He put his mug down on the desk, it seemed inappropriate to be holding both an invitation to dinner with the German Ambassador and a mug of coffee at the same time. He read it twice then handed it to Lisa to read to him just to make sure he hadn't misread it.

His Excellency, Peter Hartmann The German Ambassador respectfully requests the company at dinner of the following people:

Mister Andrew Phillips.
Doctor Robert Deville.
Mister Magnus Roche.
Miss Carrie Annis.

There were more words, but she didn't read them, she was already thinking how to tell everyone the news. This was massive and worth a lot of gossip points at the canteen.

He hadn't heard anything from the Ambassador since the meeting in London. Really all Andrew could remember was how nice he seemed as a bloke. Out of the three it was a surprise that the German was the most supportive, the Permanent Undersecretary had seemed OK but didn't ooze enthusiasm and the other guy from MI6 had just been an arsehole, a real slime ball, who appeared to want to totally undermine the whole report; he was determined to rubbish all the hard work, *Jesus wept it was irrefutable evidence*, he felt his anger rise but swallowed hard until he calmed.

"Lisa, would you mind calling the team together, looks like we have a dinner to attend."

Phillips looked at the invite once again, he was

shaking his head, ever so slightly but never the less he was shaking it. The German embassy for dinner, his father would have burst with pride if he had still been alive.

The detail he hadn't read included dress and timings: he would have to look at everyone's diaries, and at best it would be a three day trip. They were due a treat so he called his head office in Maidstone to tell them that team France was going to the ball. The public relations officer would have a fit; she would be drilling them in protocol and etiquette. He could already hear her in a total flat spin back at the office, she would be so annoyed that she hadn't been invited, but this one was his team outing after all.

Presently they all dribbled in one at a time, Carrie was first, *she had a lovely white blouse on with a tight navy blue skirt*, he shouldn't think like that he admonished himself. She was confused as to why the meeting had been called so urgently; Andrew said he would explain when the crew had all arrived. Next came Doctor Robert Deville accompanied by Magnus whom he had met in the lift.

Andrew cleared his throat with a cough, the collective quietened and looked at him expectedly.

"Right," he said, "have you all got your diaries? We have a little soiree to attend, nothing special, it's just a private dinner with the German Ambassador at the German embassy in London, right moving on." He set off to cover another subject but was instantly stopped in his tracks, as he had planned would happen.

"Whoa, back the truck up there." Said Magnus, "Did

you just say the German Ambassador has invited us to dinner at the embassy? And then just flippantly move on, you joker. What the hell is all that about?"

Andrew set about explaining everything and the reason why, he couldn't hide the excitement in his voice. "I have contacted the head office and we all have permission to go, but the PR officer wants us to drop by the head office the day before so she can run through the etiquette etc. Also, we have been allocated an expenses account so we don't embarrass anyone by being paupers." He looked at Magnus and smiled. "Fortunately the dinner is on Friday night so we travel to Maidstone on Wednesday then London on Thursday to book into the Dorchester Hotel courtesy of the German government. We then have carriages to the embassy for pre-dinner drinks and finally, dinner. We can spend the next day getting our feet back on the ground, before we come home and tell Lisa nothing. Just watch her go mad as she tries to pump us all for information." He knew Lisa would be listening in her office right next to his, slightly ajar door, she was anything but subtle our Lisa.

The trip to London was planned for the next week so diaries had to be sorted pretty quickly. Magnus was still working in a cemetery near to the battle of Loos. This had been a particularly bloody battle with literally thousands left dead; the whole area was surrounded by cemeteries full of the fallen. Recently there had been some damage and Magnus had been sent to ascertain what could be done to make it good. It was typical of Magnus that when he was there he found more work to do: several headstones were looking worse for wear and he had authorised their replacements. He was due to go back to see how work was progressing but it could wait a few days whilst he was away. More pressing for Magnus was what he was going to wear? He didn't even own a suit, never mind formal wear. Once more it was Carrie, who came to his rescue.

"Stop worrying, you can hire it these days. I can take you to the shop this afternoon after work if you like. There's one on the way home for me. It might cost you though." She had a delicate smile but it was full of intent.

Magnus, never one to miss a beat nodded in agreement. "Would dinner fix the bill? I'm staying down here anyway overnight, so it would be a perfect opportunity to kill two birds with one stone, if you'll forgive the expression! I didn't know you could hire, that's a huge relief."

The others in the office waited patiently for the two to finish their flirting.

"Have you two finished?" asked Andrew. "If so there are a couple of things we should sort before we go today." It was said in earnest but in truth he knew he had lost them.

Robert was next. "I have a white jacket, it's very French, and so very stylish. It's only fitting of a man of my fine breeding." He laughed and Phillips told them to go home.

It was agreed that they would go in two cars. Lisa booked the ferries and as ever the whole trip was planned like a military manoeuvre. Timings were given for meeting locations and where people were being picked up; suits in suit carriers would go in Andrew's car because he could lay them along the back seat of his huge Renault estate car. He was also taking Robert in his car, because he said it would mean Laurel and Hardy would be in the other car; Carrie snorted her coffee and they all laughed. He thought what a great team he had, and as he said goodnight he felt lucky to have the best job in the world with the best people he could wish for.

CHAPTER 58

Dinner at the Embassy

The German embassy in London was a magnificent four-storey Georgian building in Belgrave Square; it stood for all the things that were good about Germany. It looked strong and dependable, and since the reunification of East and West Germany it had received a facelift that made it even more impressive.

Their chauffeur-driven cars were parked outside the Dorchester Hotel: two huge black Mercedes Benz with diplomatic number plates had arrived at exactly 6.55pm with chauffeurs dressed in suits and, much to Carrie's amusement, hats. Everyone stopped to look at who was leaving in the cars. Even at a top range hotel full of visiting celebrities it wasn't every day you saw diplomatic cars picking people up.

Once the four of them had arrived at the embassy, they were met by the Ambassador himself. The men looked splendid in their dinner jackets and Carrie was outstanding as a lady dressed in a tight black dress that had cost her far too much but looked so much better than it should.

Drinks were served and the Ambassador was totally

engrossed in every detail of the finding, identifying and final report of the collapsed cemetery at the Somme. He had a grandfather who had fought in the Great War and his father had fought in the second war. Both had survived but neither was very keen to discuss the dreadful events that they must have encountered. He was fascinated at the whole process and made the four of them completely at ease before they had even sat down for dinner.

The course was a sumptuous delight of rich and then sweet foods, all local dishes to Germany and the chef came out to meet his dinner guests to warm appreciation from the diners. Over dinner the conversation changed slightly with the Ambassador's explanation of how the body they had uncovered was not that of Adolf Hitler, but was in fact that of his brother Otto Hitler who it had been believed had died of diphtheria when he was only an infant. The Ambassador explained that he personally had taken full responsibility in heading an investigation as to how this had happened and all the evidence was incontrovertible.

Andrew wasn't completely against the idea but felt disappointed that the explanation was so simple. Robert could easily understand the science behind the findings and the fact the DNA was so 100% right to the Hitler family made him rethink his initial conclusions. However, Carrie was completely unconvinced, she had been sure their initial report was correct. The Ambassador explained that in actual fact the DNA was only 99.2% accurate; this was concluded after having investigated

271

the same samples from the tooth and bone fragment from the skeleton in the museum that was believed to be Adolf Hitler. It was a remarkable discovery to learn that in fact Otto had not only survived but had never had any childhood disease that would have caused his death. He had been sent to his aunt's house to make more room in the Hitler household and had been reported dead by a neighbour, but no death certificate was issued only a temporary certificate of absence.

"You have to understand that there were literally hundreds of children dying from an outbreak of diphtheria at the time and the hospitals were under huge pressure to arrest the outbreak. Young Otto just slipped through the net, bureaucracy failed as it sometimes tended to do in those days." He was so convincing that it really didn't take long for the group to believe the tale and explanation.

"So, I am sure you will understand the delicate nature of your findings. Alas we are not totally rid of the Nazi extremism in many parts of Germany and a finding such as yours, or indeed anything to do with Adolf Hitler fuels more anti-Semitic feelings to a new brutish element. I cannot help but wonder if, given the facts as we all have them now, if we wouldn't be better to just let this entire event die down. I am sure we can arrange for the body to be reburied, with full military honours of course, it is the least we can do for poor Otto. But I think it would serve no purpose to invite controversy by evoking the name Hitler. I feel sure you will agree." He smiled as he wound his web of silky deceit around his unsuspecting prey. If he was honest, and in general he was, he wished this story was true. He had ensured that all records of Otto Hitler had either been removed from files or destroyed. But as he had agreed with Lesley Smyth there would be no benefit to any nonsense about Adolf Hitler. Germany had moved on from his vile political diatribe it was just a pity the rest of the world didn't seem so keen to forget him.

At the end of dinner more drinks were offered, indeed encouraged. The small party retired to a beautiful lounge with a string quartet playing quietly in the corner, mainly waltzes it had to be said but very enjoyable for all that.

Peter Hartmann asked Andrew to walk with him for a private word. "Andrew, you have a wonderful team there, they have done some brilliant work. I do hope you're not so disappointed in the final outcome. I have some papers for you, I thought you might like to keep something of the original papers you won't have seen them before. I have to confess, I stole them from the British, but please don't tell them, they may think I'm a spy." He laughed as he reached into a cupboard and pulled out a yellowing file he had asked Smyth to let him dispose of; it was the MI6 case notes from 1924 but modified significantly to totally dispel any thoughts or suggestion that it might have been anyone else other than Otto that was found.

Back then he would have been shot just for looking at them but now they were old news, to be destroyed; for Hartmann they served one more purpose. If they had been associated with Adolf Hitler why would he give them to Andrew Phillips? It was a brilliant double bluff. Andrew looked at them and let out a low whistle, he gave them back to the Ambassador. These files were way above his pay scale, all of them were marked 'TOP SECRET' in fading red ink on top of each page.

Following the pleasantries of coffee and liqueurs, it was time for handshakes, and fond farewells. With impeccable manners the Ambassador hugged Robert in a manner the Frenchman would appreciate, it was as if they had been friends for years, to be fair several glasses of fine cognac, and it was a first class bottle from the town of Cognac in western France, had helped the relationship bloom; there was another one in a black velvet bag marked 'Just a token Herr Doctor'. They shook hands and said goodnight. Magnus was next, he liked Peter Hartmann: he was a man's man and understood the problems Magnus had in the field, almost as well as Andrew did, it was uncanny. Before he left the Ambassador gave him a velvet bag, inside it was a bottle of Bollinger 1990 vintage champagne. Magnus frowned, what was that for? The Ambassador leaned in and whispered, "I thought you might like to share that with *Fräulein* Annis later." he winked.

As Carrie approached the Ambassador clipped his heels together and bowed his head, she nearly passed out; he was such a gentleman. She was actually swooning and blushed bright red as he took her hand and kissed the back of it. He reached back with his spare hand and was passed another velvet bag, this time the contents were a ludicrously expensive bottle of Coco Chanel from 1972, the year she was born. When the formalities of good manners had passed he hugged her closely as would a father. Finally it was Andrew's turn, he had stood in line with a huge grin on his face to see the people he cared for so much enjoying a great evening, and the ending was as perfect as he could have wished.

Peter Hartmann knew why he liked Andrew Phillips, he was a gentle man who cared about the people he worked with and shared a passion for their work. He thought Phillips would have been a great diplomat. He had all the qualities needed, he was tenacious and determined to see that the details were right before he made comment. Hartmann actually felt a little bit guilty about his need to deceive Phillips and his team, who knew, one day he might be able to make it up to them. The small gifts, although on the surface were quite extravagant were mere trinkets but he enjoyed giving them anyway; however, he had a special gift for Andrew.

As Andrew turned to shake his hand he gave him a leather document holder with the yellowing file inside and a small jewellery box that contained a Tag Heur wristwatch, it was magnificent but that wasn't the best bit on the back was engraved, *To Andrew. Thank you for finding me. Otto*. He shook the Ambassador's hand with a genuine affection, it wasn't a coincidence he felt he had found a new friend: he had.

CHAPTER 59

The Dorchester Hotel

It was quite late when they arrived back at the hotel, a nightcap was in order and everyone agreed to meet in the bar. Andrew said he would meet them back there in ten minutes: he needed to go back to his room and drop off his gift. When he got back to the room he sat on his bed and almost nervously opened the leather file holder, sat there was an envelope and inside was the whole investigation according to the Germans. A mixture of old and new paperwork, even the original document that somebody called Jack Adams had signed, he wasn't sure of the relevance of it at that stage.

Tomorrow he would have more time to look closely at the file but for now he had mixed emotions. He was disappointed in a way; he really wanted to find that in fact it *was* Adolf Hitler even though everyone told him, and to be honest they always had done, that it was not possible for it to be him. On the other hand there had always been this niggling doubt that it was, despite all the evidence to suggest it was, so he was not hugely disappointed when someone came up with a perfectly viable alternative. *Otto Hitler eh*, he thought, *how come bureaucracy always seemed to get it so wrong?* Office types sat behind desks; he really hoped he was different. He had a quick glance at his new watch, there was no doubt about its authenticity, and it came with a certificate and looked like a million dollars. He looked at the face, it told him to move his butt and get down to the bar; he was late. By the time he got there he was last, there was a drink sitting on the table where the other three were sat.

"Well, that was a night to remember." It was Robert who was thinking out aloud. "Is that guy for real? He is a great bloke, how come he's not like any German we have ever met?" He finished this thought out loud with, "What a guy, awesome!"

Magnus said he had enjoyed it as much as he could, but felt a bit uncomfortable in such high company: he was much more comfortable with a pint and a pie. He hoped his night hadn't finished; Peter Hartmann has sussed him out in seconds, he was disappointed it was so obvious. Carrie was in love, she adored the Ambassador. "Isn't he a sweetheart, a bit old for me but wow, what a gentleman?" She punched Magnus on the arm. "Not like you, lover boy, rough and ready." She knew the night hadn't finished or at least she hoped it hadn't, that's why she had ordered tonic water because she didn't want to be tipsy.

Andrew couldn't help himself, he had to ask. "Otto Hitler, are you lot ok with that or do you have any doubts? I have all the original paperwork upstairs, but I need to read it thoroughly before we can cover it, but not tonight eh, that was a superb evening." He couldn't let it go though, why did MI6 have a folder on the Hitler family? Or did they have one on everybody who might be in a position of power, he was sure that was the answer but it still niggled at him all the same.

Presently it was time to retire, Andrew could see a dalliance about to occur, and you didn't need to be psychic. They were grown-ups and he quite liked the idea that the two of them could have a good time; he just hoped it wouldn't spoil a great work team. Magnus made some pathetic excuse that he was going up, however, Carrie spoiled his plan instantly. "I'll be there in a second." Andrew just burst out laughing. Magnus at least had the decency to blush.

"Have a good night Carrie, goodnight, I'll see you in the morning. Breakfast is on until 10:30."

Robert had fallen asleep in the chair. Andrew had a huge amount of respect for Robert, he was grumpy, hard-nosed and stubborn but he didn't make mistakes and spoke it as it was. All qualities Andrew Phillips liked. He gently touched the doctor on the shoulder, who instantly opened his eyes and said, "I'm sorry, did I fall asleep? Or did I manage to avoid the lovebirds leaving?"

Andrew laughed again, it had been a great evening for laughter. "I'm going up Robert. I didn't want to just leave you here snoozing, goodnight."

With that he made his way to the lift. He might just have a quick read of that folder before he turned in, just a quick one.

Once settled in bed he leaned over and turned on both bedside lights to even out the light, it gave off a warming brightness that was easy on the eyes. He felt strangely nervous as he opened the folder; there it was right before him, the whole story. Or as much of a story the Germans wanted him to see.

He read it quickly, scanning it rather than taking in all the detail as there was a lot of detail. When he had finished he didn't believe what he had just read so he read it again, mindful of what Peter Hartmann had said to him earlier about it not being in anyone's best interest for this information to become public knowledge. Now that he had looked at the folder he knew why. It was dynamite and if this ever got out it could cause major problems with historians, politicians and the diplomatic centres all over Europe. MI6 had tried to kidnap Adolf Hitler in 1924, but they had the wrong Hitler they had picked up his brother Otto, or so this folder would have you believe and the evidence was pretty compelling, but then the cynic in Andrew Phillips thought *well it would be if that's what they wanted you to believe.*

Two names kept coming up, Jack Adams and Albert Hagerman, one English and the other German apart from that there was no detail about either. Their mission had been to capture and persuade Hitler to attend a meeting with the British government. Evidently they collected Otto and not Adolf of the Hitler family and he ended up dead, and buried in an Imperial War Graves Commission grave in France. Otto was supposed to have died of diphtheria when he was only a baby but apparently he hadn't and instead he had been used as a decoy for his younger brother of two years. Phillips thought out aloud, *you couldn't make this up, surely this is rubbish?* he then thought, *and the fact you think you found Adolf and not Otto isn't?* He was tired and crabby, it had been an extraordinary day followed by an even more extraordinary evening.

There was no eureka moment for Andrew, he just didn't believe it: it was all so convenient. Maybe if he slept on it and got a good night's sleep, he might be able to concentrate on it a little more. He leaned over and clicked off the bedside lights, just in time to hear Carrie and Magnus start to enjoy their evening but at a different party, one where they were the only two guests. He sighed deeply and buried his head into the pillows to try to drown out any noises. He eventually fell off into a deep sleep.

The next morning breakfast was quiet, it felt a little bit like after the Lord Mayor's show. Magnus and Carrie had ordered breakfast in their room. No doubt they would make their own way back, contented and satisfied with the evening before; not only with themselves but also with the explanation of the findings, however, they hadn't seen the documents which Andrew would show them back in France.

Robert was washed and packed ready to go, so over breakfast Andrew asked him if he would like to look at the folder, he didn't. He was quite happy with the findings and besides he had a pile of work back in the lab that needed sorting and although he had enjoyed last night's soiree, he was ready to get back to work.

So really when it boiled down to it, it was just Andrew

who had managed to keep any interest whatsoever in the whole thing. He shrugged his shoulders, he would be back with this later.

★

That evening back in France, the folder sat on Andrew's dining room table, it was almost calling him to take another look. He couldn't resist it now he was alone and had spent the whole day cogitating it around in his head. He took a fresh glass of red with him and sat at the table, once more he felt the same excitement when he opened the folder. It was obviously made sterile by the Germans, there was nothing that was even slightly ambiguous about the finding and conclusions they had reached, and on the face of it, that was true. But what about that Official Secrets Act form for Jack Adams? Andrew worked out the dates, was it possible Adams was still alive? He would be very old if he was.

Andrew Phillips was a resourceful man, he had contacts all over the place and it was time for him to find out. There was no point in letting this niggle away at him, he needed to find the answer once and for all, for his own state of mind. After a couple of phone calls to friends that were into genealogy, and a chat long overdue to both, he sat down and finished his wine. It took precisely forty-seven minutes for his phone to ring; it was Steve Leavis, the first of the two mates he had called earlier.

"Found him, and guess what, he *is* still alive and you'll never guess where he lives."

Andrew was stunned. He said in all sincerity that he owed Steve a large beer and he would call in on him when he came over to England next. It was a shock, and along with the long day, loads of driving, and a couple of glasses of wine he was knackered, it was time for bed.

★

The next day he was first in the office, he had slept like a log in his own bed and once showered he was raring to go. He knew there would be an interrogation from all sorts of people today, the least of his worries was the one from his main office in Maidstone. They would want to know all the nitty gritty and might even ask for a written report, he had already decided not to mention any of the gifts the team had received apart from the certificates of thanks signed by the Ambassador. No his first concern would be Lisa, she would want to know everything and the more gossip worthy the better, he knew he would have to keep most things from her.

He poured himself some coffee; the croissants would arrive shortly with Lisa so he didn't have long. Next he found an English Yellow Pages phone directory and with some slight trepidation, he looked up the number. He wrote the details on a piece of paper and readied himself to make the call.

CHAPTER 60

The Visit, Langwith

Andrew Phillips looked at the piece of paper in his hands and once again shook his head in disbelief. On this slip of paper lay the truth, or at least the name and address of where the truth might be found. A seventy-year mystery could be answered:

The Old House, (care home)
Manor Road
Langwith
Nottinghamshire

He picked up the phone and dialled the number. The phone rang three times before a polite and correctly spoken lady who declared she was the matron answered it.

"Hello, The Old House, Matron speaking. How may I help you today?"

Phillips was surprised how nervous he felt.

"Hello there, my name is Andrew Phillips and I'm from the Commonwealth War Graves Commission. I wonder if you might be able to help. I am looking for a gentleman who I believe might be a resident there with you. His name is Jack Adams."

There was the briefest pause before she answered.

"Yes, we have a resident by that name, are you a relative Mr. Phillips?"

"Er, no I'm not family. I am the senior officer of the French section of the Commission and I am in England for the next few days. I have been working on some historical events and I believe Mr. Adams might like to know the findings. I would rather like to give them to him personally, if that's possible?" The question took Phillips by surprise, he hadn't thought of that.

Matron thought for a few seconds. *She loved Jack, everyone loved him, he was a lovely man.*

"Well, I am sure he would be happy to meet you Mr. Phillips, only Mr. Adams is very elderly and we try to limit his visits to close family, he is very popular here in the village, what with him being the oldest resident. When are you planning on being in the area?"

"Tomorrow would be ideal if that isn't inconvenient. What time would best suit your routine at the home, Matron?"

This was the clincher for matron, *what a nice man to think about our routine*, she would make sure that she shared a cup of tea with Mr. Phillips when he got here.

"Well, how would just after lunch suit you Mr. Phillips? Mr. Adams has a short nap after his lunch but I would be very pleased to offer you some light refreshment until he wakes. Do you have far to travel?"

Not far, he thought, *this journey had started months ago*

*and he would walk from Maidstone to Langwith if he could find
the final answer.*

"No, it isn't far I can be with you by lunchtime,
that would be wonderful, thank you. Shall we say 1pm
then?"

There were some niceties to close the conversation,
and then he hung up the phone.

★

Linda Lesley enjoyed her position as the matron in
the home; it had been her 'home' in more ways than
one for the last thirty years. She had been here for the
last days when it had been a private house, then as an
auxiliary nurse before she went to do her nurse training.
Once she had qualified as a staff nurse she came back
to work here with the old folk. They had been called
geriatrics in those days now it was elderly care, the seeds
of political correctness had been sown. She had worked
here for twenty-five years as a nurse. Now she enjoyed
the fruits of that labour of love as she climbed the ladder
of responsibility to matron. The home hadn't lost any of
its charm over the years.

Tomorrow she would enjoy meeting Mr. Phillips,
she would ask cook if she would make some cake; tea and
cake were always welcome and she liked the sound of Mr.
Phillips. She wondered if she might get to learn some
hidden secret about her beloved Jack. He never really
spoke about the past, other than the happy times spent
here at the house prior to its conversion. Jack had been a

285

resident here for the last twenty years, having lived alone in the cottage he had been gifted as a wedding present long ago. It had been ten years before that his wife had died. He stayed in their house alone but independent. It was only after a fall and significant pressure from his children that he was admitted here. He had known the big house since he was a lad, and regaled all who would listen with stories of its grand history. The staircase with its magnificent banisters and the old colonel's office, each had a tale and Jack was always happy to tell.

All those years ago Linda was the nurse who had admitted him. Jack Adams was like a father to her. Her father had been lost when she was a child, he had died down the pit when she was only six years old and from that day on life had taken a turn for the worse. Her mother was young and attractive but never remarried. Instead she dedicated her life to making sure that her two children were looked after properly, 'No latchkey children in her house' she would say and Gerald, Linda's older brother was never to set foot down a pit. He was a painter and decorator now and had been since he left school, he had the contract to decorate the home when it needed it. Linda made sure that whenever a resident passed away their room was cleaned from top to bottom and then repainted. It was a touch that was typical of her and that ensured the home maintained its top rating in the area.

CHAPTER 61
Meeting Matron

Andrew Phillips stood at the entrance of The Old House. It stood as an imposing building and had been home to the twenty-five residents since it became a nursing home back in the 1980's. Prior to that it had belonged to a trust who looked after it as a general office block for the estate in which it sat, before that it had lain empty for ten years since the last of the Alcots had vacated the property, unable to meet the high maintenance costs that came with owning a large country house. There had been quite a lot of interest in buying the place from city businessmen but each one had fallen by the wayside.

As part of the estate, there stood four workers cottages and these were occupied by the different members of the same family. Bought over the years the children and grandchildren of Jack Adams lived a quiet if somewhat secluded life. In number one had lived Jack Adams, now an old man. His wife Alice had died more than a decade before and he remained, curmudgeonly and belligerent in his world of memories, and although he still had a very sharp mind his body was failing him and eventually he had been admitted to the hospital following a fall at home. He would never return back to his beloved home, and from the hospital he had been admitted to The Old House nursing home where he still lived today, some twenty years later.

In number two lived Albert Adams he was in his sixties and was the son of Jack, and next door to him lived his son Paul and wife Lesley with their four children.

All in all it was a happy row of houses, strong in family values and safe from the outside world and busy lifestyle that was Langwith. Elizabeth, Jack's daughter, had also returned to retire and live in the cottages after a successful career in Leeds as a post office manager. Len, her husband, had been keen to move back to Derbyshire once they retired and the cottages were a great place to live. They hadn't been blessed with children but played active aunt and uncle roles to Albert's four and there was an open door for everyone. Life had been idyllic then, right up to Jack taking a tumble.

Andrew walked in and followed the signs to the office, here a young lady met him but he didn't catch her name, she said she was the receptionist and took him to meet the matron who, she said, was expecting him. He looked at the clock on the wall it said 12.55pm, he was five minutes early.

Matron met him with a handshake and a warm smile. She showed him to a chair in her office and thanked Claire, the receptionist, who left to collect the refreshments matron had asked the cook to make ready for this meeting. Tea, coffee and cake were all brought in on a wheeled trolley and Andrew couldn't help but think it was a nice place to spend your last years.

"So Mr. Phillips, can I ask what this business with Jack is all about or is it all *hush hush*?" She giggled at the thought that Jack Adams could be involved with anything that was secret.

Andrew placed his cup in its saucer and smiled a disarming smile, "Oh there aren't any secrets, Matron. Jack was involved in a military operation a long time ago and I just wanted to confirm a couple of things with him, for my research and to close a file that has been open in my mind, for far too long. I'm sure if he remembers it at all it will just be a couple of details. It all helps though. I'm sure you understand, red tape and bureaucracy, it blights us all."

He couldn't and indeed wouldn't tell her what it was that he had taken all this time in arranging. There was no doubt that if she knew what he was going to discuss with Jack she would be on the phone to the local and national newspapers before he had time to leave.

Tea, sandwiches and cake done, it was time for the main event. Andrew looked at the wall clock behind matron's desk; he had been here for an hour already, making small talk and playing verbal chess. He knew she was fishing for gossip about Jack but in truth he didn't have any, well not that he was prepared to share.

He finished his tea and made a bit of a show by placing it back on the table with a firm *chink* and the spoon fell off the saucer and onto the carpet. He didn't mind, it just added finality to the meeting.

"Well Matron, I really should be getting on. Lunch has been most enjoyable. How considerate of you to have refreshments, you really shouldn't have. Will Jack have finished his afternoon rest, yet? I really wouldn't want to be a bother?"

Matron knew it was time to let him go, clearly there was nothing of interest she could glean from Andrew Phillips. *He is a charming man* she thought, *but he was no use as a gossip.* She loved to talk, she wouldn't ever condone gossip; however, with a feeling of the 'fly was escaping the web' she knew she would have to give him up.

She checked her fob watch, it was gone 2pm and Jack would be awake by now. He liked a nap after lunch, just in the chair, before his family visited later in the afternoon. They came every day, always at 4pm. She had never known them miss.

She rang a bell. *How quaint*, thought Andrew, *a bell, it was almost Victorian and fitted the place perfectly.* There was a knock at the door and a very smartly dressed lady entered. "Claire, would you be kind enough to let the nurses know Mr. Phillips is here and to ensure Mr. Adams is ready to receive a visitor please." Claire nodded and left.

"You know the history of this place Mr. Phillips?" She asked him as if she expected him to know but he didn't.

"I'm sorry, I don't," said Phillips

"It was the old manor house, and used to belong to the Alcot family for many, many years. When the master of the house died he bequeathed it to Mr. Adams. This is really his house, as well as his home; he donated it to the local authority to give a home to old miners and land workers. Very philanthropic man is our Mr. Adams, and we all owe him a great deal. It's his legacy, and when, one day he passes, dear God let that be never, we will all lose a great friend." She felt herself well up with emotion, and it came across as a wonderful thing to Andrew Phillips. It was obvious, many people loved Jack Adams, and although Andrew hadn't ever met him he just knew he was going to like him.

CHAPTER 62
Jack Meets Andrew

Jack was sitting in his favourite armchair, he was old, very, very old, his skin was thin and he looked fragile. That is, until you looked at his eyes. There was more life in those greying green orbs than Andrew could ever hope to achieve. He wore a *Tattersall* checked shirt and a green woollen tie covered by a cardigan made of cashmere, the whole ensemble was made complete with a pair of cavalry twill trousers all matching and perfectly suited. *Jack may well be old but he was stylish and still dapper*, thought Andrew. He wore his old comfy loafers on his feet and a twinkle in his eye that said 'butter wouldn't melt in his mouth'. All in all, he presented as the perfect picture of the retired and indeed aged, country gentleman. The second he was introduced Andrew Phillips immediately liked Jack. They were as kindred spirits.

Andrew was offered and readily accepted another cup of tea, Jack was having one to go with the digestive biscuits he so loved but was rationed by the nurses. They presently returned with a fine china pot of freshly brewed tea and a small plate of biscuits, and with the click of a closing door Jack and Andrew were alone.

Jack asked Andrew to open the bedside table and pass him the packet of digestive biscuits he always kept there, and with a wink said he still had a few secrets. It was a wonderful way to open the road for the questions Andrew had for him.

"So Andrew, what brings you all the way from London to talk to an old duffer like me? I haven't been to London in fifty years and I'm happy to say it hasn't requested me. So how can I help you?" Jack sat back with his cup and biscuit, a contented and happy man; he liked company and didn't seem to get much these days.

Andrew sipped his tea, he had rehearsed this moment a million times but now it was the main act his mouth was dry as a bone. "Well Jack, you may be able to help me with a bit of a puzzle my team and I have been working on. You won't know but I am based in France and I work for the Commonwealth War Graves Commission, you might remember it as the Imperial War Graves Commission, it changed its name in the 1960's."

Jack felt a cold chill on his neck, he checked the windows were closed and nodded his head in understanding.

Andrew continued. "As part of my role I have to ensure that all the war graves are kept safe, clean and tidy, as you would understand and as an old soldier would demand. Well, a little while ago, it was reported that a number of graves had collapsed into an old World War One bunker on the Somme. It fell to me and my team to sort the mess out, but the mess turned into a bit of a mystery and I am led to believe you might be able to shed some light on what happened." Andrew stopped talking as Jack put his hand up to stop him.

"You've found him haven't you?" said Jack, so quietly it was barely a whisper just louder than a thought really, but Andrew heard it like a cannon shot.

"Found who, Jack?" he questioned.

"Hitler." said Jack. He sat upright and looked into Andrew's eyes.

"You found him, after all these years. The good Lord has given him up, or maybe the devil didn't want him."

Andrew sat, stunned and not sure what to say next, he placed his hand on Jack's shoulder, a gentle gesture strangely full of emotion and kindness.

"Yes Jack, we found him, did you put him there?"

"I did, well we did, but I'm afraid I can't tell you any more than that Mr. Phillips because it's covered by the Official Secrets Act which I had to sign all those years ago."

Andrew opened his folder and lifted out a yellowing piece of paper. It had been sat in a folder, equally yellowing in the darkest safe in all the land, it shared it's home with secrets that would never be told and that one day would just disappear as if they had never happened.

Jack could see that the folder was yellow, but his old eyes couldn't see any detail. Not only did he need eyeglasses to read he often used the magnifying glass that was sat on his bedside table. Andrew Phillips said to him, "I'm not sure if you can see this Jack, but it is the original official secrets document that you signed in 1924. This is the only copy and when we have finished speaking we're going to destroy it. And besides which what are they going to do to you Jack you're over 100 years old! They're not exactly going to throw you in the tower are they?"

Jack smiled and chuckled quietly. "I haven't seen that document in ages. How on earth did you get hold of that when you work for the Commonwealth War Graves Commission? You must know some pretty powerful people to have that document in your hands."

Andrew said, "Jack I have a story to tell you but it is missing some vital detail. I'm hoping that by the time we have finished, you will be able to clear up the ending of the story for me. I hope that I can close this folder for the last time. My team and I have been fed a *cock and bull story* and I suspect that you are the only one who can fill in the missing details. If you are happy I'll tell you what I know and you can then put me right on any bits I have wrong."

Jack looked at the folder and the yellowing paper, he smiled as he reached out and took the thin card folder in his hand as if weighing it in his mind. Finally he said to Andrew, "You know something Andrew, I have waited all these years to be able to tell someone what really happened that night. Why don't you tell me what you think happened and I will see if my memory will allow me to fill in the missing pieces." He gently put his gnarled old hand on top of Andrew's hand like a granddad would. It was surprisingly warm and reassuring.

"Just let me put this damned contraption in my ear, I'm a bit hard of hearing these days and I wouldn't want to miss a word." He expertly and with surprising dexterity popped an hearing aid in each ear. Andrew thought he mustn't shout; it made him smile.

Andrew cleared his throat, it was a bit of a habit he had when he was nervous, in anticipation of the great mystery about to be unfolded imminently. He proceeded to tell Jack, how the whole episode had started and then unfolded and subsequently ended with a tale spun to distract him from the truth, for all that was worth.

Jack nodded, totally engrossed in the tale he was hearing. It was as though he was back in his youth and all the focus he had needed to stay alive was back, his mental agility tested once more and, as ever, it wasn't lacking. He heard and took in every single word, tilting his head at points where he either couldn't quite remember what had happened or things he knew to be untrue. When Andrew had finished Jack had some questions for him,

"So they told you it was Otto Hitler? The long dead brother of Adolf who actually died when he was but a nipper. Well I suppose it's believable, if you want to believe it. But let me tell you something that is irrefutable." Jack looked hard into the eyes of Andrew, and although misted by time they had lost none of their focus or determination. "Let me tell you, it was Adolf Hitler I put in the ground, and that is a fact. They obviously don't want you to go public with this Andrew, and if you will accept some advice from an old man, let sleeping dogs lie. There is no point in making enemies of these people, what will you gain? Nothing. You now know beyond any doubt that you and your people found the body Albert Hagerman and I buried in that grave in 1924. No one else knows the story or the truth apart from those who are telling you they don't. Well, they do. And they have good reason to leave it there. Don't rock the boat, take the pat on the back from them and take the truth from me." Jack sat back into his chair, he was worn out.

With that Andrew could see the strength leave Jack, he was tired and Andrew knew it was time for him to leave. Jack was already falling asleep when Andrew gently covered his knees with a blanket from the bed. He picked Jack's hand up and gently shook it, he whispered to Jack, "Thank you sir, thank you, Jack".

The documents folder he had brought for Jack seemed redundant now and he didn't really want to leave it here for the nurses to find. This conversation had been the culmination of that particular secret document and he owed it to Jack to keep his promise and destroy it. He tore the top off one of the pages and wrote 'Jack, the rest is shredded. Thank you for sharing. Andrew' he left his little note on Jack's bedside table.

Andrew quietly left the room and walked to the reception office to find Claire. She was sitting at her desk and when he approached she smiled and stood to meet him.

"Have you finished, Mr. Phillips?"

"I have Claire, yes. Mr. Adams is sleeping and I don't want to tire him out or disturb his nap. He was very helpful; you have all been extremely helpful. Do you have a document shredder in the office?"

Claire said that they did and he asked if it would be possible to shred some papers for Jack, as he had promised. Claire said he could pop into her office, and as he shredded the Official Secrets Act of 1924 signed by Jack Adams he knew he was closing a chapter of their lives, maybe even the whole book.

When he had finished he said, "Matron explained that the home is run by a trust, would it be possible to make a donation to that trust? If so, can I leave it with you and a little something for the nurses who are looking after the people that live here? I want to show my appreciation for the fantastic job you all do and thought maybe I could contribute to the drinks' fund for your next night out together."

Claire was very moved and said matron dealt with that kind of donation, but the trust would be delighted to accept his gift. She rang the buzzer and matron came out, with her make-up freshly applied. Andrew gave her ten five pound notes for the drinks' fund and a cheque for five hundred pounds for the trust fund.

Matron was blushing as he said, "You look far too young to be a matron. Jack clearly loves it here and you are the person he seems to love most. Thank you for your time and allowing me to visit today, it has been very helpful and Jack answered all my questions. He is asleep and I hope you don't mind but I pulled a blanket off the bed to cover his knees, I wouldn't like him to catch a chill. I would like to visit again if you don't mind, only as long as it's convenient. But I don't know when I will be back in England. Obviously I will call first if that would be ok?"

With handshakes all round, he left by the front door. As he walked to his car he turned around to look at the house once more, deep down he knew he would never return and he wondered at the stories that door could tell if only it could talk. He opened the car door and got in, as he did he looked at the lake, there on the right was the boathouse that unbeknown to him had been the place Jack had proposed to Alice in 1917. The Old House had a plethora of secrets; none would ever be given up. He drove out of the driveway.

CHAPTER 63

Heaven Open Your Pearly Gates
for One of Yours is Coming Home

Jack lay quietly in bed. He knew he was nearing the end, he hoped for it. At 103 years old he had led a full and long life: things he had been proud of like his children, Albert and Elizabeth were there; he could feel them rather than see or hear their presence. Both had grown into good people. Albert and his wife had become parents and grandparents themselves, but there had been no children for Elizabeth, still she had been happy with her lot and never complained. For the last thirty years since Alice had died he had taken great comfort from his offspring.

He opened his eyes to take in the scene; he didn't want people to be sad. He had enjoyed a wonderful life, full of love and friendships. Blessed with good health for the most of it. Albert noticed he was awake and came to hold his dad's hand. "Hello Pops, we're here, Elizabeth and me, thought you might like some company." Jack pulled his son towards him, he wanted to hug him but was weak so whispered into his ear, "I love you son, you've done me proud, but it's time for me to go.

Elizabeth you look like your mother and you're blessed with her heart and love. No man could want for better children, thank you both, remember I love you always." He squeezed their hands and felt very tired.

He felt himself drifting off to sleep and for a fleeting moment he could smell his old tobacco rub from his pipe; however, he hadn't smoked a pipe for thirty years, oh God he could do with a smoke, he never forgot how much he enjoyed a pipe. He had been told by the doctors to stop years ago. He smiled as he realised he was rubbing his hands as if rubbing a roll of tobacco ready for his pipe. He knew there would be no more nightmares, no more faces in the dark. This sleep would be restful and eternal.

In his ears he could actually hear his heartbeat slow. It was so quiet, not a single sound could be heard. He noticed even the constant swooshing in his ears had gone, and that dammed hearing aid was finally finished with. Gently his breathing shallowed and his heart slowed and finally with a deep sigh Jack Adams passed away.

It was a perfect end to a life of joy, punctuated with conflict and strife, he had seen and survived two world wars and a long line of loved ones before him had passed over and taken this final journey to a better place.

As he walked he could feel the grass under his feet, the Elysium sun was warm on his back and a gentle breeze blew across his face. He could hear a tune being whistled, it was a tune he hadn't heard since 1915, a tune his old friend Jim Cunningham had often whistled before he had been gassed in the trenches.

As he walked into the never-ending rolling hills there was a wood to his right and sitting there in the shade sat his old friend smiling. As he stood up he wandered over to greet Jack, "Hello old chum, we have all been waiting for you."

Jack looked over to a small group talking to each other resting on the grass, each known to and loved by Jack. His parents were sitting on a blanket holding hands, there were no signs of the disfiguring burns on their bodies, they looked just the same as when Jack had last seen them, healthy, such a long time before. His mother looked serine and she glowed with love. His father looked strong and pristine, a kindly smile playing on his lips. Next to them, Captain Tim Alcot a man Jack had known for all his short life. He stood, talking to his father Colonel Gerald Alcot. *Ah, the colonel, such a wonderful man* thought Jack, he had been as a father to Jack for so many years. The colonel looked sage-like and immaculate in his three-piece tweed suit, just as Jack had always remembered and pictured him.

Edith, Jim's wife was drinking fresh lemonade and as the wind caught her hair it curled and tumbled onto her shoulders; she was happy, she always had been.

As Jack looked on Albert Hagerman walked out of the woodcutter's cottage next to the trees, he spoke in German and Jack understood him perfectly as he called to Monica in the hut. Albert nodded a salute to Jack, *how typical of him* thought Jack.

Everything was so slow and peaceful. The feeling of total wellbeing had virtually overwhelmed him and the only sense he was aware of was the conscious thought he could feel everything and yet nothing at the same time: he was omnipotent. As far as the eye could see, all was peaceful and serene, everything in order and just as it should be.

Jack knew she would be there, waiting, and as he looked she spoke, like a thousand bubbles all bursting at once the joy rushed over him as he turned to see his Alice, "Hello love", he said and as he walked to reach her she opened her arms to embrace him. As he closed his arms around her he felt heavenly for the very first time.

Acknowledgements

No author produces a book alone, we may type alone but that's not writing, that's typing. The thing that makes it work are the people who share the trip with you.

First and foremost as ever, thanks to Di the long suffering lady of the house; once more normality returns to the homestead. Then a small but perfect support team who read the work before it is published and make sure I don't make a complete fool of myself.

This time special mentions go to Steve Leavis, a gem of a man who keeps me grounded, Julia Jones who never lets me take off in the first place, and finally Jan O'Leary who just makes me feel warm all over. These three are priceless. All are very passionate about seeing a new guy get it right, and all are invaluable, a simple thanks is never enough, but it's all they're getting!

Finally, I really want to thank all the people who read *The Long Shot*, my first book. Their encouragement and goodwill left me in no doubt that a follow up book was required. I trust this book will leave them fully sated but wanting some more.

The Long Shot

Michael Atherton

Enjoyed the read?
Praise for Michael Atherton's first novel, *The Long Shot*

"Can't put it down."
"A real feeling of WWI."
"A real page turner."
"Stunning first novel."

– Amazon.co.uk

Turn the page to read an extract from the prequel to
A Shot from the Shadows…

CHAPTER 1

Jack, August 22, 1916

The Somme offensive is in its seventh week, six weeks longer than planned.

Sergeant Jack Adams coughed, part of his morning routine after a breakfast of fags and phlegm. The tea he had in his mess tin stank, but worse than the smell was the taste, tainted with petrol and an oily film that floated on top.

Jack rubbed his hands together to try and get some movement into his stiff fingers. It had been a cold night, but the day promised to be warm and balmy. At home, the harvest would be starting, the rabbits running wild without anyone to stop them.

Something had changed; it had been two days since that shot, the one that had had his name on it and which had missed by less than an inch. Clearly, his name had been spelled incorrectly. The bullet had thumped into the sandbag that he'd been resting his head and rifle on. It had been heading straight for the centre of his head and. but for a splendid rat that had caught his eye and made him turn his head. It would have killed him outright.

1

A sharpshooter, like him, trained to hit first time every time, had been watching Jack for about an hour, waiting. There was something personal about snipers, not random – like with shrapnel or machine gun fire – but carefully aimed.

Loathed by the enemy and loved by his own, Jack was an excellent shot but he had a human failing: compassion. He never released the key to eternal rest (or bullet to most people) until he was absolutely certain he would kill his target, quickly and efficiently like the rabbits he shot for the pot back home.

The realisation that he would very probably die here in France, far from home, had hit him hard. He didn't want to die; he had everything to live for. He did know, however, that it would be quick: a sniper's shot to kill a sniper.

He walked, hunched over, down along the trench. His watch was due to start in an hour but he had to find a new place today. News was that the Bavarians had moved into the trench system opposite. No one liked the Bavarians, and killing their officers was easy – they were like proud peacocks strutting around.

Brave or just stupid, Jack didn't really care. As a gamekeeper on the estate back home, he had seen enough of the upper classes to be satisfied when he saw one drop, and if he was honest with himself, he didn't much mind which side the toffs were on, they were all the same: strutting, and cock sure.

He did, however, like one: Captain Alcot – known as Master Tim back home – was the son of his employer,